HARE

Praise for
Hare

"Can a serial killer ever find redemption? Peter Ranscombe follows Edinburgh murderer William Hare to the civil war-torn United States in the years after his evidence condemned his notorious accomplice William Burke to hang. Hare insists he's escaped his blood-soaked past, but Boston detective Alexander Gillespie isn't so sure, especially when bodies start turning up who've been killed by the same method used by Burke and Hare in Edinburgh. Hare seems to be the prime suspect, but as the body count rises Gillespie realises he may be the only man able to help him track down the killers. Confederate agents, ruthless industrialists and a crazed flame-haired temptress all stand in the pair's way as the book hurtles to its explosive climax. Ranscombe weaves a convincing and intriguing tale of murder, mystery and mayhem in a brilliantly realised and researched historical thriller. Wonderful premise, contains more bodies than Greyfriars Churchyard, and a tumultuous, explosive ending. Great stuff."

Douglas Jackson, author of *Caligula*, *Claudius* and the Valerius series, and, as James Douglas, of *The Doomsday Testament*, *The Isis Covenant* and *The Excalibur Codex*

"Steeped in the social foment of the young United States, Peter Ranscombe's *Hare* is a smart thriller with plenty of pace. Not just a great read, this novel reflects on our time as much as it does the murkier corners of the nineteenth century."

Craig Sterling, author of *Stealing Fire*, which was shortlisted in the book-to-film category at the 2011 Rome Film Festival

"An ingenious plot told in such a compelling way that you'll lose track of time, a vivid sense of the past, and characters you can believe in –

Peter Ranscombe's *Hare* marks the arrival of a major talent."

David Robinson, Books Editor, *The Scotsman*

"Ranscombe explores the theory that it takes a killer to catch a killer in his stunning debut novel, Hare. The grizzly tale of Edinburgh mass murders William Burke and William Hare is familiar to most people. But few will know that, while Burke was hanged for his crimes, Hare turned king's evidence and walked away a free man. This fast-paced story set against the backdrop of Boston during the American Civil War sees Hare come to the aid of his old adversary, Captain Alexander Gillespie, to help the police solve a series of mysterious murders in the city. This dark and atmospheric thriller is an absolute must-read for fans of crime fiction. Ranscombe proves himself to be the new kid on the tartan noir block and succeeds in creating a hero from one of history's most hated serial killers, showing that the darker side of human nature can exist alongside honour and conscience. The narrative is compelling and the characterisation believable, making *Hare* difficult to put down. I quickly found myself buckled in and happily racing headlong with the plot to its explosive conclusion."

Morag Bootland, Staff Writer, *Scottish Field*

HARE

A NOVEL

Peter Ranscombe

**KNOX ROBINSON
PUBLISHING**
London & New York

KNOX ROBINSON PUBLISHING

34 New House
67-68 Hatton Garden
London, EC1N 8JY
&
244 5th Avenue, Suite 1861
New York, New York 10001

First published in Great Britain and the United States in 2014 by
Knox Robinson Publishing

A CIP catalogue record for this book is available from the British
Library.

ISBN HC 978-1-908483-83-6
ISBN PB 978-1-910282-97-7

Typeset in Trump Mediaeval

Printed in the United States of America and the United Kingdom

www.knoxrobinsonpublishing.com

For Sam

HARE

PART ONE
BOSTON, 1863

1

"Stop in the name of the law!" screamed a nightwatchman as Collins reached the bottom of the slope and began weaving his way between gravestones, heading for the south gate. The gnarled old trees in the southern part of the cemetery gave him more cover from the light of the full moon and the pursuing men, but the bullets from three of the guns still peppered the ground and gravestones around him in quick succession.

Collins flung himself at the gate, climbing up the iron railing then hoisting himself over and dropping to the street on the other side before any of the bullets could find their mark.

"Which way did he go?" barked the lieutenant as his men reached the foot of the slope. The nightwatchmen shook their heads and panted to regain their breath.

"Adams, Franklin, get out onto the street," ordered the officer. "The rest of you search these stones."

The lieutenant lumbered back up the slope and crossed the graveyard to where two nightwatchmen were waiting for him.

"Did she see anything?" he asked one of the men, who was crouched beside a sobbing woman at the side of the freshly-dug grave. A smashed lantern lay by the headstone.

"Dunno sir, she won't stop her crying," replied the patrolman.

"But we got one of them," added the other officer, kicking the boot of the body that lay at his feet.

"You fool, he's not going to be much use to us dead, is he?" the lieutenant snapped.

Bending down, the lieutenant grabbed the shoulder of the grave robber, turning the body over so he could inspect the man's face. The supposed corpse let out a gasp as his head lolled on the ground.

"He's alive. Bring those lanterns closer," the lieutenant barked as the man lying on the ground slowly opened his eyes.

"Tell me your name son," the lieutenant said calmly to the dying man. The amount of blood seeping from the gunshot wound in the man's chest meant he would never make it back to City Hall for questioning.

The dying man coughed and shook his head.

"He'll kill me," the man groaned.

The man looked up at the lieutenant for a moment. "Brandon," he said. "Fergus Brandon."

"And why then Brandon were you trying to rob this grave?"

Brandon coughed again but the movement made his body convulse as the pain from the wound increased its hold over him.

"Tell me!" the lieutenant shouted this time.

Brandon's lips moved but only a gurgling sound came out, accompanied by a trickle of blood from the corner of his mouth. The lieutenant leaned in closer.

Later, as the coach carried him back to the detectives' office, the lieutenant retrieved his notebook from the top left-hand pocket of his jacket and, with a frown, jotted down Brandon's dying word: "Resurrectionist".

Collins banged on the door and then doubled over, his lungs aching as he gasped for breath. He could hear a bolt being removed and then the door swung open to allow the Irishman sanctuary in the dark interior. Outside on the cobbles, he could hear the echoing footsteps of the two nightwatchmen as they pounded the streets in search of their quarry.

Bent-double and panting, Collins tried to catch his breath. He reached up and wiped the sweat from his eye.

"Where's Brandon?" a voice asked from across the darkened room.

Collins turned his eye to focus on the speaker.

"Dead," he spat.

The man handed Collins a glass bottle, from which the Irishman gratefully took a long slug. He could feel the whiskey warming his belly as he slowly tried to get his breathing back under control.

"And the police?" the man asked.

"They followed. But I think I lost them."

There was a pause.

"You led them here?" asked the man.

"Where else could I go?" Collins replied, taking another swig from the bottle.

"No matter," the man said. "Here, you should rest," he added, pointing towards a cot in the corner of the room.

Collins handed the bottle back and lowered himself on to the bed as his companion turned to place the whiskey on the table. He was vaguely aware of a movement on his blind side but before he could turn his head a pillow was forced down onto his face. As he struggled with his attacker, Collins felt an immense weight on his chest as a second assailant pinned him down in a vice-like grip. After a moment his struggling lessened, then his body convulsed and was left limp on the cot.

2

"Goddammit O'Malley, these newspapermen can't even get their facts straight anymore," cursed Captain Alexander Gillespie as he threw a copy of the *Boston Post* down onto his desk.

Lieutenant Patrick O'Malley looked up over the top of his *Boston Daily Advertiser* at his commanding officer and sighed heavily. O'Malley was amazed at the deterioration of his colleague and friend, with whom he had worked for twenty years. The civil war was taking its toll on all of the staff at Boston's police department, which seemed to be haemorrhaging officers to prop up the Union's front line. Gillespie was taking the extra workload harder than most.

"They don't even know their history," complained Gillespie, scooping up the newspaper to show O'Malley and pointing an accusatory finger at a column headlined *Boston's own Burke and Hare*.

"Burke and Hare were murderers, not grave robbers."

O'Malley nodded. He had heard the rant before.

"They killed sixteen souls in Edinburgh and sold their bodies to the medical college for profit. I chased them through the streets myself. These newspapermen seem obsessed with blurring the lines between the facts and some strange fiction they want to concoct for their readers."

O'Malley let the words wash over him. Gillespie was the finest detective he had ever served under and, out of respect for his boss, the lieutenant let Gillespie's anger blow itself out.

O'Malley paused for a moment after Gillespie finished speaking. "You've got to admit sir, it makes for a better headline," he offered in his soft Irish brogue.

There was a moment's hesitation as Gillespie glared before the pair burst out laughing together, easing the tension in the cramped office.

Though civil war was tearing the country to pieces, civic life in Boston continued unabated. The mayor had laid the cornerstone for the new city hall on School Street the previous year and, while the blocks of white Concord granite were being chiselled and raised into place on the site of the former Suffolk County Courthouse, the police department awaited its new home in City Hall.

While the mayor and his officials remained in the red brick Old State House at the junction of King and Cromwell streets, the police department had been forced into temporary accommodation on School Street, labouring under the constant noise from the building site opposite.

And just as civic life continued, so did the life of Boston's murderers, rapists and other criminals who Gillespie and O'Malley were charged with catching.

"What about the *Advertiser*?" Gillespie asked. "Are they still carrying the body snatching story as well?"

"Aye, that they are," O'Malley replied, spreading the broad sheets of the newspaper flat across his own desk, "although they've not got any of the details of what happened last night in the graveyard."

"Just as well, I guess," Gillespie mused. "If they knew that one of the suspects is dead and the other one is missing then their editors would call for our heads."

There was another pause and O'Malley grimaced then looked down at his newspaper.

"You're kidding me," Gillespie said.

"Nope," replied O'Malley. "It looks like the *Advertiser* has made the Burke and Hare connection too."

He ran his finger down the lines of the column until he found the passage he sought.

"'Are Boston's finest really so devoid of wit and intelligence that they are unable to apprehend the callous fiends who would rob the graves of our fathers and mothers, husbands and wives?'" O'Malley read from the newspaper.

O'Malley frowned. "They use the word 'Resurrectionist,'" he muttered. "What does that mean, sir?"

"It was a sobriquet given to the body snatchers in Edinburgh," Gillespie replied. "A blasphemous play on words."

O'Malley fished his notebook out of his coat pocket and flicked through the pages, skimming over the details of three recent murders they were investigating down at the docks and a spate of grave robberies. He still couldn't tell if the incidents were connected. At last he found the pages containing his notes on the previous night's attempted grave robbery. The screams of the dead man's daughter, who had come to visit the grave, had alerted O'Malley and his passing patrolmen, who had shot one man and pursued the other.

"Brandon, the dead man, I could have sworn that was his last word."

"Are you sure?"

"Positive," O'Malley nodded.

Gillespie leaned back in his chair and stared at the ceiling.

"Maybe he picked the word up from the newspaper," Gillespie mused. "What else does the *Advertiser* have to say?"

"'The desecration of the graves of our loved ones brings to mind the heinous crimes of the villains Burke and Hare, who left the residents of Scotchland terrified to bury their dead for fear of their immortal souls being disturbed from their eternal slumber.'"

Before Gillespie could answer the charge against his officers or correct the newspaper's misspelling of his homeland's name, his thoughts were interrupted as the door to the detectives' office flew open and a giant of a man stepped in from the street, accompanied by two shorter figures wearing the regulation grey suits and small bowler hats of the police's administrative division.

Gillespie and O'Malley sprung to their feet and stood to attention, their newspapers left crumpled on their desks.

Every inch of Police Chief Isaac Blackstone's six-foot-six height commanded the respect of the officers who served under him.

"Where are we with these murders, Gillespie?" Blackstone asked without preamble. He threw his hat down onto Gillespie's desk and paced the cramped confines of the office.

"As you will have seen from my report, sir," Gillespie replied, "we're continuing to question the dock workers in the hope of finding the person or persons who may have been responsible for the murders of the three men."

Blackstone had read through Gillespie's latest report but the police chief did not waste the opportunity to stamp his authority.

"It's not good enough!" Blackstone yelled, forcing the men in the room to jostle nervously.

Gillespie stood his ground and kept his eyes fixed on those of his commanding officer. His ability to hold a stare was one of his greatest assets.

"You know how the mayor feels about these murders," Blackstone continued to berate his captain. "Any restlessness among the workers in the city could seriously hamper the war effort."

From the way Blackstone raged about the war effort, one could be forgiven for thinking it was his own personal efforts on the battlefield that would win the day for the Union, Gillespie mused. Yet Blackstone was a Boston blue blood, part of the ruling elite, and had never served as a soldier, unlike Gillespie and O'Malley.

"But we have made progress on the grave snatching case," Gillespie offered. O'Malley lowered his head to hide the smirk that wound its way across his lips as the captain bated his superior. "One of the suspects is dead and I firmly believe we are closing in on his accomplice."

"This body-snatching saga is a bloody side show," Blackstone shouted. "I want all of the scant resources we have focussed on solving these murders."

Blackstone took a step closer to Gillespie, still standing beside his desk.

"I want this murderer caught, Captain. The last thing we need is to be made a laughing stock by the worthless simpletons who write these pieces of trash," Blackstone said, sweeping his hand across the newspaper lying open on Gillespie's desk.

With that, the chief snatched up his hat and stormed back out of the office, his two silent minions following behind.

O'Malley watched him go, raising his eyebrows and shaking his head.

"What now, Inspector?" O'Malley asked, using the informal nickname that he and the other officers used for their captain. Though Gillespie had served in America for most of his career, the nickname was a throwback to his time as a police officer in Scotland.

Gillespie slumped in his chair and smoothed down the dark bristles of his moustache before running his fingers across the stumble on his chin, both flecked with grey. The captain was a creature of habit and O'Malley recognised the tell-tale signs of his mind mulling over a problem.

"Take as many men as you can find and head for the docks," Gillespie instructed, as he rose to his feet and retrieved his dark military-style greatcoat from the back of his chair. "If Blackstone wants us to divert more resources to this murder inquiry then that's exactly what we'll do. I want you to question every dock worker and canal navvy you can find, whether he's Irish, Italian, Russian or whatever. And take Fletcher with you," Gillespie added, referring to his other lieutenant, who had transferred from New York City more than a month before.

"No buts O'Malley," Gillespie cautioned him. "He may be full of himself but we need every pair of hands we can get."

O'Malley's brow creased into a frown. "Aren't you coming too, Inspector?" he asked.

"No," Gillespie replied, placing his hat on his head and turning for the door. "I have a doctor's appointment."

3

"Gentlemen, as our Lord said during his all-too brief time on this Earth, 'Ye shall know the truth and the truth shall make you free'."

The rich timbre of Professor Seymour Cartwright's voice easily filled the main lecture theatre of Harvard University's Massachusetts Medical College. More than one hundred young men sat on the steeply-tiered benches, leaning forward on their desks and scribbling down notes as they hung on the professor's every word.

Gillespie slipped into the back of the lecture theatre and stood leaning against the rail behind the final row of benches, gazing down at the professor, who stood before a table at the front of the theatre, at the foot of the tiered seating. Cartwright gave an almost imperceptible nod of his head, acknowledging the police officer's presence.

Gillespie's strict Presbyterian upbringing kicked in and he subconsciously identified the passage from Holy Scripture as the thirty-second verse of the eighth chapter in the Gospel according to St John. The detective recognised Cartwright was taking the quote out of context but the professor's liberal use of Scripture came as no surprise to him as the gulf between science and religion – and those who practiced in each field – appeared to be growing wider. Nevertheless, he was intrigued by Cartwright's selection of the passage.

With a flourish of the professor's hands, his unspoken question was answered. Cartwright lifted the white blanket that lay on the table in front of him and, with a flick of his wrists, tossed it clear over his shoulder, as if he was a magician performing a trick. Beneath the blanket lay the remains of a human cadaver, which Gillespie noted from the remaining appendages had once been a man.

"And where better to look for truth than inside our own bodies?" Cartwright mused. "The soul of this individual may have thrown off its mortal coil but this earthly form before us can reveal not only how this man lived, but how he died as well."

Gillespie watched as Cartwright lectured his students. Before the lesson, the flesh of the cadaver's chest had been sliced open in a perfectly straight line from the throat all the way down to the naval. The two pieces of the man's skin had been drawn back as if it were the front of a shirt, revealing the ribcage and internal organs beneath. Cartwright proceeded to elucidate the procedure for opening the ribcage to examine the heart and lungs and then launched into a comparison of the rival techniques of Bohemian pathologist Carl von Rokitansky and Rudolf Virchow, his German compatriot.

While Blackstone frowned upon Gillespie consulting with Cartwright – and even the normally unshakable O'Malley had been given cause to leave the professor's laboratory on more than one occasion at the sight of a post-mortem examination – Gillespie knew the techniques being employed before him were the future of policing.

Employing the scientific disciplines practiced by Cartwright had helped Gillespie to solve many cases over the course of the previous twenty years and the detective held high hopes that the professor's insight could lead him to catch the culprits in his current inquiries too.

As Cartwright brought his lecture to an end, he told a joke in Latin that flew straight over Gillespie's head but elicited a ripple of laughter from the students. Cartwright was replacing the white sheet over the top of the corpse when a hand was gingerly raised from the front row of benches.

"Professor?" the student said tentatively, encouraged by the persistent elbowing of the students either side of him.

Cartwright smiled and raised an inquisitive eyebrow. "Yes, Saunders?" he asked.

"Sir, the latest paper from the Royal Society in London arrived last week and it contained an interesting treatise on the human body – and on reanimation in particular sir," said the student, taking his time to reach his point but emboldened by the sea of heads turning in his direction from the benches that surrounded him.

Cartwright tilted his head to one side as he considered what the student was telling him. "Go on, Saunders," he said.

"Well, do you believe that such a feat could be achieved professor?" the student asked. "Could a doctor bring a dead patient back to life?"

Cartwright appeared to ponder the question for a moment before replying, but the professor's sharp mind had already pieced together an answer before the student had finished asking the question.

"You are, of course," Cartwright began, "referring to the writings of the eminent Prussian scientist Herr Professor Kristophe van der Waal. I too devoured his latest paper with much interest. But his conclusions, I feel, are wide of the mark."

Cartwright turned his attention to the rest of the assembled students in the lecture theatre.

"In his latest paper, Professor van der Waal postulates that as well as pumping blood around the body, the heart is also traversed by electrical signals, such as those that now cross our nation through Samuel Morse's telegraph system.

"While I have read other work that confirms his theories on the heart's electrical system – indeed, I know of colleagues in London who are studying the same phenomenon – his assertions that these electrical signals could be restarted after death to bring a patient back to life are, I feel, a step too far."

"But why, sir?" asked Saunders, the student who had posed the initial question.

"We have known since the days of the ancient Greeks that the heart is the pump that drives blood around the body," Cartwright explained. "Once that action has ceased, I see no way of restarting it. A physician may be able to restore electric order to the heart in the moments after such signals cease but to reinitiate the pump itself seems a far-fetched notion to me."

A thought suddenly seemed to occur to Cartwright and he ended the lecture as he had begun, with a passage from Scripture.

"'Thy dead men shall live, together with my dead body shall they arise: awake and sing yee that dwell in dust: for thy dew is as the dew of herbs, and the earth shall cast out the dead.' Only Christ can raise the dead."

After the students had cleared out of the lecture theatre, Gillespie walked down the steps in the aisle at the centre of the benches to join Cartwright beside the demonstration table.

"Bravo, maestro," he said, giving a slow clap with his hands as he descended the stairs. "Another good turnout for your show to boot."

"I'd like to see more of them," Cartwright explained, shaking the detective's outstretched hand. "Before the war, it was standing room only in my classes. Paying students had to stand around the edges just to hear my lectures. Now it seems that more and more young men are enlisting as field surgeons. They're desperate to wet their hands in the butchery that goes on at the front and make a name for themselves. Week after week, it feels like there are fewer and fewer of them remaining here to learn their craft."

"That was you once," Gillespie offered, reminding the professor of his own time as a field surgeon nearly twenty years before in the war between America and Mexico.

"I saw sights in the desert that I would not wish on any other man," Cartwright said. "As did you, I have no doubt," he added. The pair had served together in the United States Army, Cartwright as a medic and Gillespie as a soldier.

Cartwright's gaze shifted around the empty lecture theatre and he shook his head. There was a moment's pause as he was lost in thought before he turned back to Gillespie. He looked as if he was about to say something but then thought better of it.

"That will be all for today, Jamie," he said to his assistant. The tall young man who was standing behind the trolley with the cadaver nodded in silent acknowledgement and slipped out of the lecture theatre. Jamie Taylor had been rendered mute after a shell exploded in the trenches, showering him in shrapnel. But Cartwright had taken pity on his former student and had hired him as one of his research assistants to prepare bodies for examination and help him perform autopsies.

Once Taylor had left them, Cartwright turned back to Gillespie.

"You've come about the bodies no doubt?" he asked.

"I wish it was a social call," Gillespie replied. "But I need to confirm if the latest killing is linked to the previous two."

Cartwright nodded. "As well as the strange branding on the chest, this victim was also asphyxiated, just like the others."

"And the branding came after the man was dead?" Gillespie checked.

"Yes, just like the others – you can see for yourself if you like. I was using the latest victim as a demonstration for the students."

Cartwright gingerly folded back the white blanket as far as the body's waist this time, his showmanship contained for the moment as he led Gillespie through the science of his investigation.

"Don't worry," said Cartwright, noticing the pensive expression on Gillespie's face. "I made the initial incision before the lecture. None of the students would have seen the marks on the chest."

Cartwright carefully placed the skin from the man's chest back into place, revealing two circular brands on his upper body. Gillespie peered again at the marks he had become so familiar with from the two previous corpses.

"Why brand the victims after killing them?" Gillespie's rhetorical question was left unanswered as the two men considered the body.

"And you said he was killed in the same manner as the other two?" the detective asked.

"Yes," replied Cartwright, reaching onto his table of instruments and passing a magnifying glass to Gillespie. "Look at the mouth."

Gillespie did as he was instructed and Cartwright gripped the dead man's chin and forehead, overcoming the rigour mortis that had set in to part the corpse's lips.

"I found the same fibres inside this victim's mouth as with the other two. There's also bruising across the ribs, which could indicate that two assailants were involved. It's a technique that I believe is called – ".

"Burking," Gillespie interrupted the professor, tearing his eyes away from the corpse and beginning to pace the floor.

"Of course," Cartwright nodded, remembering what Gillespie had told him when he had explained how the first two men had died. "A little bit too close to home for you?"

"It feels like a lifetime ago," replied Gillespie, as images from his first case as a police officer in the Scottish capital flashed through his mind. The murders committed by Burke and Hare had brought a new word into common usage: "burking" to describe how a victim was smothered by one man while having his chest compressed by another.

"Well, it nearly was a lifetime ago now," smiled Cartwright. "Neither one of us is as young as he once was."

Gillespie sighed, feeling every one of his fifty-one years as he so often had of late.

"I still don't see it," Gillespie said. "Three bodies, all Irish canal navvies, all dumped down at the docks. No families, no quarrels with friends or other labourers, no obvious reason to brand them in such a manner.

"Then there are the body snatching cases too," Gillespie added. "I have a feeling they're linked to the murders but I just can't see it."

"The branding is certainly highly unusual," agreed Cartwright, who had picked up the hand lens and was staring at the two circular marks on the man's chest. "From the way in which the skin has been marked, I can tell the injuries came after the victims were dead – but for what purpose I can only speculate."

A thought struck Gillespie.

"You were talking to the students about…"

Gillespie struggled for the right word.

"Reanimation," Cartwright offered.

"Yes. Could whoever is exhuming these bodies be investigating the same field as this Prussian scientist? Or could he have come to America?"

Cartwright thought for a moment before answering.

"It is feasible," he conceded. "But you would need enormous resources to carry out research such as this. From what I understand of his studies, the electric currents van der Waal was generating were not inconsiderable.

"Plus, I can say with absolute certainty that van der Waal has not travelled to the United States," Cartwright added.

"How can you be so sure?" Gillespie asked.

"He's dead," Cartwright replied simply. "Killed when his laboratory burned down. The electrical equipment he was using could not have been as reliable as he would have wished. It's morbidly ironic, don't you think? An electricity researcher killed by an electrical fault?"

Gillespie paused on the steps outside the Massachusetts Medical College and gazed across North Grove Street to the city's jail. How many ghouls had Gillespie locked away in the prison? And how many more could he catch before the strains of the job finally took their toll on his aching body and mind?

He walked past the police carriage that had brought him across the city to the college and signalled to the driver to wait for him as he walked down to the end of the street.

Gillespie gazed out across the Charles River to the town of Cambridge, which spread out back towards the main campus of Harvard University. He knew that, as well as his office at the medical college, Cartwright also had rooms at the university's main buildings out in leafy Cambridge. While Blackstone wanted everyone to know he was part of Boston's elite, Cartwright wore his pedigree and wealth in a much lighter and more reserved manner. It was one of the reasons why Gillespie had got on so well with the surgeon during their army service together and why he had sought out the professor to help with his murder inquiries down the years.

Gillespie let his mind wander. He looked across at the more gentile streets of Cambridge and became even more aware of the contrast with Boston itself. The city felt like a powder keg ready to explode. The war was not going the Union's way; conscription for men aged between twenty and forty-five had been introduced in March, but richer men had been able to buy themselves out of service for the princely sum of three hundred dollars or by naming a substitute to take their place. The cash exemption led to the cries of "The blood of a poor man is as precious as that of the wealthy" from those living in poverty in the northern states, an injustice surprisingly taken up by many of the otherwise Union-loyal newspapers.

With the evening's sun beginning to sink behind the far bank of the broad river, Gillespie pondered the huge divisions in his adopted country, between rich and poor, slaves and freemen, immigrants and Americans. The deep-seated fault lines had finally burst open into a civil war that had already cost the lives of thousands of men.

As more and more men marched off to the front, Gillespie felt that any spark could ignite Boston's powder keg and he prayed earnestly that the series of murders he was investigating would not lead to unrest. Though he found a small amount of pleasure from taunting Blackstone, Gillespie knew as well as his commanding officer did that any problems at the city's docks or factories could bring the Union's faltering war efforts to an abrupt halt.

4

Gillespie's head was no clearer when his carriage reached the temporary detectives' office and his mood was not helped by the scene of pandemonium that greeted him when he opened the door.

A mixture of uniformed officers and Gillespie's own depleted squad of detectives were questioning several dozen Irish canal-building navvies, with the din from the labourers' answers filling the small office. Behind the rows of crowded desks, Gillespie could see even more navvies being moved in and out of the makeshift interview rooms that the captain had encouraged his men to use.

Andrew Fletcher, the officer who had transferred from the New York City police force, walked over to greet Gillespie. Fletcher's clean-shaven features made him look even younger than his twenty-eight years but Gillespie noted the hard determination in the young man's eyes.

"We've nearly finished questioning all of the canal workers, Inspector," explained Fletcher, who still stumbled over the use of the British title used for Gillespie.

"But it's not good news, sir. We know that the final navvy to be murdered, O'Driscoll, disappeared between seven o'clock and eleven o'clock on Monday night. But all of the navvies have the same alibi – they were all at a union meeting on Monday evening."

Gillespie sighed and nodded. "Where's O'Malley?" he asked. Fletcher pointed towards the back of the room, where the corridor led down to the cells in the basement beneath the office.

As Gillespie headed to the stairs, he met O'Malley coming up from the holding pens.

"They were all at the same union meeting?" Gillespie asked.

"All but one," O'Malley replied. "I had the union clerk bring along his log book. All of the workers signed in to the meeting – even though they're not citizens they still wanted to come up with some kind of protest against the Union draft – and were there all night. All the workers except for one of the foremen, a man named Laird."

"Do you have him here?" Gillespie asked.

"Aye, down in the cells. He wouldn't give an alibi for the time of the murder so I threw him downstairs to think about it some more."

Gillespie knew the evidence was circumstantial at best but the absent canal navvy was the best lead so far.

"Right, I'll come with you to question him again," Gillespie decided and followed O'Malley back down the stairs to the cells.

"He's a right queer one this Laird," O'Malley explained as they walked down the poorly-lit corridor, with a dozen cells leading off each side. "One calm bugger. He just sat there giving one-word answers when I asked him about the murders. There's something funny about his eyes too," O'Malley muttered.

The officers reached the final cell and O'Malley slipped his key into the lock. The lieutenant pushed open the door and led the way into the cell.

The only light to illuminate the cell came from the gas lamp out in the corridor and at first Gillespie could only make out the vague shape of the figure who sat on the bench, the sole piece of furniture in the small cell. He was tall, around six foot, but wiry. His salt and pepper coloured hair was long and swept back from his high forehead.

But it was the eyes sunk deep into the face above the high cheekbones that Gillespie was drawn to. One blue, one green. And a flash of recognition passed across those eyes as Gillespie gave a murderous cry and launched himself across the cell at its inmate.

Gillespie swung his arms in quick succession, raining a stream of blows across the face of the prisoner, who brought his arms up to shield himself. But apart from the defensive gesture, Laird didn't return the blows and sank to the floor as the attack continued.

"Inspector," O'Malley cried as he lunged to grab Gillespie by the coat and pull him back from the prisoner. The lieutenant dragged his commanding officer out of the cell and threw him against the far wall of the corridor before quickly locking the cell again, watching Laird lift his head to look at the small window in the door.

"What the hell's gotten into you?" O'Malley demanded.

Gillespie's breath came in short gasps after the exertion of hitting the cell's occupant. His knees gave way and he rested his back against the wall, slowing sinking to the floor.

"That man," Gillespie panted. "His name isn't Laird. It's William Hare. And he's a self-confessed serial killer."

EDINBURGH, 1829

Wednesday, 28 January 1829

The morning's rain had turned to constant sleet, whipping across the city from the Firth of Forth and chilling members of the huge crowd as they stood huddled around the scaffold hastily erected on the High Street, at the very heart of the Royal Mile that ran between Edinburgh Castle and the Palace of Holyroodhouse.

From his vantage point on the flat roof of Parliament House, Patrolman Alexander Gillespie gazed down at the throng of more than twenty thousand people gathered to watch the prisoner swing from the noose.

Down to his left, he could see the crowd spilling down Libberton's Wynd, the tiny lane that led from the High Street into the Cowgate below, which in turn snaked its way through the Grassmarket and along to the West Port, where the convict's heinous crimes had taken place.

For weeks since he had been found guilty by a jury of fifteen of his peers at the High Court of Justiciary and sentenced to death by the Lord Commissioner of Justiciary, residents of the West Port had been braying for blood. And within the hour they would have it.

Gillespie pulled his hat down lower over his head against the wind and adjusted the black cape he wore over his shoulders to protect his neatly-creased police uniform. He drew his wooden baton from his belt with his right hand and began tapping it against the outstretched palm of his left as he paced backwards and forwards behind the balustrades, peering down at the crowd below. He paced his way between the two soldiers who stood lazily on the roof, their rifles trained on the scaffold below in case any members of the massive crowd tried to storm the platform. The pair of soldiers ignored Gillespie as he strode across the rooftop, repeating the same pattern he had adopted all morning long as they waited for the execution.

Again Gillespie cursed his inspector under his breath. His senior officer had seen the toll that the West Port murders had taken on Edinburgh's newest and youngest police recruit and had stationed him on the roof of the nearby Parliament House rather than down on the street with the other officers, ready to pounce if the crowd got out of hand. From his position on the roof, Gillespie knew he would be next to useless if trouble kicked off – but it had given him the chance to formulate his plan.

He felt a cold hand tightening around his stomach each time he thought about how the two killers had got away from him. That night in the Grassmarket, when he and his sergeant had been out on patrol and had found the pair dragging a young man between them, had continued to haunt his dreams and occupy his every waking thought. But they had got away. A scuffle between two whores had torn his sergeant's attention away from the pair of Irishmen and Gillespie had been dragged away to help break up the fight.

The young man was James Wilson, better known as "Daft Jamie", one of Burke and Hare's victims. If Gillespie had stopped them that night then a life would have been spared. That morning, the hangman would dispense justice to one of the murderers. And, before the day was out, Gillespie vowed he would serve his own form of justice on the other.

As he looked down on the giant crowd milling about in the weak early-morning light, Gillespie's gaze was drawn to an innocuous wooden door on the corner of Libberton's Wynd and the High Street. Behind the small door lay the tiny gaol or jail in which Gillespie knew the prisoner had been brought the day before by coach from the main prison on Calton Hill, so as to avoid a lynching on the journey across the town's centre. There would be no chance of the prisoner being snatched by the crowd in the few short paces between his cell in the Libberton lock-up and the scaffold on the High Street.

From speaking with one of his police colleagues earlier in the morning, Gillespie knew that the condemned man had been strangely calm in the weeks leading up to his execution, reading religious tracts left for him by the Roman Catholic priest who had been attending to him at the gaol on Calton Hill. During his final night, chained to the wall of the lock-up, the prisoner had begged for his manacles to be removed and the magistrates' guards had taken pity on him and complied with his request.

"Thank God these are off and all will be off shortly," the murderer had lamented, according to Gillespie's colleague, who had heard the words from one of the guards. Soon, that final wish would come true.

Now, in the tiny cell, the prisoner would have had his arms pinioned, ready to be led out for the execution. The patrolman absentmindedly wondered if the prisoner had accepted the final glass of wine offered to those about to lose their lives.

The crowd was swelling even further now as workmen streamed across from the New Town to Edinburgh's Old Town. Large sandstone edifices were slowly taking shape on Princes, George and Queen streets, named after the monarch George IV's visit to the city only seven years earlier. The old turgid waters of the Nor Loch had been drained and a new district was developing on the far bank, large homes for those who could afford such luxury. A New Town with new houses for Enlightenment minds, away from the squalor and poverty of the Mediaeval Old Town.

But the separation of the towns had not stopped the lawyers and doctors and teachers and clergymen of the New Town rubbing shoulder-to-shoulder with their workers as they crossed back to the Old Town to watch the execution. Burke and Hare may have sold the corpses to Dr Robert Knox's medical school – where he taught the very modern science of anatomy to his students – but their crime of murder was as old as time itself. New reason, same old crime.

Knox had avoided prosecution because there was no evidence to show he knew where Burke and Hare were getting the bodies, but Gillespie planned to make sure Hare did not go unpunished.

Involuntarily, his hand dipped beneath his cape and caressed the cold blade of the long knife he had slipped into one of the pockets of his uniform. Soon he would see that justice was done.

His revere was broken by the shifting of the gathering crowd below, which had fallen ominously silent. Gillespie saw the soldiers on either side of him tightening the grip on their rifles. While he was out on patrol the night before, he had seen the crowd assemble to watch the workmen erect the platform and gibbet that formed the scaffold standing on the street below him now. Around midnight, three cheers had been called out by the crowd when the workmen had finished attending to their duties and the throng had begun to disperse.

But the first of them had been back again by six o'clock the following morning, braving the rain and the sleet and the flurries of occasional snow to grab the best spaces behind the metal chain that had been erected on poles around the scaffold, giving room for the soldiers drafted in to help the police guard the execution site. The infantrymen's bright red tunics stood out against the grey stones of the cobbles and the white blanket of snow that still covered many of the rooftops.

Gillespie had heard that people had spent between five and twenty shillings to book a space at one of the windows overlooking the head of Libberton's Wynd. From the mixture of accents Gillespie heard, he knew that the execution had not only attracted spectators from Edinburgh itself but also a host of visitors from the surrounding towns. In the throng below, Gillespie could also pick out the familiar sight of news reporters he recognised from *The Daily Scotsman* and *The Caledonian Mercury*.

The crowd's silence was broken by the striking of the bell inside St Giles' Cathedral, off to Gillespie's right, as the hour tolled eight o'clock. Shortly after the clock finished its morbid wail, the door to the lock-up was thrown open and bailies Crichton and Small from the town council led the procession out of the tiny cell and across the street to the scaffold. Following behind them came the condemned man, supported on either side by two Roman Catholic priests, who helped guide his pinioned body towards its final destination. As soon as he stepped out onto the street, the crowd began sending up a tumultuous roar of shouts and cries, hurling insults at the murderer as he walked his final steps.

Dressed soberly in a black suit – no doubt supplied by Captain Rose, the governor of the Calton Hill gaol, or one of the clergymen – the prisoner walked in a determined manner towards his fate until the path guarded by the soldiers narrowed and his pace appeared to falter, as if he was half-closing his eyes to block out the view of the crowd around him.

The bailies led the execution party up onto the platform, where the murderer and the two priests knelt down and prayed with him. Once they were finished, Rev Marshall, a Church of Scotland minister, led a prayer, his loud voice booming out over the hushed crowd. No sooner had the minister finished his prayer then the crowd took up with its cheers again, intermingled with hisses and boos from those closest to the scaffold.

Stepping forward, the executioner began preparing the prisoner, passing the noose of the rope around his neck and unfolding the black hood ready to slip it over his head.

"Burke him, Burke him, give him no rope," came the cry from the crowd. Gillespie's mouth twitched into a brief smile. How quickly a new word can enter the language, he thought. The masses wanted the condemned man to be smothered, ending his life in the same way he had slaughtered his victims.

Gillespie stared hard at the face of the prisoner, its angular features already burned deep into his memory. For his part, the murderer continued to look composed and calmly gazed around at the massive crowd, resigned to his fate.

The hangman threw the black hood over the condemned man's head, plunging his world into blackness, and placed a plain white handkerchief into his hands. Gillespie knew the piece of fabric was used as a signal – when the prisoner dropped the handkerchief, the executioner would pull the lever to open the trap door beneath the condemned man's feet, plunging him to his death.

Once the hood had been drawn over the murderer's head, the crowd let up another massive cheer as the magistrates, ministers and their attendants began to leave the platform.

"Hare, Hare, where is Hare?" came the call from one part of the crowd, only to be taken up by another segment of the audience with "Hang Hare too".

The chorus died down and, from his vantage point on the roof, Gillespie could just make out the final words that one of the priests told the prisoner.

"Now, say your creed and, when you come to the words 'Lord Jesus

Christ', give the signal and die with his blesséd name in your mouth," said the priest.

As the clergymen descended down the wooden steps from the platform, the crowd began chanting again, "Burke him, Burke him, do the same for Hare". Once silence had descended again, Gillespie watched as the prisoner stretched out his hands as best he could with his arms pinned to his sides. Though the black hood masked any sound escaping from his lips, the patrolman could tell that the murderer was reciting his final prayer. After a brief moment, the convict dropped the white handkerchief and the hangman pulled back the lever, opening the trap door on the stage and sending the man to his death.

The rope had enough give so that the prisoner's neck didn't snap but instead he was left dangling from the noose, drawing loud "Hazzas" from the crowd to accompany each convulsion from his writhing body. As the final twitches came to an end and the prisoner's body fell limp, the masses let up an enormous cheer that echoed around the Old Town. William Burke was dead.

The soldiers on either side of Gillespie visibly relaxed as the hangman cut down Burke's body and the crowd began to disperse with further cries of "Hang Hare too" and "Wash the blood from the land". The infantrymen's shoulders sagged, relieved that no one had tried to storm the scaffold or stab Burke as he passed along his path through the crowd.

As the throng of people began to clear from the High Street, Gillespie caught sight of a face that made his blood freeze. There, standing on the steps of the High Court watching the proceedings was the man on whom he planned to dispense justice. Not in hiding, not fleeing for his life, but watching his accomplice hang for the crimes they had both committed. The figure began making his way through the crowd, unrecognised by the masses with his newly-shaven head but noticed by Gillespie thanks to his strange eyes, one blue and one green.

As the figure passed through the crowd and headed down Libberton's Wynd, Gillespie ran across the roof and set off in pursuit.

Even in the narrow wynds and closes of Edinburgh's Old Town, the fierce wind was whipping the sleet and snow into Gillespie's face as he searched for his prey. Branching off from Libberton's Wynd, he began making his way along the back passages and lanes that linked the narrow streets.

His efforts were soon rewarded as the crowds thinned and he picked out a solitary figure making his way along a deserted wynd towards the West Port. Since his release by the authorities, Hare must have been hiding in plain sight, remaining in the community he had terrorised for months on end.

A despicable move from a despicable man, but one that Gillespie would soon put to an end. As he caught up with his quarry, he pulled the sharp blade from his pocket and placed his hand firmly on the man's shoulder. One quick slit across his throat and it would all be over.

"William Hare," he snarled as he tugged on the man's shoulder, swinging him round to face his fate.

Hare's face broke into a twisted smile as he turned to face Gillespie. The patrolman drew back his arm to slash Hare with the knife but his face froze in horror as Hare parried his thrust with his arm, knocking his aim off so that his blade only scratched Hare's cheek. The blow sent Gillespie crashing to the floor; Hare had sensed the younger man's approach and had been ready for the attack.

Gillespie picked himself up off the cobbles but Hare was already on him, raining down a series of blows to Gillespie's head and chest. The young patrolman gasped for breath as the hail of blows from the well-built Irishman, eight years his senior, knocked the wind out of him.

Gillespie swung his leg around and caught Hare behind the knee, bringing the Irishman crashing down onto the cobbles. Hare brought his arms up to protect himself from Gillespie's onslaught, knocking the knife from the police officer's hand and sending it slipping across the wet cobbles. Hare smashed his fist into Gillespie's jaw and then broke his nose with an uppercut from his other hand.

The patrolman sank dazed to his knees for a brief moment as Hare scrambled away but it was all the Irishman needed. Sweeping the knife up with one hand and slamming Gillespie into the wall with the other, Hare held the police officer pinned against the side of the narrow wynd.

"And who do we have here?" Hare hissed as he used the handle of the knife to prise Gillespie's lank, wet fringe of hair away from where it had become plastered against his face. "Trying to be a hero boy?"

Hare paused as he looked into Gillespie's eyes, then an evil grin spread across his face.

"Ah, the police patrolman," Hare nodded. "You were the one who taunted me in the cells, weren't you boy?" Hare added as he remembered the long nights spent awaiting trial, being held by the police and beaten by its officers.

"You deserved far worse," Gillespie spat, squirming to get away from the murderer but managing to keep his resolve firm enough to reply.

"King's evidence, boy," Hare retorted. "I'm a free man."

"You'll never be free from what you've done," Gillespie wheezed, struggling for breath as Hare lent his full weight into pinning him against the wall.

"We'll just have to see about that," said Hare, as he plunged the sharp point of the knife into Gillespie's midriff, before pulling the blade back out again.

Gillespie slowly sank down the wall, crippled by the blow and quickly losing hope of rescue. The cold wind began wrapping its icy fingers around him as Hare drew back to survey the damage he had inflicted.

"What are you going to do now, Hare?" came a voice from the dark shadows of the wynd.

Hare spun round. "Who said that?" he screamed, spinning round and round again on the spot but still unable to locate the source of the voice.

Through the hazy thoughts that were fogging his mind, Gillespie looked up at the Irishman, confused by why he had stopped his attack.

"Who's there?" Hare yelled. "Did you bring someone with you boy?"

"What do you mean?" Gillespie croaked.

"That voice. Who's there?"

"What voice?" Gillespie managed as his energy continued to ebb away.

"You don't hear that?" Hare scowled, turning round and round again as he searched for the source of his torment.

"*Of course he doesn't hear me,*" came the voice again. "*Only you can hear me.*"

"What do you mean?" Hare frowned, lowering the knife.

"*I mean I'm here to haunt you, Hare, you double-crossing piece of Newry shite,*" replied the voice.

Hare watched in horror as a ghostly spectre dressed in a black suit emerged from the shadows and stood before him, untouched by the falling sleet as it began turning into a torrent of rain.

"Burke," Hare whispered.

"*The very same,*" came the reply. "*You betrayed me and now I'm going to make you pay.*"

"What do you mean?"

"*I'll be there each step of the way. Every move you make, I'll be watching and waiting. I'll lead them to you. I'll lead every police officer and grieving relative I can find. They'll make you pay for your crimes, just like you made me pay.*"

Gillespie watched in confusion as Hare appeared to carry out a conversation with himself.

"*And what about him?*" Burke asked, pointing down at the stricken police officer. "*One more murder? One more corpse? What difference is one more going to make when it comes to the eternal damnation of your soul?*"

"You found faith?" Hare shook his head in disbelief.

"*No, Hare, faith found me,*" Burke scoffed. "*And it's going to find you too.*"

"I can change," Hare said blankly, his face a mask of confusion. "I can mend my ways."

"*Once a piece of scum, always a piece of scum,*" Burke yelled at him. "*You'll never change and I'm here to make sure you get what's coming to you.*"

Hare's reply was interrupted by a loud blast from Gillespie's whistle as the injured police officer used what was left of his strength to signal for help. Much to his relief, his call was answered by two blasts from three other distinct whistles, as his fellow patrolmen converged on his position.

"*What you going to do now?*" Burke snarled. "*Are you going to kill all these coppers?*"

A final look of consternation flashed across Hare's face before he dropped the knife and turned tail, fleeing to fetch his wife and child before quitting Edinburgh for good.

As Hare ran through the pouring rain, the voice cried after him: "*You can't run from me Hare. There's no escape now. I'll always be with you.*"

PART TWO
BOSTON, 1863

5

O'Malley had a talent for finding whisky. As the rotund Irishman lowered himself into the chair opposite Gillespie, he placed a tall glass bottle and two tumblers on the desk in between them. The bottle wasn't the usual Irish whiskey that O'Malley kept secreted in the bottom drawer of his desk; instead, the resourceful lieutenant had procured a bottle of 12-year-old Highland malt whisky from Glendronach distillery in Aberdeenshire.

"Just don't tell the Chief," O'Malley told Gillespie in a mock whisper. "It won't be too long before he misses this and tries to find out who took it."

Gillespie smiled at the small piece of home that sat on the desk between the two men. But then a cloud passed across his face as he remembered the other reminder of his homeland who lay curled up in one of the makeshift cells in the cellar beneath their feet. O'Malley noted the change in the captain's expression as he poured each of them a healthy measure of Scotch.

"Are you sure it's him?" O'Malley asked, giving voice to the unspoken question he had carried with him as he had cleared the office of the other policemen, until only he and Gillespie were left, save for the two guards below in the cellar. "It's been such a long time since you saw him."

"I'd know that face anywhere," Gillespie replied, raising the glass to his lips and taking a slug of the spirit. He let the warmth of the whisky trickle down the back of his throat and into his chest before sighing heavily.

"He may be thirty years older but I'll never forget those eyes. His eyes are just the same. And that scar across his left cheek? I gave him that scar the night he fled Edinburgh after Burke was hanged."

Gillespie involuntarily ran his fingers along his left flank, touching a long forgotten scar of his own.

"Why are you taking this so personally?" O'Malley asked. There was no sense of criticism in the question and Gillespie had worked with O'Malley long enough to know that there was no malice attached to the inquiry. "I remember you saying that Burke was hanged during your first year with the police but why has finding Hare again unsettled you so much?"

Gillespie swirled the Scotch around in his glass and took another swig before answering.

"I let him get away," Gillespie replied.

"I don't understand," said O'Malley. "I thought Hare turned king's evidence against Burke. He traded his partner's life for his own. Surely you had no choice but to let him go?"

"I don't mean after the hanging," Gillespie said. He leaned back in his chair and he recounted the story of a murder hunt, thirty-four years earlier and three thousand miles away.

"Burke and Hare killed sixteen men, women and children over the course of a year. Most of the victims were suffocated at the lodging house run by Hare's wife, Margaret Laird. It wasn't until some of the other lodgers became suspicious that we caught them. They had been selling the bodies to a surgeon named Robert Knox at his medical school but the evidence against them was circumstantial at best. We didn't have enough to hang them both so Sir William Rae, the Lord Advocate, offered Hare a bargain."

"Lord Advocate?" O'Malley frowned.

"Scotland's chief prosecutor," Gillespie offered. "Unlike Ireland, Scotland has its own judicial system that's independent of English law."

O'Malley nodded and sipped his Scotch while Gillespie continued.

"Hare confessed to the killings and implicated Burke as his partner," he said. "In return he walked free. But..."

Gillespie's voice trailed off as he lost himself in his thoughts and memories.

"But what?" O'Malley asked.

Gillespie looked blankly at the top of the staircase that led down to the cells.

"I could have had them both," he replied. The lieutenant waited patiently for his commander to continue his story, staring down into his whisky so not as too pressurise Gillespie.

"I was on patrol with my sergeant in the West Port, the part of Edinburgh where Burke and Hare lived," the captain explained. "The sergeant had stopped to speak to a pair of whores plying their trade when three figures started stumbling down the stairs and into the close where we were on patrol. At first I thought they were just drunk and I was going to reprimand them. But then I saw the two larger men on either side were man-handling the younger figure in between them. I recognised him – it was James Wilson, a simpleton known as 'Daft Jamie'. I approached them but they just carried on walking. I was about to stop them when the whores started playing up and the sergeant called me over to help him restrain one of them.

"But one of those men stared at me the whole time as they made their way down the close. He wouldn't take his eyes off me, nor me off him. His stare made me feel like I had a cold hard ball in the pit of my stomach, as if I was going to be sick. I later found out he was Hare – he probably thought I was on to him. But I wasn't and they sold Daft Jamie's body to Knox like all the rest."

"It sounds like you didn't have much of a choice," offered O'Malley. "If your sergeant gave you an order then you had to follow it. Besides, how were you to know what they were up to?"

"I should have trusted my gut," Gillespie replied.

"What about Hare's scar?" O'Malley asked.

"That was the day Burke was hanged," Gillespie said. "They had already released Hare. But he turned up to watch the hanging, waiting in the shadows. Afterwards, I followed him, ready to finish the job that the hangman had started. Only one of them paid the price that day when it should have been both of them.

"But he got away with just that scar on his face and I was left wounded on the street. My cut healed but the memory stayed with me. It's haunted me for thirty years, the murderer who got away."

"But he signed a deal," O'Malley protested.

"Aye, Hare had his freedom and we signed a deal with the devil."

Gillespie drained the last of his whisky and stood up.

"And now that devil is sitting in one of my cells again and I'll be damned if he's going to escape this time."

The two uniformed officers guarding Hare pushed the prisoner into the small room that Gillespie had set up for the interview. While other police forces questioned their suspects wherever the mood took them, Gillespie had trained his detectives in Boston to carry out their inquiries in an ordered and methodical manner.

The detectives were already waiting in the room when Hare arrived, O'Malley leaning against the far wall and Gillespie sitting on a chair in front of the table in the centre of the room, with his back towards the door. Before they had entered, O'Malley had grabbed Gillespie's arm.

"Hold it together in there, ok?" he said. Gillespie had simply nodded and slid into his seat.

Without being instructed, Hare took a seat opposite Gillespie at the table. The two uniformed policemen stood either side of the closed door. Gillespie swung round to address them.

"Wait outside," he told them.

The guards snatched a furtive glance at O'Malley, who nodded that it was ok to leave Gillespie with the prisoner. The captain waited for the two uniformed officers to leave before he began his questioning but, before he had chance to commence the interrogation, Hare spoke.

"I know you," he said. Though his Irish accent was all but gone after countless years away from his homeland, Gillespie still recognised the nasal tones of Hare's diction. "Gillespie," Hare said, before crinkling his brow in thought and adding, "Alexander Gillespie."

"And I know you, William Hare," Gillespie replied, his tone measured and even.

Hare shook his head. "That's not a name I've been called in a long time," he said. "That man you knew is dead. He died back in England when God washed away my sins."

The hairs on the back of Gillespie's Presbyterian neck bristled. "Washed away your sins?" he repeated. "God doesn't wash away the sin of murder Hare; once a killer, always a killer."

"'To him give all the prophets witness, that through his name whosoever believeth in him shall receive remission of sins'," Hare quoted.

"Acts, chapter ten, verse forty-three," Gillespie nodded. "How about we try something a wee bit more basic, Hare? How about Exodus, chapter twenty, verse thirteen? 'Thou shalt not kill'."

Hare fell silent and slumped back in his chair.

"You're not the only one who can quote Holy Scripture," Gillespie said, pushing back his seat and beginning to pace the room.

"I haven't killed for a very, very long time," Hare said, shaking his head.

"Is that right?" Gillespie asked. "So the fact that this city is struck by first a spate of grave robbing, next by three murders and then you turn up is simply just a coincidence?"

"We never robbed any graves," Hare protested. "We did so many wicked, wicked things but we never desecrated a grave."

"That was then, this is now. Who knows what depths you would plumb?"

Hare shook his head. "I'm a changed man, Gillespie," he said.

"Bullshit," Gillespie yelled, slamming his fist down on the table. "We found fibres from a hessian sack in the mouths of all three victims. Exactly the kind of sacks you'd have access to at the canal. It looks to me as if you've found a new Burke to complete your wee partnership and spark off a fresh murder spree."

"I don't know anything about those murders," Hare protested.

"Then where were you on Monday night when the first navvy disappeared?"

The question came from O'Malley who pushed himself forward off the wall where he had been positioned and leaned over the table, arms wide apart, staring hard at Hare.

The suspect turned to face his fellow Irishman for the first time during the interview.

"Like I told you before, I was at home," came the reply. "My wife, she'll be worried. I need to send word to her. I need to tell her I'm here."

"First you start giving us answers about these murders and then we'll see about what we'll do for you," O'Malley told him.

"Let's leave it there for tonight lieutenant," Gillespie declared brightly, a smile spreading across his face. "We'll pick this up in the morning."

A look of confusion passed over Hare's face, echoing the puzzlement O'Malley was feeling.

Gillespie pulled open the door to the interview room. "Throw him back in the cells overnight lads," he told the two uniformed officers waiting outside. As they led Hare back down to the cellar, O'Malley perched on the corner of the table.

"What was all that about?" he asked.

"Don't you see?" Gillespie retorted with a grin. "We've got him. We need to check out this wife he purports to have at home. I reckon there'll be no such woman. Ideally, we need a confession and I think a night in the cells is a good start to softening him up."

6

Gillespie sat listening to the ticking of the grandfather clock in the hall of the mansion house as he fidgeted with the starched collar of his shirt. He hated the high formal collar, much preferring his light-weight work shirts. The elation of the night before had been short-lived and the detective's black mood had descended once more. Too many questions about Hare's guilt were rearing their heads in Gillespie's mind.

"For the love of God, will you stop your squirming, Gillespie," Blackstone hissed. The police chief sat to Gillespie's right and the captain exchanged a glance with O'Malley, who sat to his left. Next to O'Malley, Fletcher looked up and down the hall at the sepia photographs of the Barron clan arranged neatly on the oak-panelled walls of the long corridor. The New Yorker seemed at ease with his starched collar and well-tailored coat, much more fashionable than the suits worn by the other three police officers.

Mayor Patrick Augustus Barron was the first mayor of Boston of Irish descent and had swept to victory during the election in December. As the civil war continued, it seemed to Gillespie that Boston's Irish immigrants were becoming further and further integrated into the city's political and social establishment.

At the end of the corridor, a door was opened and a sea of bright sunlight swept over the dark wooden panels. Gillespie could just about make out the silhouette of a butler standing in the doorway.

"Mayor Barron will see you now," the servant announced.

Blackstone led the way along the corridor, each man carrying his hat and his walking cane as he entered the bright sunroom. Gillespie almost had to shield his eyes from the strong afternoon sunlight that was flooding through the glass panels on the ceiling and walls of the solarium where Barron and his guests were taking their morning tea.

Gillespie took in the group sat around in a circle on the green-painted wrought iron furniture, sipping at their cups of tea as a pair of maids weaved in between them, refilling the china vessels from their long-necked tea pots. The dozen or so guests were made up of the city council's senior aldermen, several captains of industry and some of the more outspoken of Boston's clergy, along with their wives. Blackstone and Gillespie sat down in the two vacant seats and were promptly handed cups of tea by the maids, while O'Malley and Fletcher remained standing behind the senior officers, unsure where to loiter.

Blackstone helped himself to three sugar lumps using the tweezers proffered by one of the maids, quite at home among Boston's upper class, while Gillespie sipped at his tea and took in the faces of the assembled great and good of the city. The heat from the sun cascading in through the glass did little to ease Gillespie's discomfort but the temperature appeared not to bother the mayor's guests.

He recognised several of the industrialists and aldermen but his gaze came to rest on one of the women in the group. While most of the ladies were sat together on one part of the circle, talking amongst themselves, the woman in the high-necked black dress was seated between two men and was holding court. Her flame-red hair was tucked under the brim of her tight-fitting black bonnet and the strong sunlight picked out her bright green eyes. Gillespie looked away as she turned to face him, only too aware that she had caught him staring. The captain tried desperately to remember where he had seen the woman before.

The mayor finished his conversation with the minister sat to his left and turned to face the two policemen, who were seated to his right.

"Chief Blackstone, Captain Gillespie, so good of you to join us," Barron said. "I hope you have an update for me on these ghastly murders."

"Indeed we do, Mr Mayor," Blackstone began. "We have been working tirelessly on this case for many days now and last night we reached a breakthrough."

Gillespie sipped his tea, noting Blackstone's use of the pronoun "we", as if the chief himself had been patrolling the graveyards and pounding the cobbles in an effort to catch the killer or grave robbers or both.

"We have detained one of the Irish labourers working on the canal-building project," Blackstone continued. "A man known to Captain

Gillespie as a murderer with previous form for such heinous crimes."

Blackstone turned to his captain and gestured for Gillespie to tell the assembly about Hare. Gillespie shot the chief a dark look as he leaned forward and placed his tea cup and saucer down on the low wrought-iron table in front of him. He had pleaded with Blackstone not to make the details of Hare's arrest public until his detectives had been able to find proof that Hare had murdered the canal workers.

"Mr Mayor, our inquiries are still continuing but, as the chief said, we believe we have found the killer," explained Gillespie, choosing his words carefully. "He has no alibi for the night of the first killing and would have had contact with all three of the murdered workers."

"And the name of this villain?" the mayor asked.

"I'd rather not say for the moment, sir," Gillespie replied, provoking an even darker look in return from Blackstone.

"May I remind you of the office you are addressing, Captain?" the mayor responded. "Now spit it out man, who is this creature you have in custody?"

"He had been working on the canal-building project as a foreman, going by the name of Edward Laird. But his real name is William Hare and, along with his accomplice, William Burke, he murdered sixteen men, women and children in Edinburgh during 1828."

There was an audible intake of breath from the audience gathered in the mayor's sunroom, who had all ceased their own conversations when Barron had begun to question the police officers.

"But why did he not hang for such crimes?" the mayor asked.

"He struck a deal with the authorities to turn king's evidence against Burke and fled Edinburgh on the night that his accomplice went to the gallows," Gillespie answered, lifting the cup and saucer and taking another polite sip of tea.

"Wait, did you say Edward Laird?"

The question came from one of the industrialists, an unfeasibly tall man that Gillespie knew as Arthur Tate, who controlled much of the cotton imports into the city of Boston. Clumps of Tate's white hair were combed back at the sides of his head but the length of his face was exaggerated by the lack of covering on the dome of his skull, with wispy strands of stray hair still arching over his scalp where a full head of hair had once resided. He wore glasses with very thin wire rims and pushed them back up his nose as he leant forward in his chair to question Gillespie.

"Yes, that's correct, Mr Tate," the captain replied politely. Gillespie's path had crossed with Tate's on more than one occasion, through brawls and the death of workers in his factories to the demise of his business partner, Arnold Proctor, a death that Gillespie still regarded as unexplained. While he had tried his best to probe the circumstances surrounding the death of the man whose body washed up on the banks of the Charles River five years earlier, Boston's upper classes had closed ranks and Gillespie had found it hard to prise apart the puzzle.

"But that's preposterous," Tate protested. "Laird is one of my very hardest working men. He runs a tight ship. His team of navvies is one of the most productive that I have working for me."

Realisation dawned too late for Gillespie; Tate was among the consortium of industrialists building the latest canal in Boston, designed to bring cotton into the city more quickly and ease the shipment of finished goods out of Massachusetts. Gillespie silently cursed Blackstone again – briefing the mayor with so many of the so-called great and good of Boston in attendance had been a fatal error.

"I can't imagine a man such as Laird carrying out these crimes," Tate continued. "His nature is nothing but civil. And as for him being a mass murderer as you suggest – well, I'm sorry captain but I think this is an obvious case of mistaken identity."

"I can assure you, Mr Tate, that this is Hare," Gillespie replied, keeping his tone even despite the slur against his investigative abilities.

"No, no, no captain, I agree with Arthur, you are obviously sadly mistaken," chipped in one of the ministers. Gillespie turned to face Father Declan O'Conner, the Roman Catholic priest whose parish covered much of Boston's docks and industrial areas. "Edward Laird is one of my most devoted parishioners. He prays in church every morning before his work and never misses mass, he brings his wife and children every Sunday. He even works in one of my church's soup kitchens, dolling out gruel to the poor. No sir, you clearly have the wrong man."

Gillespie was taking mental note of O'Conner's assertion about Hare's family – perhaps not a hastily constructed alibi after all – just as Lieutenant Fletcher, who had been waiting quietly with O'Malley near the door, took a step forward to the edge of the circle of chairs. "Gentleman, and ladies, as Captain Gillespie has explained, our inquiries are continuing and you can rest assured that the Boston police force will do everything in its power to keep your streets safe and the war effort going," said the policeman from New York.

Fletcher's honeyed and educated tones washed over the audience, soothing their concerns and inviting a chorus of nodding heads and murmurs of approval from Boston's upper classes. Gillespie knew that Fletcher had stepped out of line by intervening on the captain's behalf but he could see Blackstone nodding along with the rest of the assembly, pleased that one of his officers had stepped in to reassure the leaders of the community.

While Gillespie knew that Blackstone had been instrumental in transferring Fletcher from New York to Boston, it was not until he was squirming in the stifling heat of the solarium that he realised the chief had also been looking to groom someone to replace the captain.

"I may have only served in this fair city for a few months but you can take it from me that the Inspector here is one of the finest officers that I've ever had the pleasure of serving with," Fletcher added, patting the seated Gillespie on the shoulder. The captain did his best not to throw the remainder of his tea over the junior officer.

"Inspector?" the mayor's wife asked. While her husband was of Irish descent, Clara Burton-Barron was descended from "good Puritan stock" and was an integral member of what Gillespie often referred to derogatorily as the "Boston blue bloods", the city's almost aristocratic upper class. It was her family's money that had bank-rolled Barron's election campaign the preceding December.

"I served in the police force in Great Britain before I moved to the United States," Gillespie offered by way of explanation. "I brought an old title with me."

"Oh, I see, I thought I recognised your strange accent," Clara beamed. "You're Irish, aren't you?"

"Scottish," Gillespie corrected. Silence fell on the room. The mayor's wife was not used to be scolded and certainly not by members of the working class.

"Ah, so that's why you're convinced that Edward Laird is this Hare character," nodded O'Connor. "I see that time has maybe played tricks on your mind, leading to this case of mistaken identity," the priest added, tapping his temple.

"With due respect, Father, I don't think that's the case," said Gillespie calmly. "When you have stared into the eyes of a killer, it's not something you can forget."

"Nonsense," scoffed Tate. "You must have come into contact with dozens of killers in your time, Captain. What makes this one so different?"

"Yes, Captain, tell us what makes you think Laird is this Hare?" O'Conner chipped in.

"Tell us about Hare," the mayor's wife added, not wanting to be undone.

"I have pursued killers on both sides of the Atlantic," Gillespie began, hushing the chatter that had broken out between members of the audience. "I've chased down men who have slit the throats of their lovers, smugglers who have shot at me to protect their stolen whiskey or coffee or tobacco and drunken dockers who shot at their comrades during a brawl.

"I have caught scum who have killed two, three or even four gentlemen in their pursuit of riches. But only once have I had the misfortune to face a foe as evil as William Hare," Gillespie continued, deciding that if he was in for a penny then he was in for a pound. The cat was out of the bag thanks to Blackstone and so if the Boston blue bloods wanted gossip with which to shock their friends over morning coffee then he would be only too happy to supply it.

"Burke and Hare didn't kill out of anger or to protect their wives or through some kind of drunken excess – they killed for money," Gillespie said, his voice low.

"They intoxicated their victims at the lodging house that Hare and his wife ran in Edinburgh's West Port and then smothered the poor souls.

"One pushed a pillow down over their faces while the other squeezed the life out of their chests so they wouldn't struggle free. Imagine that; being dazed and confused and gasping for air as these two men hold you down.

"But these weren't random killings. Burke and Hare sold the bodies to Doctor Robert Knox at Edinburgh's medical college for dissection. Men and women, old or young, workers or jobless, it made no difference to them. They even killed an eighteen-year-old simpleton for Christ's sake."

Gillespie realised the volume of his voice had been rising as he delivered his shocking diatribe until he was shouting the final words at his silent audience.

The uncomfortable silence was broken by a knock at the oak-panelled door that led from the corridor of the main house into the solarium. A black-suited butler entered and crossed the room to deliver a telegram to the mayor, having seated the folded piece of paper on a silver platter. Gillespie absentmindedly wondered if he really had swapped Edinburgh for the New World after all, with the United States having adopted so many of Great Britain's customs.

The mayor nodded to the butler and took the telegram from the outstretched platter, perching his reading glasses on the end of his nose before unfolding the paper and peering at the short lines of printed text. His eyebrows arched before he folded the paper in half again and passed it to Blackstone.

"I think it may be time for you gentlemen to take your leave of us," the mayor observed.

Blackstone rose to his feet as he read the note and snatched up his bowler hat from the wrought-iron table.

"Indeed I think it is, Mr Mayor," the police chief replied. "If you will excuse us?"

Blackstone passed the telegram to Gillespie as he led his trio of officers from the room and down the long hallway. As he left, Gillespie could feel the green-eyed stare of the woman with red hair burrowing into the back of his head, just as it had done all the way through the briefing.

He read the telegram as they walked down the corridor to the front portico and the waiting carriage outside on the gravel strewn drive.

"Did you put on that little show in there to shock those poor people or just to embarrass me?" Blackstone yelled at Gillespie as the four men crossed the drive and climbed up into the back of the black carriage.

"Any embarrassment was just a bonus sir," Gillespie muttered under his breath as he re-read the note before passing it to O'Malley.

"To Chief Blackstone. Stop," the telegram read in the police operator's clipped tone. "Two more bodies found. Stop. Both dock workers. Stop. Both disappeared last night. Stop. Hare still in custody. Stop. Request further instructions. Stop."

7

As the carriage turned onto School Street, Gillespie caught a waft of the acrid smoke that was billowing out of the windows of both the temporary detectives' offices halfway down the street and one of the houses next door. The captain cursed under his breath as the carriage pulled up behind where three of the Boston fire department's new steam-powered engines clogged the road. Gillespie weaved his way between the fire appliances at a run, closely followed by O'Malley and Fletcher. The carriage had dropped off Blackstone at the Old State House, pressed into service once more as the city hall, before continuing on to School Street.

"What happened?" yelled Gillespie over the sound of the steam engines starting up, ready to pump water through the leather hoses and into his burning offices.

"Fire, sir," replied Sergeant John MacLeod, one of the uniformed officers who had been assigned to Gillespie's squad. "Looks like it started in that house next door," added the sergeant, pointing to the building next to the police office. Over MacLeod's shoulder, Gillespie could see teams of firemen working the manual hand pumps on two of the older horse-drawn fire engines, preparing to tackle the blaze next door, where flames were licking the window frames.

"First thing we knew about it was when the smoke started filling the office," MacLeod continued.

"Did you get everyone out?" Gillespie asked, his gaze flitting backwards and forwards between the office and the horde of firemen preparing to tackle the blaze.

"All the day watch are accounted for, sir," replied MacLeod.

"What about Hare?" Gillespie demanded. The sergeant looked blank.

"The prisoner in the cells. The one called Laird," Gillespie offered.

"Still down there, sir," MacLeod replied. "Him and two drunks we picked up for brawling down at the docks."

Gillespie turned away from the sergeant and addressed his men, who had congregated around their captain.

"Hare's still inside, along with two other prisoners," Gillespie told them. "We need to get them out. O'Malley, Fletcher, you're with me."

Before either of his lieutenants could protest, Gillespie ran the few paces across the street and barged open the main office door with his shoulder. The sight that greeted him inside was far less chaotic than the scene out on the street. Although the main body of the office was filled with black smoke, the flames from the fire next door had not yet penetrated through the walls, leaving the furniture and fittings in the detectives' room untouched.

With O'Malley and Fletcher following close behind him, Gillespie led the way across the office to the stairwell, hunched over in a half-run to avoid the smoke billowing above their heads. He snatched the keys to the cells from a peg at the top of the stairs before leading his officers down into the cellar.

The smoke had not yet penetrated the basement of the building and so the three policemen were able to quickly locate the cells in which the prisoners were being held. Gillespie tossed the keys to O'Malley and Fletcher, who quickly unlocked the doors and began leading their detainees up the stairs. The captain tightened his grip around the key that sat in his hand and looked down the corridor at the door to Hare's cell.

O'Malley turned around and watched Gillespie for a moment.

"Quickly, Inspector," he called, before turning and pushing his prisoner up the stairs.

Gillespie stood in front of the door to Hare's cell and sighed deeply. Would it be so bad to leave him here? To let the fire consume his evil? But then the doubts at the back of his mind about Hare's guilt jolted the policeman back to the present and he turned the key in the lock.

Hare was still sitting on the bench in the corner of the room but Gillespie guessed he must have heard the commotion further down the corridor as his head was tilted up expectantly as Gillespie threw open the door.

"On your feet," Gillespie commanded as he retrieved a length of rope from the pocket of his greatcoat.

"Turn around," Gillespie instructed Hare before binding his wrists behind his back.

"There's really no need for this," Hare said as Gillespie pulled the knot tight.

"I'll be the judge of that," Gillespie replied, drawing his Colt 1860 army model from the holster around his waist and levelling the revolver at Hare. "Now move it. The building's on fire and we've only got minutes before the gas lighting goes up."

Hare didn't need to be told twice; he led the way out of the cell and along the corridor towards the staircase. As they reached the top of the stairs, Gillespie felt Hare recoil and step back as the wooden top of the banister exploded and sprayed him with splinters. It took Gillespie's mind a split-second to register that they were being shot at before a second bullet embedded itself in the doorframe at the top of the stairs.

"Get down," Gillespie yelled above the noise from the creaking building as the fire started to take hold. He pushed Hare to the ground behind the nearest desk and pulled at the far legs, bringing the desk crashing down as a shield. A further two bullets struck the top of the desk, showering the pair in splinters before Gillespie poked his head above the defences to locate their assailant. He managed to crack off a shot at the tall figure in the long coat who was running towards the far end of the office before losing sight of him in the smoke.

"Come on," he shouted to Hare as he grabbed the man's arm and led him in pursuit. Gillespie was halfway across the office when there was a loud hissing sound followed by a thunderous explosion as the gaslight reservoirs embedded in the walls caught fire, showering debris across the room. The initial explosion threw both men to floor, before bringing parts of the ceiling down into the office. One of the beams supporting the floor above came crashing down on Gillespie, pinning him across the back. Wedged between the floor and beam, Gillespie squirmed to try and free himself from the fallen timber. At the edge of his vision, he thought he saw the gunman disappearing into the house next door through a gap in the collapsing wall.

Despite the smoke and increasing heat, Gillespie saw a shadow pass in front of his vision.

"Untie me," Hare said.

"What?" Gillespie answered.

"I can help you, but only if you untie this rope," Hare replied, crouching down in front of the immobile policeman and pushing out his hands. Gillespie weighed his options – Hare could have saved himself without being untied. The captain grabbed at the ropes and tugged the knot open.

His hands free, Hare grabbed the end of the timber that pinned Gillespie to the floor and gave a great heave. He managed to raise the wooden beam only a few inches before dropping it. Again he yanked at the strut but again it dropped back to the floor. Hare paused for a moment and, in amongst all the smoke, Gillespie could have sworn he saw Hare closing his eyes in prayer. Then, with an almighty heave that demonstrated unexpected strength for a man of his advancing years, Hare pulled the beam clear of Gillespie's body and threw it several feet across the burning office, before it came crashing down on one of the burning desks.

Gillespie looked up at his rescuer and, for a brief moment, he was back in the rain-soaked close on the dark Edinburgh night after Burke hanged and Hare was standing over him again with his own blade.

But then Hare bent down and did something that Gillespie never expected to see: he smiled. Gillespie grabbed Hare's outstretched hand and dragged himself to his feet. The captain stumbled unsteadily and so Hare slipped his arm under Gillespie's shoulder and led him towards the door.

The cold night's air came as a relief to Gillespie as he sucked in lungs-full of fresh oxygen while lying crumpled on the hard cobbles of the street. O'Malley and Fletcher rushed to his side but neither made an effort to restrain Hare, who was bent double next to the captain, heaving gasps of air into his own lungs to fight the effects of the smoke.

"Thank God you're ok, Inspector," O'Malley said, bending down and helping Gillespie to his feet. Gillespie's mind was reeling from what had just happened: the fire, the gunman in the office and collapsing ceiling all fought for space in his head. But the overpowering thought that clouded his judgement was that he was still alive – thanks to Hare.

His revere was short-lived as, with a mighty crash, one of the windows from the house next door exploded, showering the cobbled street and the nearby firemen in shards of glass. Through the gaping hole, the tall figure in the long black coat emerged from the burning building.

"Look, there," shouted Hare as the gunman pushed past two of the firemen, throwing a third to the ground with a well-timed roundhouse punch.

The gunman stood and looked at the group of police officers for a moment, as if weighing up the odds against him, before taking off at a sprint away from them down School Street.

Without warning, Hare set off after the gunman, almost matching his fast pace.

"No!" screamed Gillespie, still gasping for breath. "Fletcher, get after them!"

The New Yorker threw off his overcoat and legged it down the street after the two escapees. The gunman began by running straight and true down the centre of the road but his route was blocked by the older hand-pump fire engines and a crowd of firemen. He feigned left to avoid one and then broke right across to the other side of the street, before disappearing between the stone gateposts of the building site where the new city hall was being constructed.

The first two levels of the four-storey central structure had already been completed and the wings were slowly being added at either side. At night, the building site was deserted making it easier for Fletcher to follow the sound of first the gunman and then Hare racing up the front steps and between the columns on either side of the empty doorway. He followed them up the stairs and into the main foyer, just in time to see the pair racing one after the other up the staircase to the first floor.

O'Malley and Gillespie arrived outside the partially-built city hall with their revolvers already drawn. A crowd of uniformed officers, detectives and firemen crowded around them but O'Malley signalled for them to keep their distance and remain by the gateposts. Above them, Gillespie saw a dark shape moving between the columns on the first floor, just behind a line of balustrades above which glass-panelled windows would be placed. He could hear muffled shouting and then, from the gaping hole in the front of the first floor, a figure came hurtling through the air. The body seemed to hang for a moment in the open air before coming crashing down onto the paved entrance to the building, smacking into the hard slabs face first.

O'Malley rushed forward and gingerly turned the man over to reveal the crushed face of the gunman who had shot at Gillespie inside the burning detectives' office. Gillespie looked up to the first floor of the building and saw Fletcher leaning over the side, his revolver drawn but not smoking. Beside him, Gillespie saw Hare leaning on the edge of the balustrade staring down at him. For the second time that night, Gillespie thought he saw Hare close his eyes in prayer.

8

The cold morning light did little to relieve the grim scene in which Gillespie found himself standing the next morning. Stood at the centre of his former temporary office, the captain was surrounded by the smouldering remains of his murder and grave robbing inquiries. Though he could not yet make the connection, Gillespie's instinct told him that the two cases were linked. The presence of an arsonist and gunman the night before also told him that he was getting close to unravelling the mystery behind the series of deaths and finding the culprit.

The captain poked at the remains of where his desk once stood with the end of his walking cane and shuffled his feet around in the ashes.

Weaving his way between the few remaining firemen who were beating out the final flames in some smouldering piles of debris, O'Malley came to stand beside Gillespie. Although Fletcher and the other detectives had been sent home in the early hours of the morning, the Irish lieutenant had stayed with Gillespie throughout the night as they sifted through the remains of the office and questioned the uniformed officers who had been on duty when the fire broke out.

"You should get some sleep," O'Malley offered as he rubbed his hands together and blew on them, the cold morning air turning his breath to steam.

"No time," Gillespie muttered. "Whoever was behind these murders knew that we were getting close otherwise they wouldn't have done all this," he added, waving his cane around the scene of destruction.

"But the only lead we have so far is Hare and we know he was locked in one of our cells when the latest two deaths occurred," O'Malley said. "It just doesn't make any sense."

"I know that Hare is still the key to this," Gillespie said. "You can't have a series of murders like this and then a known felon turning up at random."

"That known felon saved your life last night."

"I know, I know," Gillespie sighed. "What about the gunman?"

"Fletcher maintains he threw himself off the building. He got to the top of the stairs and saw Hare closing in on the man but then he flung himself off rather than be caught."

Gillespie stared at the ground for a few moments.

"He might be a pain in the arse but Fletcher's no liar," O'Malley added. "If he says Hare had nothing to do with it then I'm inclined to believe him."

"Like you said, it just doesn't make any sense," Gillespie protested. "If Hare isn't involved in these murders then why send someone to try to burn down the office and kill him? Or when the assassin fails, why does Hare chase after him unless he knows that gunman can finger him for the murders?"

"I don't know," O'Malley sighed.

The two men stood in silence for a few minutes while Gillespie proceeded to poke and prod more of the ashes, in the vain hope of recovering some of his files.

"Anything else?" he asked eventually.

"One more thing," O'Malley said, signalling for the captain to follow him. "They found the two uniformed officers who were missing after the fire."

"I thought they'd accounted for everyone last night?"

"It was chaos, it's no wonder more men didn't go missing."

"Did they die in the fire?"

O'Malley shook his head. "Not exactly," he replied.

The pair walked across to MacLeod, the old uniformed sergeant who had not gone home either overnight. The sergeant was standing over two blankets, underneath which Gillespie assumed lay the bodies of the dead officers.

"They were two of my best nightwatchmen," MacLeod said, shaking his head. Boston's night- and day-watches had been brought together nearly a decade earlier to form the current police department, modelled on Sir Robert Peel's metropolitan police in London, but Gillespie knew that old names and habits died hard among men like MacLeod.

"How did they die?" Gillespie asked.

With a shaking hand, MacLeod leaned over and pulled back the blanket from the first body.

"Clarins' body is so badly burned that it's hard to tell how he died," the sergeant offered, pointing at the charred skin and scorched clothing that covered the first dead officer. MacLeod threw back the sheet and bent over to pull back the cover from the second body.

"But Porter was found buried face-down under some rubble over there," MacLeod indicated with a vague wave of his hand. Gillespie absentmindedly thought that he could have shared Porter's fate if it hadn't been for Hare's intervention.

Gillespie looked down at the face of the young policeman lying before him. At first the amount of soot covering the body made it hard to distinguish what O'Malley had wanted him to see. But then his eyes fell on the man's face.

Gillespie and O'Malley bent down in unison and Gillespie patted his pockets looking for his black leather gloves.

"Sergeant, pass me your gloves please," Gillespie commanded after being unable to find his own.

MacLeod fished his white dress gloves out of his pocket and passed them to the detective. Slipping the gloves on, Gillespie leaned forward and began examining the wound on Porter's face. The mangled mess of pink flesh and congealed red blood didn't look like an impact mark from a fall. Gillespie poked his fingers into the wound and began slowly fishing his fingers around in a circular motion, distorting what was left of Porter's face in the process.

A small crowd of police officers had gathered around the bodies now, watching Gillespie at work.

"Sweet Jesus man, have you got no respect for the dead?" MacLeod muttered as Gillespie continued to examine the wound. Suddenly, the captain leaned back on his haunches and held a piece of metal up to the light.

"A bullet?" O'Malley asked.

"Aye," nodded Gillespie. "This man didn't die in the fire, he was murdered."

Gillespie leaned forward again and pulled the buttons of Porter's uniform open to reveal his chest. Two more gunshot entry wounds had peppered the right side of his chest and Gillespie set about removing what was left of the bullets, which had been flattened on impact. He cleaned the blood and gore from the bullets on the dead man's uniform and handed them to O'Malley.

"Hang on to these for now," he instructed. "I want Professor Cartwright to examine them along with these two bodies."

He handed the gloves back to MacLeod, who gaped at him open mouthed.

"What next?" O'Malley asked as he rose back up to his feet with Gillespie and helped the captain to throw the blanket back over the corpse.

"City Hall," Gillespie replied. "We need to brief Blackstone and work out what our next move is."

Despite Blackstone's presence in the Old State House being only a temporary measure as he, along with the rest of the city's administrative hierarchy, waited for the new city hall to be completed on School Street, the police chief had still managed to make himself seem at home behind the huge mahogany desk in his dimly-lit office.

While the new City Hall – being built in the French second empire style from pale granite blocks – had been designed to be open and spacious, the eighteenth-century redbrick Old State House at the junction of Washington and State streets was cramped. O'Malley and Gillespie found Fletcher already waiting for them in Blackstone's office and the three officers took seats on the opposite side of the desk from their chief.

Blackstone dispensed with any preamble. "For the love of Christ Gillespie, the bloody office is burned down and two of our men are dead," he scalded his junior officer, taking a healthy swig of whisky from a tumbler of Scotch on his desk. Gillespie noted that, despite the early hour, Fletcher also had a half-drunk glass of whisky in his hand, while neither he nor O'Malley had been offered a drink from the decanter sat on a sideboard next to the desk.

"I'm well aware of those facts, sir," Gillespie replied, trying not to snap at the chief. "I think this means we're getting close to whoever is behind these murders. Last night someone tried to kill Hare, which I believe means he's at the heart of this matter."

"Hare!" Blackstone barked. "Don't talk to me about your theories. I had telegrams from Tate and that priest O'Connor yesterday evening when we were back from the mayor's place. And then a telegram from Barron himself this morning urging me to release the man."

"We can't do that yet, sir," O'Malley interjected. "He's our only lead."

"Yes, he's all you've got after you let that arsonist escape last night," Blackstone bellowed.

"Sir, if I may," Fletcher began, cradling the Scotch in his hands. "I believe that was my fault, Chief. If only I'd been on to him more quickly then perhaps he wouldn't have thrown himself from the construction site."

"Nonsense, Fletcher, I'm sure you did your best," said Blackstone, dismissing the lieutenant's protestations with a wave of his hand. "From what I hear, it was down to Captain Gillespie to detain the suspect in the office and he let him get away."

"Now wait a minute," protested O'Malley, weighing into the argument. While the Irishman may have only been a lieutenant, he wasn't beyond speaking his mind when the mood took him.

Gillespie sat quietly and listened as O'Malley argued with Blackstone and Fletcher. His faithful lieutenant would not let the chief walk all over the captain but Gillespie knew that Blackstone's hands were tied when it came to releasing Hare, especially with pressure bearing down on him from the mayor. And that was when a plan began to formulate in Gillespie's mind.

"Perhaps we can satisfy the mayor but still continue this line of inquiry," Gillespie mused. The three other police officers turned to face him.

"What now?" asked Blackstone, his tone more measured.

"Hare is a foreman on Tate's canal-building project," Gillespie began. "He has access to the workers. But if he isn't killing them, as the latest set of murders would suggest, then maybe he's our way of catching the real killer."

O'Malley began nodding enthusiastically. "Use him as bait you mean?"

"Yes, exactly," Gillespie replied. "Burke and Hare killed to order. They murdered their lodgers and sold their bodies to the medical school for cash. Maybe we can use Hare to find out who is killing these dock workers."

"But wait, you said you've already checked out the medical school and they can account for the origin of all their corpses," Blackstone snapped.

"Yes sir, but I don't think the killer is trying to sell these corpses to the medical school," Gillespie explained. "All of the bodies are dumped not long after the men go missing. I don't know who wants these men dead but if they're after bodies then maybe we can set Hare up as a supplier."

"It's worth a try," agreed Fletcher, weighing in on Gillespie's side. The intervention of the New York officer seemed to be enough to convince Blackstone.

"Alright Gillespie, but you'll need to get Tate to agree to this scheme," he cautioned. "And Hare too for that matter. As far as we're concerned, he's a free man now, you've got nothing to hold him on."

Blackstone drained the last of his Scotch and waved his hand in dismissal, indicating he wanted the detectives to clear out of his office.

9

Gillespie gripped both sides of the tin bath and lowered his aching body into the warm water. He had heated the bath as best he could with the large cast-iron kettle from the stove but he would still have liked the water to have been hotter. In his mind, he needed the hotter water to wash away not just the dirt and grime of the day but also the doubts about Hare that were surfacing in his mind.

Gillespie sighed deeply as he leaned back and rested his head against the edge, letting the water slosh around his shoulders and up the back of his neck, caressing away the tension in his upper body.

The captain reached across to the stool he had placed beside the bath and plucked the bar of Robertson's soap from where it lay next to his shaving razor. He tore at the cream-coloured wax paper, unwrapping the bar of translucent green soap before tossing away the packaging. Rubbing the soap between his hands, he slowly built up a lather and raised his hands towards his nose so that he could sniff the familiar aroma, a smell that reminded him of childhood baths in his family's cramped tenement flat in Edinburgh.

Joining the police had seemed the perfect use of his talents: his teacher at the primary school at the top of Edinburgh's Royal Mile had always described the young Alexander Gillespie as "sharp", a keen young mind destined for the city's university and a career in medicine or as an advocate at the bar. But long before Gillespie first stepped into a classroom, the journey to university and the professions had already been closed off to him. With his soldier father lying dead on the battlefield at Waterloo and his widowed mother left with six children, Gillespie's association with the classroom and its rigid form of learning was brief. He left at thirteen and was taken on by a local coal merchant, heaving hessian sacks of fuel around the city's Old Town until he was sixteen and old enough to enlist in the police force.

But an education with the coal carriers in the wynds and closes of the Old Town had taught him more about people and their lives than any number of hours inside a school classroom or a university lecture theatre could ever have done. Living and working with the poorest people of Edinburgh had sharpened his instincts to the same level of refinement as his naturally-inquiring mind.

Though Gillespie could barely remember his father, who had died when he was only three years old, the policeman felt that the old soldier with the handlebar moustache – revered in a single sepia photograph that sat enshrined above his mother's fireplace – would have been proud of his son's chosen career. While his father's musket barrel fell silent while trying to protect his homeland from a threatened French invasion, Gillespie had protected first the streets of Edinburgh and then of his adopted home in Boston from the threat of crime.

And it was at the beginning of that fight against crime that Gillespie's path had first crossed with Hare. The inspector sat up in the bath and began working the lather of soap across his chest and arms as his mind returned to the subject of the serial killer in his custody. He winced as he passed the bar of soap across his shoulders and upper arms, the muscles built up through three years of lugging coal nearly four decades earlier were aching worse than ever after the day's ordeal. His hands came away black with soot as he worked the soap into nape of his neck and up into his hair, removing the marks that the smoke from the fire had left across his body. Even though confusion over Hare's actions raged through his mind, an unexpected thought suddenly grabbed hold of Gillespie's consciousness. His memory rolled back to the hours before the fire and the meeting at the mayor's house – and the flame-red hair of the woman whose stare had bored into Gillespie. He pictured her now, her long hair cascading down over the pale skin of her exposed neck and shoulders and his imagination conjured up an image of her there in his apartment, standing naked beside the bath. In his mind he watched as she dipped a toe into the tub to test the water before sliding first one slender leg and then the other into the opposite end of the bath from him. Goosebumps spread across her naked flesh as she eased herself down into the water with him, her legs curling around his waist to catch him in a pincer movement, bringing her face close enough to him to see the freckles spread across her nose and cheeks. He watched her gasp as the water enveloped first her waist and then her chest as she sank lowered into the bath, the water covering the rounded swell of her pale breasts and covering the pink of her nipples. Gillespie felt himself harden at the thought but, as quickly as it came, the image was gone, to be replaced by the haunting memory of Hare's face staring down at him in the blazing detectives' office.

While Gillespie knew only too well about Hare's past crimes, he also knew that, without the murderer's help, he would have died that night. The investigator in Gillespie tried to square Hare's past with the events of the evening: the Irishman's hatred for human life turning into compassion for his fallen captor; his thirst of murder turning into a hunger to preserve life.

Gillespie sighed deeply again before plunging his head backwards and down into the water, washing the soap out of his hair. He paused for a moment below the surface, allowing the gurgling sound of the water to flood his hearing in a vain attempt to wash his mind clean. He raised himself back up above the waterline and then sank back down into the now murky bathwater so that his neck and shoulders were covered again.

Sitting in the cooling water, his mind was no clearer about what to make of Hare's actions. Could a leopard really change its spots? He asked himself the question again and again but, when the answer wasn't forthcoming and the water had cooled to the point of being tepid, Gillespie shook the thoughts from his head and raised himself out of the bath, dripping across the wooden floorboards of his apartment to grab a towel from where it hung next to the stove. After patting himself dry with the coarse towel, Gillespie sat naked on the stool, the gaslight turned down low as he liked it, the darkness creeping from the corners of the room, leaving just the red glow of the stove to illuminate his thoughts. After nearly an hour of sitting alone, Gillespie tossed the towel on to the floor and strode across to his wardrobe, dressing quickly before heading for the door. Having puzzled over the question of whether or not Hare could have changed enough that he could now be trusted, Gillespie now knew where he would find the answer.

LONDON, 1830

The summer's sun beat down on the workers as they filed out of the building site and onto the cobbled streets of London's East End, laughing and joking after a day's hard graft. Leaning against a wall opposite the gates to the building site, William Hare contemplated the structures standing all around him. Whereas Edinburgh was hewn from yellow and grey sandstone, London seemed to be etched out in red bricks, with the baked orange colour extending across the city's buildings for as far as the eye could see.

"So what's the plan, Hare?" asked Burke, as he leant against the wall next to his former partner in crime.

Hare sighed and turned away from where the apparition stood, trying to blot out Burke's words, just as he had been doing for the past eighteen long months.

Hare's eyes fell back to the stream of workers flowing out of the gates until he picked out the character for who he'd been waiting. Telling jokes at the centre of a line of bricklayers walked his brother, Thomas.

"Tommy," he yelled across the throng of men, several of who turned to stare at the Irishman.

"So who's this dumb mug then?" asked Burke, adjusting his cap and creasing down his black mourning clothes.

"Can it really be?" shouted back Thomas as weaved his way through the crowd. "As I live and breathe, if it's not my brother William."

A rare smile spread across Hare's face as he held his arms open and his brother came crashing into him, grabbing his shoulders and gripping him as the siblings shared a hug.

"How are you brother?" Hare asked as Thomas pulled away.

"Surviving," Thomas grinned. "And what about you William?"

Thomas cast his eyes up and down his younger brother, the pair only separated by ten months in age and even less in looks. Both of a similar build and height and with the same colourings and complexion, the only distinct difference in their appearance was their eyes, with only Hare sporting the differently-coloured irises. During their childhood, the pair had often been mistaken for twins and had been as thick as thieves, driving their mother wild when they stirred up mischief among her eight children.

"God William, you look like hell," Thomas exclaimed as he took in Hare's soiled clothes and unshaven face. "Are you on the run or something?"

"You could say that," Hare replied flatly. "You're a hard man to find Thomas. I've been in London a week, asking round every Irishman I could find if they knew Thomas Hare. And here you are now. I never thought I'd see you working for a living."

"Aye, an honest day's graft," Thomas chuckled. "You should try it sometime."

"What you doing here?"

"A brickie," Thomas replied. "If you're looking for work, then maybe I can help you out."

"That would be grand, Tommy," Hare nodded.

"But how on earth did you get into such a state?"

"That's a long story."

"Aye, a long story indeed," Burke smirked from his position against the wall.

"Well, long stories always go down better with a pint or two of stout at The Harp – what do you say, guys?" asked Thomas, turning to his mates who had gathered around the pair. "This here's my wee brother, William, and never before has a fellow Irishman been in more need of a brew."

"Aye," the other bricklayers chorused as Thomas threw his arm around Hare's shoulders and led him through the East End to their favourite pub as Burke trailed behind them, whistling an Irish melody as they walked.

Pint after pint of black Irish stout flowed in The Harp as Thomas regaled his friends with tales of his escapades with William back in Ireland, provoking much laughter and merriment as the sun sank slowly behind the red-brick buildings of the East End. As the party dispersed to each corner of the pub or out into the street, Thomas was left alone at the bar with Hare and the pair drew their stools closer together. Thomas's face turned solemn.

"What the fuck are you doing here?" he hissed at his brother.

Hare was taken aback by the sudden loss of warmth from his brother's voice. "How do you mean?" he asked slowly.

"Don't play games with me William, I may be dumb but I'm not stupid. I can read you know and I read all about those goings on in Edinburgh."

Hare's shoulders sagged as he realised that his brother knew all about his past crimes.

"Maybe he's not as thick as he looks then," mused Burke from the barstool on the other side of Hare. "At least not as thick as you anyway, Hare."

"Murdering women and children William, for Christ's sake, have you no shame?" Thomas hissed in a hushed whisper, anxious to keep his voice low enough to avoid the prying ears of the other drinkers in the tavern. "Our father would be turning in his grave if he knew what you'd done."

Hare paused for a moment and fixed Thomas with a hard stare.

"If we'd not killed him together," Hare replied pointedly.

Thomas glared at him and then a wicked smile slowly spread across his face as he raised his stout to his lips once more.

"The old man had it coming to him," Thomas nodded after draining his drink and wiping the thick white foam from his lips. "If we hadn't done it then I dare say dear old mother would have done the job for us. Beating her and beating us kids was no way for a grown man to act."

The pair fell into a silent revere, which Thomas eventually broke with more questions.

"Why'd you do it?"

"Money," Hare replied simply.

"Always the same," Thomas nodded.

"What about you?"

Thomas shook his head. "That's all behind me now. Like you said so yourself, I've got myself an honest job. And me a brickie too," he shook his head, as if he was trying to convince himself.

"What about Margaret and that bairn of your's?" Thomas asked.

A shadow passed across Hare's face.

"Aye Hare, what indeed?" Burke snarled. "Go on Hare, tell him. Tell him how you abandoned your wife."

"I didn't abandon them," Hare yelled, staggering up from his seat and knocking over the stool. He cursed himself for rising to Burke's baiting yet again.

"All right, all right, nobody said you did, okay," Thomas cooed, picking up Hare's stool for him. "Now sit yourself back down and stop your shouting."

Hare sagged back down onto his barstool. "We ran from Edinburgh after Burke was hanged," he began.

Thomas nodded his head and signalled for two more pints from the barman.

"We ended up in Dumfries, near the English border. We took lodgings but it was still too close to Edinburgh and some of the locals worked out who we were and what I'd done.

"So I took them home to Ulster with me," Hare sighed. "Back home, back to Newry."

"Ah, so you went back to the old shit hole then," Thomas nodded.

"But that didn't work either," Hare shook his head. "They knew who I was and they knew what I done. I left Margaret and young William there. No one knew her there and she can start again. As for me, the boys from the village chased me off into the woods with their clubs and bats and made to strike me down.

"But I escaped. And came looking for you," he added, draining the end of his own stout and starting on the next.

"Aye, and a smart move that was too," Thomas laughed.

"We'll soon see about that," muttered Burke.

Later, as they staggered arm in arm down the cobbled streets, singing old songs of their homeland, Hare felt a pang of hope for his future, reunited with his brother once more. But the sight of Megan, Thomas's wife, as they threw open the door to their single room in an East End tenement and Thomas's reaction to her scolding plunged Hare back into the past and a pit of despair.

"Drunk again," Megan cried in her Cockney brogue as Thomas slammed the door behind him. "I should've known it. And who's this character you're bringing into my home?"

Hare wasn't prepared for the force of the blow that Thomas landed across Megan's face, sending her staggering backwards into the small wooden table at the centre of the room. The flame from the candle on the table flickered as she bumped into the furniture, casting an eerie shadow across the whole of the room.

"I've told you before, don't you dare talk to me like that woman," Thomas yelled at the top of his lungs. "I slave away all day long and this is the only thanks I get when I come home."

"Keep the noise down," came a cry from the room upstairs, accompanied by a loud banging on the ceiling.

"Slaving away?" Megan mocked as she dabbed at the stream of blood trailing from her split lip. "I should be so lucky. Any money you make you drink away at The Harp."

Thomas slapped his wife again, this time sending her to the floor before he bent down and unleashed a series of hammer blows to her outstretched arms as she desperately tried to protect her head and face.

Even through his drunken haze, Hare surprised himself by leaping to Megan's defence. He launched himself at his brother, dragging his dead weight off the top of his wife and landing him a hard punch square to his jaw before Thomas realised what was going on.

"That's enough, Tommy," Hare yelled. "Leave the poor bitch alone."

Burke stood with his back to the closed door slowly clapping, the weak light from the candle making his pale skin look even more deathly cold.

"Bravo, bravo," Burke applauded. "Well, I didn't think you had it in you, Hare. If you'd asked me before, I would have put money on you laying into poor Megan here as well."

Hare glared at the spectre before turning back to Thomas, who had dragged himself into a sitting position on the floor and was nursing his bruised jaw.

"All right, all right," Thomas moaned. "Megan, this is William. My brother. Throw that spare blanket of yours on the floor for him. And find yourself somewhere else to sleep while you're at it – I'll be taking the bed," Thomas added as he slowly rose to his feet and slouched across the bare room to the low bed against the far wall. Thomas lowered himself onto the cot and almost immediately began snoring his way through his drunken stupor.

Megan gingerly rose to her feet and glanced across at Hare before tip-toeing over to the bed and removing a pale blue blanket from the side on which Thomas wasn't sleeping.

"Here you go," she whispered as she handed it to Hare, who paused for a moment and looked at the blanket before handing it back to her.

"I think you need it more than I do," he said, resting his hand on the back of Megan's as he handed her back the blanket. He felt a tingling sensation as their flesh touched but he quickly pulled away and threw his coat down on the floor against the wall, making a simple cot for himself.

Megan stood staring blankly at him for a moment before blowing out the candle and finding her own space against the cold wall.

Hare woke late the next day, stirred from his deep stout-induced sleep by the rattling of a spoon in a bowl. He rolled over to face into the centre of the room and caught sight of a scene of domestic bliss. Megan was standing over Thomas's shoulder as if the previous night's beating had never happened, while Thomas sat at the table and devoured a bowl of cold porridge-like gruel.

"Ah, William, you lazy gobshite," Thomas cackled in between mouthfuls. "You always were a late riser but some of us have work to do. This bricklaying may never make me rich but it gives me enough to put food on the table," he added, polishing off the end of his breakfast and heading for the door.

"You stay here today," Thomas said as he slipped his arms into his greatcoat. "I'll have a word with my foreman and see what we can do about finding you gainful employment while Megan here will get you cleaned up."

Megan handed Thomas his cap and kissed her husband on the cheek before he left, favouring the side of her mouth without the scab from the night before.

Hare shook his head and stiffly raised himself up from the floor before stretching and then plonking himself down on a seat at the small table.

Megan passed him a bowl of her porridge and then turned to leave, slipping on her coat as she went.

"Where are you going?" Hare asked.

"Out," she replied simply and shut the door behind her.

Once he had eaten, Hare let his gaze wander around the room, taking in his brother and sister-in-law's simple possessions. Burke was strangely absent as Hare let his mind muse over the previous evening's events, the first time in months that he had been free of his former accomplice's ramblings.

Hare's gaze stopped over an old tin bath in the corner of the room and he suddenly had the fiercest desire to clean himself. He dragged the bath out from the corner of the room and found a bucket inside.

After several trips down to the stand pipe at the end of the close in which the tenement stood, Hare had managed to fill the bath and he quickly stripped off and lowered himself into the tepid water. The cool liquid made him shiver but he forced himself down until his whole body was submerged and his teeth began to chatter.

After letting the cold water lap around his naked form, Hare pulled himself into a sitting position and used a cake of soap borrowed from among Megan's sparse toiletries to quickly scrub himself clean. Using a razor he had found buried beneath a pile of Thomas's dirty clothes, Hare set about scraping the thick stubble from his chin and cheeks, shaving off weeks of excess growth until he was as smooth and clean as he could manage.

Hare slept again in the afternoon, taking the time to recover from months sleeping rough and surviving on what food and drink he could beg or steal as he travelled from Ulster to London in search of his brother.

He woke from his slumber to find Megan had returned home and was silently preparing food for an evening meal. Outside, the last rays of the summer's sun was turning the brickwork of the close a burned orange again.

Megan turned and gasped when she saw Hare's clean-shaven face.

"I almost didn't recognise you," she said, tilting her head to the side to take in the sight of Hare in one of her husband's old blue shirts.

She turned back to her work as Hare got up from the bed and sat at the table.

"Does he do that often?" Hare asked. Megan looked at him for a moment, weighing up whether she could trust this stranger in her house.

"Most nights," she nodded eventually.

"Why do you put up with it?" Hare frowned.

"What choice does a girl like me have?" Megan spat back. "If I tried to leave him he'd kill me. You've seen the temper he's got on him."

They lapsed back into silence, Hare watching Megan as she reheated a stew from the night before, when Thomas had taken Hare to The Harp rather than returning home for his supper.

"Are you really his brother?" Megan asked.

Hare nodded.

"Funny, he's never talked about you," she continued. "But you look so alike. It's uncanny."

As she finished stirring her stew, Thomas ambled back into the single room, his voice booming as he wished them both a good evening and slipped into a chair with Hare at the small table. Megan doled out bowls of stew for them and sat and listened as Thomas regaled them both with tales of his day at work and the latest jokes and wheezes the brickies had found to tell one another. As Megan cleared away the empty bowls, Thomas rose to his feet and tapped Hare on the shoulder.

"We're heading out, Megan," he told her as the pair headed for the door. "I have things I need to discuss with my brother here."

Megan's face fell as he said it. "Well, don't you be late again you hear," she retorted, years of beatings having failed to dim her spirit.

Thomas grunted a reply as they headed out the door and into the darkening night.

"It may be harder to get you onto the site than I'd thought," Thomas said at last as the pair sat again at the bar of The Harp.

"How do you mean?" asked Hare, matching Thomas's sup from his pint with a mouthful of his own stout.

"Some of the boys got a wee bit suspicious last night," Thomas said slowly. "They've read the papers too and they think they know who you are. One of them must've said something to my foreman because he wouldn't even talk to me about it. I was hoping to get you in there before anyone put two and two together but it looks like your wee outburst last night might have put pay to that."

Hare peered down into his drink.

"Maybe I could try somewhere else," he mused.

"It's not that easy," Thomas shook his head. "London's no place for an Irishman who's down on his luck. Feinian scum they call us. We're like second-class citizens. It's far worse than you'll have had it up in Edinburgh."

"Oi, Thomas, is that your murdering brother you're having a pint with there?" came a cry from the back of the bar.

Thomas swivelled round on his stool and cast a scowl over at the owner of the voice. Hare noticed the barman's ears had pricked up at the mention of murder and the landlord now stood with his thick muscular arms folded across his broad chest.

"You watch your mouth, Cormack," Thomas called back. "That's my flesh and blood you're talking about there."

"What of it?" Cormack replied, standing up from his booth and dragging his small frame across the pub to stand beside Thomas's stool. "Here's me just asking if this is the same William Hare that killed all those wenches and babes-in-arms up in Scotland."

"Now Cormack, no-one nowhere is making any mention of murder except you," retorted Thomas, rising from his stool and standing over the smaller Irishman. "Where do you get these daft ideas into your tiny wee head?"

"Do you want a piece of me, Thomas Hare?" Cormack snarled.

"Cormack, you can't even handle me on my own and you've found that out the hard way in the past. What makes you think you're going to have any better luck when there's two of me?"

Hare rose from his stool and stood beside his brother, mimicking his stance with his hands on his hips.

"Evening, Cormack," he said. "Now what's this you're saying about me being some kind of filthy murdering scumbag?"

Two of Cormack's friends slipped out of their booth and came to stand beside the smaller man, evening the odds if a fight was about to start.

"Trouble, Thomas?" asked the landlord in a loud voice from behind the bar.

"No trouble, Pat," Thomas replied. "Me and my brother were just leaving."

Thomas spat on Cormack's shoe as he pushed his way past but Cormack's friends grabbed his arms and held the angry man back as Thomas and Hare slipped into the dark night.

Thomas and Megan slept in the same bed that night, the Hare brothers' drinking session interrupted by Cormack's accusations. After Thomas left for work the following morning, Megan stayed, sitting on her bed and watching Hare at the table.

"How long will you stay?" she asked.

"I don't know," Hare shook his head. "If Thomas can't get me onto his site then I'll have to look for work elsewhere."

"That's a shame," Megan sighed. "It's been good to have you around. You seem to bring out a better side of him."

Hare stared at her for a long time before speaking again.

"Has he always hurt you?" he asked at last.

Megan shook her head, the thick blonde curls of her hair bouncing from side to side.

"He was a lovely sweet man when I first met him," she said. "But he soon changed when he fell in with those other damn brickies."

"If you're unhappy, you could leave him," Hare offered.

Megan let out a hollow laugh.

"You know he'd come after me," she shook her head. "Besides," she added. "Who would have me now? I'm soiled goods me. Bruises from head to toe."

Megan rose from the bed and paced out the few short steps to the centre of the room and stood before Hare. Slowly she untied the lace at the top of her white blouse and let the ends of the ribbon fall away before easing the garment off her shoulder and down her arms until it was left limp around her waist, revealing her full breasts with their pink nipples and large areolas. Slowly she turned round in a circle, revealing the dark bruises that plastered the length of her arms and the sides of her torso.

Hare let his eyes wander over the dark blue, purple and yellow blotches that covered her back until she turned full circle and stood before him again. He knew she was deliberately tempting him but he couldn't help himself.

"Who would have me now?" she asked again.

"I would," Hare swallowed hard as he kicked back his chair and grabbed Megan roughly by the shoulders. He kissed her long and hard on her lips, which soon parted to let his tongue probe inside her mouth. Megan kissed him back with equal passion and depth, running her hands up and down his back.

Hare reached down and pulled her blouse up clear over her head and threw it down on the floor, before grabbing Megan's waist and pulling her close to him again. He worked his hands higher and grabbed her breasts, kneading them with his rough hands as he kissed her hard against the mouth again.

Megan pulled away from him and walked backwards towards the bed and lay down on the blankets. Hare joined her and quickly yanked off her skirt and underskirt, tossing them to one side and then stripping his own clothes off. Megan pulled Hare down on top of her and kissed him on the mouth again, letting out a low moan as she began working her hips backwards and forwards.

Hare lost himself in the fast rhythm of their love making, until a voice over his shoulder almost broke the spell.

"William Hare, what the Hell are you doing?" asked Burke. "If Thomas catches you he's going to skin you alive."

"Argh," Hare screamed at the top of his lungs, shaking his head to clear Burke's voice from his mind.

Megan thought it was part of Hare's passion and let out a cry of her own, digging her fingernails into his back and pulling him closer. Their rhythm grew faster and faster until both reached climax with more screams of ecstasy.

They made love three more times over the course of the day, only rising from the bed for comfort breaks. Hare wasn't sure how long they lay together after the final time, but when he awoke again it was growing dark again outside.

Megan made no effort to uncurl herself from his arms and start preparing the supper.

"What happens if Thomas comes home?" Hare asked. "What happens if he finds us?"

"Let him find us," Megan mumbled. "I don't care anymore."

Before Hare could protest again, the door was pushed open and Thomas stood in the doorway, his mouth agape.

"What the hell is going on here?" he yelled, slamming the door behind him.

"This won't end well, Hare," Burke snarled, perched on the edge of the small table. *"I tried to warn you."*

"I bring you into my home and you betray me like this," Thomas screamed.

Hare rose from the bed and raced to put himself between Thomas and Megan.

"You whore," Thomas shouted. "You filthy cheating whore."

"Leave her, Thomas," Hare snapped. "It's me your quarrel's with."

Thomas launched himself at Hare, wrestling him to the floor and aiming his punches at his brother's face. But Hare was ready for him and lashed out with his own fists, making contact with Thomas's ribs and breaking one of his bones with a sickening crack.

The pair carried on fighting on the floor while Burke shouted encouragement for Thomas, trying to distract Hare.

Megan slowly stood up from the bed and edged round the rumpus in the middle of the room until she reached her stove and grabbed her black cast-iron frying pan. Turning round, she paused as she picked her moment before swinging the frying pan and landing a blow to the back of Thomas's head.

Her husband collapsed forward, the blow knocking him off the top of Hare, who was quickly back on his feet and slugged his brother another blow to the jaw, laying him out on his back.

Hare jumped on top of him, sitting on Thomas's chest and pinning his arms to his side.

"Quick, grab that pillow," Hare yelled at Megan, who dropped her frying pan and snatched up a pillow from the bed.

"His head," Hare gasped. "Smother his head with the pillow."

Megan hesitated, looking from Thomas's blood-splattered face to Hare's manic stare.

"Ah, if in doubt, resort to the old classic eh, Hare?" Burke cried *with an expansive sweep of his arms.*

"It's too late now," Hare said firmly, ignoring Burke's ramblings. "We've got to finish him off. Now quickly, burke him."

"I'm so proud," Burke sniggered. *"Named after me that move was, Megan."*

Megan swallowed hard and then bent down and placed the pillow across Thomas's face before pushing down, pinning it tight against his nose and mouth.

"Press harder," Hare panted. "Push it down."

Megan pushed harder and harder and slowly Thomas's struggling ebbed away until his body stiffened and fell back against the bare floorboards. Hare sat panting for a few moments longer, taking in the sight before him. If it hadn't been a struggle for life and death then the scene would have been almost comical; a naked man and women smothering a fully-clothed man on the floor of his own home.

Megan caught his eye and couldn't help but smile. They both burst out laughing at the sight of each other and the corpse between them.

"What do we do now?" she asked.

Hare's mind was racing and he knew he had to come up with a plan quickly. Suddenly an idea dawned on him.

"I can't stay," he began. Megan nodded slowly. "There would be too many questions. But we need a way of getting rid of Thomas's body that doesn't leave any of the suspicion resting on you."

"The coppers won't be worried about another dead Irishman," Megan offered. "One less for them to kill with their clubs."

"No, I was thinking more of Cormack and the other Irish brickies from The Harp," Hare muttered. "But I think I know how we can solve two problems at the same time."

"How?" frowned Megan.

"I'll explain on the way," Hare smiled. "Go and find some sacks and then help me wrap up Thomas's body. We're going to have to move him tonight while it's dark."

Standing outside The Harp in the darkness of the next night, Hare struck a match and lit his dead brother's pipe. After getting the body in position the night before, Hare had helped himself to Thomas's clothes, coat and tobacco while Megan cleaned the blood from the floor.

As he took a long draw on the pipe and slowly let the smoke out between his teeth, Hare knew that his plan would work. Across in the tenement, he knew that Cormack or one of the other brickies would turn up in the evening to find out why Thomas hadn't gone to work that day. They would find Megan alone and wailing in the small room, tears streaming down her face.

In between sobs, she would tell the brickies that Hare had murdered Thomas and taken his body away. The brickies would be furious and would set out to find Hare, who was lying in wait for them in the most obvious place he could find – standing outside The Harp.

True to form, Hare didn't have to wait long for the trap to be sprung.

"There he is," cried Cormack as he rounded the corner at the end of the street, a flaming torch in his hand. Behind him, seven of the other brickies paused and watched as Hare stepped out into the centre of the cobbled street to get a look at his would-be assailants.

After making sure they had got a good look at him too, Hare turned tail and ran, heading for the building site.

Climbing over the locked gate, Hare paused on the other side to give his pursuers time to see that he had scaled the defences and was now inside.

Hare turned and jumped back in fright as a dark figure blocked his path.

"And where do you think you're going?" asked Burke.

Hare ignored the spectre's question and instead stood and waited for his pursuers to follow him.

"There he goes, in the site," Cormack shouted as the team of brickies closed in on the gate. As they clambered over, Hare set off again, heading for the rear of the site, with Burke in close pursuit. As Hare rounded a pile of bricks, he saw Megan waiting for him, just as he had planned.

"Quickly, they're not far behind," Hare panted as he helped her drag Thomas's body out of the brown hessian sack and lay it out beside the open lime pit used by the builders to mix their mortar for the bricks.

"Ready?" he asked.

"Ready," Megan smiled as together they kicked Thomas's corpse into the lime pit.

"No," whispered Burke, grabbing either side of his head in horror as Hare's plan dawned on him. "No, you can't do this."

Hare grinned and nodded and Megan let out an almighty scream at the top of her lungs, the sound reverberating around the empty building site and out into the dark night. She grabbed Hare and kissed him hard on the lips before pushing him away.

"Thank you," she said simply. "Now go."

Hare flashed Megan a final smile and then ran off to the right, getting ready to circle back round to the gate. He crouched behind one of the many piles of bricks that peppered the yard and waited to hear what would come next.

Megan's scream had attracted the brickies, who quickly found her standing by the lime pit.

"What happened?" asked Cormack, gasping for breath after the chase.

"It was Hare," Megan stammered. "I came looking for my Thomas's body. I was trying to find out what that monster had done with my husband. But I found him instead. He tried to grab me but I pushed back and he fell into the lime pit," she added, pointing to the body the lay face down in the shallow dip.

"Get a hook boys," Cormack commanded. "Let's fish this bastard out."

Two of the brickies found a pair of poles and quickly scooped Thomas's body up under its shoulders and dragged it to the edge of the pit. Avoiding the quick burning lime, three more of the brickies hauled the body out and left it lying in the dirt.

The lime had done its job just as Hare had planned. Thomas's face, the only thing that distinguished him from Hare, had been burned away by the lime, horribly disfigured and now beyond recognition. For the brickies, Hare was dead.

"Good riddens," muttered Cormack, as the brickies turned to leave. Hare knew that Megan would play her part and help to spread the rumour that he had died in a lime pit, a lie that the brickies had no reason to doubt and would confirm to anyone who asked.

Behind the pile of bricks, Hare raised a wry smile at his good fortune and quietly slipped away into the night, out of the building site and out of London. For the first time in his life, he felt free.

PART THREE
BOSTON, 1863

10

The carriage bounced across the cobbled streets of Boston, illuminated by a mixture of the pale moonlight from high above and the seeping blue-tinged glow of the streetlights. The driver urged the horses on with his whip, racing past the tall office blocks of the city centre and out into Boston's Irish immigrant quarter, where most of the dockworkers and canal navvies lived, cramped together into tenement houses that made the squalid conditions of Edinburgh's Old Town look veritably spacious. Street after street sped past the windows but, inside the carriage, Gillespie didn't tear his gaze away from the man sitting opposite him.

The custody sergeant on duty overnight in the police station had been puzzled by the order but he recognised Gillespie and so quickly led the captain to the cell he had requested. Unlocking the door, a pair of bright eyes, one green, one blue, looked up from the cot in the corner of the small room.

Now Hare sat on the bench across from Gillespie in the back of the carriage, a loaded Colt revolver sitting across the captain's lap, its safety clip off and the hammer cocked back ready to fire.

"You don't need the gun, you know," Hare offered, as Gillespie's finger traced a line back and forth along the length of the revolver's grip. It was the first time the prisoner had spoken since the pair left the police station and climbed into the waiting carriage.

"I'll be the judge of that," Gillespie muttered back, his icy stare fixing Hare with a menacing gaze. Though the detective knew he was employing a risky strategy, he also knew that his plan was the only way for him to find out if he could trust the man who sat opposite him in the darkened carriage.

"Where are we going anyway?" Hare asked.

"You'll see," Gillespie replied. He needed their destination to be secret so that he could judge the murderer's reaction when he realised where he was being taken.

The carriage bumped on through the night until Gillespie could hear the driver shouting "woe" and the horses slowed to a trot.

As the driver pulled on the reigns to bring his steeds to a halt, Gillespie allowed himself a quick glance out the window to see where the carriage had stopped. He saw that the tall tenements had given way to a row of simple red-brick terraced houses, all of their windows darkened in the middle of the night save for the one outside which the carriage had pulled up.

Gillespie swung open the carriage door and lowered himself backwards, first onto the metal step and then onto the cobbled street below, all the time keeping his revolver trained on Hare. He motioned for the prisoner to follow him and Hare duly obliged, stepping out into the crisp night air. He was met with the barrel of a second gun, as the carriage driver stood behind Gillespie with the sights of his carbine rifle lowered on Hare's chest. The captain slipped the safety catch back onto his revolver and holstered his weapon, grabbing Hare by the arm and leading him towards the door to the terraced house.

Hare looked up and surveyed the scene for the first time and, realising where he was, let out a gasp of delight.

"Thank you," he stammered, grabbing Gillespie's hand and shaking it enthusiastically. Hare's sudden movement caught both policemen by surprise and the muzzle of the carriage driver's rifle was quickly rammed into Hare's back, pushing him forward.

"It's just for a few hours," Gillespie cautioned, letting go of Hare's hand and thumping the door loudly with his fist. As soon as he saw a shadow pass by the lamp-lit window, Gillespie knew he could have wrapped lightly and the figure awaiting them on the other side of the doorway would still have heard him.

As she opened the door, Gillespie was taken aback by the woman's appearance. Though she was short and was carrying more than her fair share of the pounds of middle age, he could clearly see that the woman must have been very attractive in her youth. Even behind the dark circles that lined her sleepless eyes and the worried crinkles across her forehead, Gillespie could see that her ruddy skin must have glowed in the past and that the dirty blond ringlets of her hair could have shone like the sun.

"Edward," she exclaimed, throwing her arms around Hare and pulling him tightly towards her. Their embrace lasted several moments, during which Gillespie trusted his instincts and signalled for the driver to step aside into the shadows, so the woman would not see his rifle.

Pulling away from the embrace, the woman turned back into the house when she heard a noise from inside.

"Oh God, the children," she said, disappearing back behind the door.

Hare made to follow her inside but Gillespie turned back to the driver.

"Stand guard here," he instructed. "No-one enters or leaves without my say-so."

Though he doubted they would be disturbed in the middle of the night, Gillespie didn't want to take any chances.

Stepping over the threshold, Gillespie's eyes quickly drank in his surroundings in the small, one-roomed house. He saw a simple wooden table and four chairs set beside the window to the left of the doorway, with a fireplace and range on the wall to his left. Opposite him, two young children had been woken from their cots by the noise of men's entry and their mother was stroking their hair, whispering soothing words into their ears. A larger bed took up the other corner of the single room, with a curtain covering a door that Gillespie surmised led to a backyard with an outside toilet. The adults' bed clearly hadn't been slept in that night.

"Daddy," screamed the little girl, slipping through her mother's arms and running to wrap her arms around Hare's leg. The girl buried her face into her father's thigh, swinging her head from side to side and letting the blond curls she had inherited from her mother cascade down around either side of her face.

The boy, older than his sister, eyed Gillespie suspiciously but the relief at seeing his father again helped him to overcome his nerves and he threw himself around Hare's other leg.

Gillespie watched Hare as he carefully bent down and scooped up his children with ease, one small bundle in each arm. The father giggled with joy as he hugged the children close to his body before depositing them on the chairs by the table.

"Tilly," said Hare, bending down in front of his daughter and stroking her blonde hair. "Have you been a good girl for your mother?"

The child nodded enthusiastically, beaming from ear to ear, unable to contain the delight of having her father home again.

"And what about you, William?" Hare asked, turning to the boy who sat quietly on the chair next to his sister. The boy had dark hair like his father and the same long, solemn features. "Have you been working hard at school?"

Gillespie bristled at the mention of Hare's real first name, which he had shared with Burke, his accomplice in the West Port murders.

"Yes father," the boy replied, nodding his head. Gillespie saw the same sad look in the son's eyes that he had noted in Hare's expression, as if the weight of the world had landed squarely on those young shoulders.

Comparing the children's night attire with the modest surroundings of the house, Gillespie could tell that Hare and his much-younger partner had gone without luxuries themselves to meet their children's needs. While their mother's dress was worn and stained, the children wore simple but new cotton nightdresses. Hare's own attire, even though it was still sooty from the fire, had clearly seen better days too.

Suddenly the woman launched herself at Hare again, wrapping her arms around him.

"Where have you been, Edward?" she demanded, tears streaming down her cheeks. "Larry Stephenson, from the canal, said you'd been taken away by the police," she continued, her words mixing in with the deep sobs that wrenched through her chest. "You've been gone for days. I thought I'd never see you again."

As quickly as they had started, her sobs ended and she backed away from Hare, fixing Gillespie with a steely cold gaze.

"And who's this man?" she demanded, her Irish accent becoming more accentuated as she became angrier and angrier.

"Molly, this is Captain Alexander Gillespie of the Boston police department," Hare explained. "And he's welcome in this house," he added, as the expression on his wife's face turned from anger to outright hatred. She stood for a moment, obviously weighing her next words carefully.

"Then the Captain'll take coffee no doubt," she said after a moment, moving across to the range and sliding a large cast-iron kettle onto the heat.

"Coffee would be fine, thank you," Gillespie nodded.

"You're Irish?" Molly frowned.

"Scottish," Gillespie corrected, wondering for the second time in as many days if his speech had really lost so much of its accent that even other Europeans were being confused.

"Ah, Scotland," Molly nodded. "Edward, lived there for a while, didn't you?"

Gillespie frowned and turned to Hare.

"Molly knows everything," Hare replied in answer to Gillespie's unasked question. "You can say anything in front of her."

Gillespie opened his mouth as if to speak but the sight of Hare's children sitting at the table caused him to stop and seal his lips again.

Molly poured three mugs of coffee and they sat down at the table by the window, Molly scooping Tilly up in her arms and sitting her daughter on her lap.

"So, tell me, Captain, why did you snatch my Edward off the streets with not so much as a word to his family about where you were taking him?" Molly demanded, bouncing Tilly up-and-down on her knee.

"Your husband has been helping us with our inquiries," Gillespie replied, choosing not to use Hare's real name for the time being.

"And what inquiries are those?" Molly pursued. "What's so important that you'd take a man away from his wife and children?"

"We are investigating a series of murders of canal-building navvies," Gillespie answered. "As foreman, your husband would have known all of the victims and is the only suspect who can't provide an alibi for the time of the most recent murder."

"Not the most recent, Captain," Hare corrected. "You'll remember I was incarcerated in one of your cells when the last man was murdered."

"Daddy, what's murder?" interrupted Tilly, reaching her arms out towards her father and letting him scoop her up and transfer her from her mother's lap to his.

"Well, Tilly, if you murder someone then you kill them, you take away their life," Hare explained, his voice calm and flat.

"But that's wrong daddy," Tilly protested. "It goes against the Ten Commandments."

"Thou shall not kill," nodded William, his gazed fixed on Gillespie. "Thou shall…"

The hairs on the back of Gillespie's neck stood on end as the young boy repeated the Ten Commandments in full.

"Good boy," Molly said, tapping her son on his knee. "There's my clever lad."

"Not everyone believes in living by the Ten Commandments like we do, Tilly," Hare continued.

Gillespie bristled again, swallowing hard, the Presbyterian bile rising at the back of his throat. This time he couldn't control his questions.

"But if you're so committed to the commandments then why take a second wife and have these children out of wedlock?" he said, drawing confused looks from both William and Tilly but not from Molly.

"Ah, we don't need some fancy piece of paper to tell us that we're married," she replied. "I don't need to get dressed up in some white dress to know that my Edward loves me."

"Molly, it's ok," Hare shook his head, before turning to Gillespie and replying: "Molly is my common-law wife. You won't find any record of our marriage down at City Hall but I love her and I love my children, Captain."

"And what about Margaret Laird?" Gillespie spat back. "Do you still love her too?"

Hare paused for a moment. "I don't know what happened to Margaret, Captain," he replied. "Our paths drew away from each other a long time ago.

"But I've served my penance for the crimes I've committed. My sins have been forgiven and I am right with the Lord again."

"And what about the sins you're committing now? What about living in sin with this woman and having these bastard children with her?"

"How can raising two such beautiful children be a sin?" Hare asked, running his fingers through Tilly's golden curls.

Gillespie drank the rest of his coffee in silence, the bitter taste warming his throat as his mind soaked up the domestic scene in front of him. Hare filled the silence by questioning William about his classes at school and asking Tilly if she had been helping her mother around the house.

Later, when the children were back in their cots, Gillespie set his mug down on the table and began questioning Hare and Molly in hushed tones. Their replies came from equally quietened voices, all too aware that their son would more than likely still be lying awake, straining his ears to hear their hushed answers through the dark.

"How can you live with this man after all the crimes he's committed?" Gillespie began.

"Edward saved me," Molly replied. "He took my broken and dirty life and brought me to the Lord."

Gillespie frowned. "What do you mean?"

The reply came from Hare. "When I left Edinburgh, I left behind the life you're talking about, Captain. I had to come to terms with the sins I committed. I prayed for forgiveness and I served my penance. Then I crossed the ocean to start my life again here."

"When I met Edward, I was working the street, bedding frontier men for a dollar a time," Molly picked up the story. "I was a lady of the night in a fort on the border with Lower Canada. Edward saved me and showed me the error of my ways. He brought me back to the light."

Gillespie watched the couple who sat across the table from him. Had Hare really changed so much?

"How can you share your bed with a murderer?" Gillespie demanded. "How can you trust this man with your children?"

"That was all a lifetime ago," Molly protested. "If you knew my Edward, if you knew what he's like, you'd understand. He's a changed man."

Gillespie shook his head, his mind racing at the image of Hare as protector, as saviour.

"If you don't believe me, you should speak to Father O'Connor, our priest," Molly offered. "He'll vouch for all the hard work Edward has done in the parish."

"Don't worry, I'll be speaking to Father O'Connor, and to Mr Tate as well," Gillespie replied, picking his hat up from the table.

"Time for us to go," he added. Molly began protesting but Hare kissed her long and hard on her mouth and her anger subsided again.

"I'll be back, my love," he promised as Gillespie led him towards the door and back out into the cold night air.

After he bundled Hare back into the carriage and cocked his revolver again for the ride back to the police station, Gillespie paused and looked back at the terraced house. At the window, he could see Molly staring back at him. From the domestic scene he had witnessed in the small house, the captain knew there was no evidence that Hare was still the monster he once was.

On the way back to the station, the two men sat in silence. Through the darkness, Gillespie could tell that Hare's eyes were burrowing into him, trying to determine whether the policeman believed him or not.

As the carriage pulled back up at the city centre police station, the first rays of dawn's light were breaking out over the eastern docks and eeking their way between the tall buildings and into the sleeping heart of Boston. Hare paused as he stepped down from the carriage, the driver's rifle still trained on his chest.

"Thank you for that, Captain," he said, holding his hand out again. Gillespie looked hard at him. Despite the lingering doubts at the back of his mind, Gillespie's gut told him that he needed to trust Hare if he was to catch this new murderer who was stalking the streets of Boston. He had to put aside his concerns over how the man running from the fire had fallen to his death; instead, he had to trust the man who had saved him from a burning building when he could just have easily have left him to die. He had to let one killer loose to catch another.

"You're welcome," said Gillespie, shaking Hare's hand. "Now come on, we have work to do."

"We?" Hare asked.

"You'll see," replied Gillespie, leading Hare back up the stone stairs and into the police station.

11

From his office on the third and highest storey of his company's warehouse on Boston's western wharf, Tate could survey nearly half of his business interests in the city. The industrialist could watch ships bringing in his cotton before his dockhands took it to his vast mills for processing. Wagon after wagon then took the finished material back down to the docks for loading onto ships sailing out to all four corners of the globe.

Below him, Tate could also see the workers in his munitions yard, taking guns and shells from his vast armoury and loading them onto the goods wagons of trains destined for the Union's front lines.

Despite the trouble in taking cotton out of the southern states, business was brisk during the Civil War for Tate.

A knock on the thick oak-panelled door to his office snapped Tate out of his reverie. He stepped away from the window and sat down in the leather-padded chair behind his desk.

"Come in," he called.

The door slowly opened and an elderly clerk shuffled in.

"Begging your pardon, Mr Tate, but there's a Captain Alexander Gillespie to see you, sir," the short grey-haired man said.

Tate sighed heavily. "Send him in," the industrialist conceded.

The clerk shuffled out again and reappeared a few moments later with the police officer following behind him.

"Captain Gillespie, twice in the same week, to what do I owe the honour?" asked Tate, forcing himself to smile as he stood up and rounded his desk to shake Gillespie's outstretched hand.

"Mr Tate, thank you for seeing me at such short notice," Gillespie replied, taking a seat in front of the desk as indicated by a sweep of Tate's hand. "I need to speak with you again about William Hare."

Tate scowled and his expression darkened. "I thought we'd been through all this at the mayor's house?" he said.

"Just a few more questions, I assure you," Gillespie said with a shrug.

Tate walked across to his drinks cabinet. "Well, if there are going to be more questions then I'm going to need a drink," he smiled through gritted teeth.

"Bourbon?" he asked.

"I'll take a Scotch if you have any," Gillespie replied, settling back in his padded chair.

"I said bourbon, didn't I?" Tate snapped, not bothering to ask Gillespie again but instead sliding the bottle of Tennessee whiskey back into the cabinet after pouring only a glass for himself.

"When did you first meet William Hare?" Gillespie asked.

"I first met Edward Laird," Tate began pointedly, "more than ten years ago when he came to work for me. He was given an honourable discharge from the army after serving with the first Massachusetts dragoons along the border with Lower Canada."

"Do you often recruit from the army?"

"Whenever I can," exclaimed Tate after taking a long swig of his drink. "Men coming out of the army understand discipline and take instruction well. They work hard and they don't answer back, which is more than I can say for half the worthless immigrants in this town."

Tate paused, looking at Gillespie over the rim of his half-raised glass.

"No offence, of course," he offered.

"None taken," replied the Scotsman, holding Tate's gaze and fixing him with an icy stare. "Plus, Hare had previous experience building canals I suppose?" Gillespie added.

Tate looked confused.

"Oh, didn't you know? Hare and his partner, Burke, had each worked as navvies on the Union Canal in Edinburgh before they launched their murder spree."

Tate shook his head and drained the rest of his bourbon before rising to refill his glass.

"Whatever Laird's crimes, they weren't committed against me and they weren't committed here in Boston. You said yourself that he was set free.

"America is a land of opportunity, Captain, a land for fresh starts. You should know that better than anyone."

Tate slid back in behind his desk but shaking an accusing finger at Gillespie, ramming home his points.

"You've had more fresh starts than most of us. In the nightwatch, in the army, back to the police again."

Gillespie kept his anger in check but couldn't stop the colour from flushing his face. He had forgotten how much Tate must have learned about him when the captain had investigated the death of his business partner, Arnold Proctor, five years earlier.

He turned the subject back to Hare. "And what does Hare do for you?"

"He's a foreman on one of my canal-building teams," Tate explained, sensing he had struck a raw nerve with Gillespie and enjoying the small victory.

"I would have thought the last thing Boston needed was another canal."

"On the contrary captain, my new canal will bring cotton directly in from farms all over the continent, cutting down on our losses at sea and speeding up our production processes.

"Plus, if the south continues in its attempts at secession then the canal will aid in the war effort too."

"Thousands of men are lying dead on the battlefield and all you can talk about is profit," Gillespie shook his head.

"Don't lecture me on patriotism," Tate snarled. "My family helped to build this city and I don't need an immigrant pressing me on the finer points of civil duty during war time."

"You're all immigrants," Gillespie barked back. "All your ancestors stepped off a ship at some point. And now you slaughter more and more of the Red Indians week by week, killing the only native Americans."

Both men sat in silence for several minutes before Tate pulled his gaze away from Gillespie to drain his glass.

"I'm a busy man, Captain, and I have business to attend to this afternoon so please do me the courtesy of getting to your point and bringing this interview to an end."

Gillespie weighed up his options; he needed to know if he could trust Hare and antagonising Tate, however enjoyable, had got him nowhere so far. Tate obviously trusted Hare, Gillespie reasoned, but if Tate was somehow connected to the murders then Hare would be an obvious ally to the industrialist.

"I need to borrow Hare," Gillespie said eventually.

"Borrow him?"

"I haven't ruled out Hare's involvements in these murders but, whether he's connected or not, he knows your canals and docks better than any man and he knows how a murderer thinks. He could be a real asset to my investigation."

"But I don't understand," Tate began, "how exactly do you plan to use one of my foremen to catch a killer?"

Gillespie rose and picked his hat up from the desk.

"That will have to remain between me and Hare for the time being."

Tate made to protest but Gillespie stopped him.

"If you have an objection then I'm sure Police Chief Blackstone can take the matter up with your common friend the Mayor. You did see how much emphasis the Mayor put on this investigation, didn't you?"

Tate grimaced and then forced a grin to spread across his face.

"Then it looks like you have my foreman at your service, Captain," he hissed.

12

"No way, Captain, no way on God's sweet Earth," Hare shook his head.

Gillespie sighed and pinched the bridge of his nose, battling in vain to ward off the headache that had been growing stronger all day since his meeting with Tate.

"I've turned away from the darkness, Captain, and there's no way I'm going back now," Hare added, fixing Gillespie with a determined stare.

"We're not asking you to kill anyone, Hare," Gillespie snapped. "All we need is for you to help us find whoever is killing these men – your men," he added to ram home his point.

Gillespie, O'Malley and Fletcher were back in Blackstone's office, a location selected to put Hare at ease and reassure him that he was no longer a suspect being questioned in his cell but was instead simply being asked to help the police with their inquiries. Hare had so far failed to warm to the plan.

Blackstone shifted uncomfortably in his large chair behind the giant mahogany desk. The police chief had remained unusually silent during the interview, letting Gillespie and O'Malley, who sat in seats next to Hare, ask the Irishman for his help. Fletcher was perched against the sideboard, casting occasional longing sideways glances at the expensive Scotch in Blackstone's whisky decanter.

"For the love of God man," Gillespie barked. "Five of your canal navvies are dead, two of my officers have been slain and our temporary headquarters have been burned to the ground. How much more serious does this have to get before you'll do your civic duty – and your duty before God – and help us catch this villain?"

"That's enough," Blackstone interjected. "Mr Hare has said he is not prepared to help you and that is the end of the matter."

Gillespie guessed correctly that more pressure was being applied to the police chief by the mayor to have Hare released.

"My name is Laird rather than Hare but thank you, Chief," Hare nodded.

"In which case, Mr Laird, you are free to go," Blackstone added, rising from behind his desk to shake Hare's hand.

Gillespie sprang to his feet. "I'm sorry sir, but I've not finished with Hare yet."

"What now, Captain?" the chief asked angrily. "You know very well that Mr Laird was in your custody when the last of the abductions and murders took place and so he's no longer a suspect."

"I believe Hare's..." Gillespie paused, searching for the right word. "Experience of such matters may prove invaluable in understanding how this killer's mind works."

Blackstone sighed heavily and the two police officers fixed each other in a stare. The chief knew that the captain still suspected Hare's involvement but he also knew that the police would need all the help they could get if they were to catch the killer and stop the unrest that was spreading in Boston's docks before it could destabilise the war effort.

Reluctantly, the chief nodded his consent. "Very well, Captain Gillespie. Mr Laird, you will be staying with us a bit longer it seems."

Hare stood open-mouthed but did not move towards the door. He had come so close to freedom only to have his desire scuttled again.

"Sergeant MacLeod," Blackstone called. The door open and the old uniformed officer stepped into the office. With the temporary station burned to the ground, MacLeod and some of his uniformed men had been attached to Gillespie's staff to help with the murder inquiry.

"Take Mr Laird here up to the aldermen's meeting room so he can speak to Captain Gillespie in private. And find him some coffee too."

The sergeant nodded his silent acceptance of the order and led Hare from the room.

"Thank you, sir," Gillespie said earnestly. Though the two men argued at great length over much of the police's casework, Gillespie knew that Blackstone shared his desire to see justice done.

Blackstone dismissed the captain's thanks with a wave of his hand. He frowned at the mountains of paper on his desk before looking up at the three officers.

"What now? If Laird, or Hare, or whatever he's called, won't help you then what's your next move?"

"We stick with the plan," Gillespie said, surprised at his own certainty.

"Fletcher, your face isn't well-known at the docks, I think you should pose as a supplier of bodies and see if you can find out who's willing to buy them."

The young lieutenant beamed at Gillespie's vote of confidence in his abilities.

"I won't let you down, sir," Fletcher grinned.

"I know and, just to make sure, O'Malley here will go with you."

The Irishman frowned but then slowly nodded his consent.

"If we play on my Irish roots then we might get further with the navvies," he agreed.

"And I could use my Irish accent," Fletcher added, drawing odd looks from his companions. "I trod the boards on a stage off Broadway as a younger man," the New Yorker explained. "I think I could revive my acting skills for one more performance."

Gillespie suddenly felt very old, faced with the next generation of police officers who had attended university or entered the force from the higher ranks of society rather than by serving time in the nightwatch or the army.

"Very well," Blackstone interrupted Gillespie's chain of thought. "Now get out of here all of you and get me some results."

As the three officers walked down the corridor outside Blackstone's temporary office, Gillespie issued his two lieutenants with their orders.

"Take what you need from the supplies store at the nearest police station and get changed into some dockers' work clothes," he instructed them. "We need to get started straight away."

"What about you, sir?" O'Malley asked.

"I've got an appointment to keep," Gillespie replied, as he turned and bounded up the staircase to the meeting room where MacLeod had delivered Hare.

13

"We've been through this already," Hare cried out in exasperation, throwing his arms up into the air again. "I've told you about every single docker and navvy I know in Boston and no, I don't think any of them are capable of committing any of these heinous crimes."

Gillespie folded his arms and leant back in his chair, rocking the seat on its rear legs. After two days of questioning, he thought he finally had Hare where he wanted him. Gillespie questioned him late into the night on their first day together, watching the tall candles set up on the long meeting room table burn down through all their wick and wax before allowing Hare a few hours of sleep. Yet Gillespie hadn't let up in his interrogation, throwing open the deep red velvet curtains to let the bright sunshine stream into the room and wake Hare from his short slumber.

Again, Gillespie went over every detail of Hare's life in Boston, from his work during the day on the canal-building project through to his service at the local Roman Catholic church at night and his time spent with his young family.

Dismissing Hare's protests that Blackstone had only given permission for Gillespie to consult with Hare instead of interrogating him, the captain had pushed on, going over the same ground again and again and again.

The Scotsman pushed on during the second morning, much to the annoyance of a secretary, who had tried to get them to vacate the room so she could set it up for a meeting of the city's aldermen later that day. Gillespie had chased her from the room and posted MacLeod as a guard on the door to make sure they were not interrupted again.

And now Gillespie had Hare where he wanted him. Tired from two days and nights of incessant questioning and longing to return home to his family, the Irishman was at his most malleable and most likely to slip up. Though Gillespie knew the past two days and the lack of sleep would have taken their toll on him too, he felt energised and alert, more in control of his faculties than he had felt in a long time.

"Heinous crimes?" Gillespie repeated Hare's words back to him. "Come on, Hare. It's just you and me now. These are murders we're talking about. Murders. Just like the kind you committed back in Edinburgh. In fact, just like the murders you committed in Edinburgh."

Hare scowled at the police captain but said nothing. Gillespie's mind had flitted between suspecting Hare was at the very heart of the grave robbing and murders – which he knew had to be linked – through to trusting that the Irishman had truly changed. But either way, his gut instinct told him that Hare could help him catch the killer that was stalking Boston's docks.

Gillespie let the silence hang between them for a long while before speaking again.

"Why did you do it Hare?"

The prisoner looked up from the table, where his gaze had fallen during the lengthy pause. He tilted his head to one side, as if seeing Gillespie for the first time, a quizzical look on his face.

"Do what?" he asked simply.

"Kill those people in Edinburgh," Gillespie explained. "Kill Mary Patterson and Elizabeth Haldane and Daft Jamie and all those others."

"Do you know, I don't think you've ever asked me that before?" Hare frowned. He eyed the captain suspiciously but his answers came more freely now, without the hesitations that had accompanied his explanations about his life in Boston.

"We were poor and we were hungry," Hare replied. "The canal was finished and there was no work to be had. Or at least no work for two Irishmen and their wives."

"Bullshit," Gillespie spat back. "Your wife Margaret ran the lodging house that belonged to her dead husband. You could have made a descent, honest living but instead you were bewitched by the money Dr Knox had to offer you."

"No one could have eeked out a living running lodgings in the West Port," Hare shook his head.

"After the New Town was built, all you rich dandies moved out of the Old Town and left us to our slums."

A bitter tone had entered Hare's voice, which Gillespie noted hadn't been there before.

"You left us to live and work and die among the filth and the disease and the overcrowding."

"You forget one thing, Hare," Gillespie interrupted his tirade. "You're not the only one who lived and worked in the Old Town. I was born and grew up in those slums and I didn't turn to a life of crime."

Hare fell silent again and watched Gillespie intently.

"Do you know what I think, Hare? I think it comes back to the money. The thirty pieces of silver, which that Judas Dr Knox paid you to keep his classes in cadavers. Knox may have got away with it, being a gentlemen as he was, but I know it was that cold hard cash that drove you on."

Still Hare sat silently watching Gillespie as the tension in the room continued to rise.

"How did it feel to kill a man?" Gillespie asked. "How did it feel to smother his mouth with a pillow or throw yourself across his chest to constrict his breathing? Did it feel good, Hare? Did it feel so good that you just had to do it again? Swap Edinburgh for Boston? Who's paying the cash now, Hare? Who are you killing for?"

"For the last time I'm not a murderer," Hare yelled as he threw back his chair and rose to his feet. The two men stood on opposite sides of the table from one another, Hare squeezing his fingers into fists while Gillespie stood with his revolver levelled at the Irishman's chest, the hammer eased back and ready to fire. Gillespie had even surprised himself with the speed at which he had risen from his seat and taken aim at his prisoner.

The pair stood breathing heavily, neither breaking their stare. Eventually, Gillespie raised the revolver so that it was pointing at the ceiling and eased the hammer back into place so the gun was no longer cocked and armed.

Hare lowered himself back into his chair while Gillespie retrieved his own seat from where it lay on the floor and slid back into his place at the table.

"Besides, Captain," Hare sighed. "I think you know well enough how it feels to kill a man. You handle that weapon like you've used it more times than you'd care to remember, I'd wager."

Before Gillespie could reply, a sharp tapping at the door broke the tension and snapped the captain back into the present. Without waiting for a reply, MacLeod opened the door and stepped into the meeting room, accompanied by a short man wearing a black woollen workman's suit and a flat cap.

It took Gillespie a moment to clock the tufts of the walrus-like moustache that identified the man as Lieutenant O'Malley.

"Sir, we've done it," the Irishman announced. "Fletcher's made contact with an agent who wants to buy bodies from him. He's set up a rendezvous for tonight."

Out in the hallway, Gillespie heard a babble of deep males voices and above MacLeod and O'Malley's heads he could see the black top hats of the city's aldermen as they gathered for their council meeting.

"Then we have no time to lose," said Gillespie with a grim smile. "MacLeod, take Hare back to the police station and hold him there till I'm ready for him again."

Hare made to protest but Gillespie cut him off with a wave of his hand.

"O'Malley, you come with me."

14

The horse-drawn carriage clattered noisily along Boston's cobbled streets at high speed as Fletcher and O'Malley briefed Gillespie on the events of the previous two days. Fletcher explained how he had been able to find an agent who wanted to buy bodies from him and that he had arranged a meeting for that night in one of the warehouses on the dockside.

As the carriage pulled onto the dockside, Gillespie craned his neck out of the window to take in the scene that greeted them. A crowd of several hundred men had gathered in front of a hastily-erected wooden platform, decked out in red, white and blue bunting. On the stage, Mayor Barron stood with a bullhorn, addressing the gathering of dockhands, navvies and other workers assembled before him. The workers' boss, Tate, stood next to Barron on the platform, with Police Chief Blackstone, flanking the mayor's other side. A group of trade union shop stewards and a brass band completed the platform party.

Gillespie was surprised to see one other figure on the stage, standing next to Tate. Amelia Proctor – the widow of Tate's business partner and, by all accounts, the real brains behind the pair's joint ventures – was wearing a close-fitting black dress, with black laces tying up the front bodice to a high point around her neck. Her long fire-red hair was platted and pinned up inside a small black hat, revealing the pale skin of her neck. Gillespie fought of the fantasies of her in his bathtub.

The carriage pulled up alongside the other horse-drawn vehicles behind the wooden stage and the three police officers climbed out. O'Malley and Fletcher remained behind the platform in case they were recognised by any of the dock workers, while Gillespie proceeded to stand at the foot of the wooden ladder leading up onto the stage, from where he could hear the mayor address the crowd.

"Remember, your efforts are essential to the war effort," Barron boomed through the bullhorn, eliciting a round of applause and loud whoops and cheers from the crowd gathered below.

"Our proud city's great police force is here to protect you and catch this foul fiend who seeks to disrupt the best efforts of our loyal Union workers here in Boston."

From his vantage point, Gillespie could just about make out the brief frown forming across Blackstone's forehead before the police chief remembered where he was and began clapping enthusiastically at the mayor's speech along with the rest of the platform party.

The mayor stepped back from the edge of the platform and passed the loud hailer to Tate, who coughed to clear his throat before addressing his workers.

"You heard the mayor: back to work boys. The more shells you produce, the more guns we ship out to our troops and the faster you complete our canal then the quicker we'll gives those Dixie dogs the kicking they deserve and reunite our great country. God bless America."

His final clarion call was taken up by members of the crowd, who began chanting "God bless America".

Tate turned and signalled to the brass band, which struck up with "The Star-Spangled Banner". As the unofficial national anthem played, the mayor led the platform party from the stage and down the wooden ladder to where Gillespie waited.

"Mr Mayor," said Gillespie, tipping his hat as the politician walked passed and gave him a curt nod before being swallowed up by his entourage.

Tate was next down the steps and Gillespie intercepted him as the industrialist reached the bottom rung of the ladder.

"A word if I may, Mr Tate," he said, leading the taller man by the arm off to one side.

"What's the meaning of this?" barked Blackstone, who was next down the wooden ladder and joined his captain at Tate's side. Gillespie noticed that Amelia Proctor had also clocked his presence and was heading towards the small group of men.

"Mr Tate, I must request that we have use of one of your warehouses tonight," Gillespie said, ignoring the chief's question.

"A warehouse?" Tate frowned. "First you want to borrow one of my foremen and now you want one of my warehouses too. What the hell is going on, Gillespie?"

"My men have found the agent who we believe has been buying the bodies of your men," Gillespie explained. "If we capture the agent then I believe he can lead us to the killer or killers who have been disrupting your operations."

"But that's brilliant news," exclaimed Tate, his giant head bobbing up and down above his narrow shoulders. "Why didn't you say so in the first place? Which warehouse do you need?"

Gillespie consulted the pencil markings in his notebook. "Storage unit number RB-211," he replied.

"It's yours," Tate beamed, an uncharacteristic smile fixed to his features. "I'll have my men stay away from that area of the docks for the duration of the night."

"Thank you," Gillespie said. "Now, if you'll excuse me, there is much still to prepare. Gentlemen, Mrs Proctor."

Amelia smiled at the captain and held out her hand for him to shake. Gillespie successfully fought back the temptation to kiss it.

"I'm flattered that you remember me, Captain Gillespie," she purred, the thin line of her red-lipsticked smile contrasting against her pale skin. Did he imagine it or did he feel a spark of something more than a cordial greeting pass between them?

Tate led Amelia by the arm back towards their carriages, while Blackstone accompanied Gillespie to where Fletcher and O'Malley stood waiting.

"This is good work, Fletcher," Blackstone said, clapping the young officer on his shoulder. "Keep this up and we'll need to make you Captain," he added before climbing into his own carriage and leaving the three officers to plan that night's mission.

The afternoon disappeared in a blur of activity as Gillespie outlined his plans for the ambush. Using the details Fletcher provided, he arranged for the uniformed police at his disposal to take up position surrounding the warehouse's entrances and exits, with all the men either disguised as dockworkers or placed in hidden positions, ready to storm the building at his signal.

With only minutes to go before the 8pm rendezvous, Gillespie found himself back in the coach, parked a short distance away from the warehouse.

"I still don't understand why we had to bring him," grumbled Fletcher, pointing his pistol across to Hare, who sat slouched in the corner of the carriage.

"I want him here when we collar your contact," Gillespie repeated. "If there's even as much of a flicker of recognition passes across that agent's face then Hare here will be spending some more time in the cells."

Hare sighed heavily but knew better than to try protesting his innocence again. Gillespie knew it was a high-risk strategy to bring a prisoner out into the field with him but as long as O'Malley kept his revolver trained on Hare's chest, the captain did not expect the Irishman to give them any trouble.

"It's time," said O'Malley after consulting his pocket watch. Gillespie took a deep breath and then led his men out of the carriage and along the perimeter fence that surrounded the brick-built warehouse. His men silently crossed the work yard at speed and took up their positions on either side of the large wooden warehouse doors.

Gillespie paused and tried to calm his hammering heart. Had he made the right decisions? Did he have enough men? He knew the only answers lay on the inside of the warehouse.

With a quick wave of his hand, Gillespie signalled for two uniformed officers to heave open the giant doors, while he slipped his police whistle into his mouth. His three long blasts pierced the silence of the freezing cold night and the uniformed officers began pouring into the warehouse, carrying their cocked firearms in one hand and lanterns in the other.

Gillespie and Fletcher quickly followed the first wave inside, their revolvers drawn in front of them.

"Armed police," Gillespie yelled. "Surrender and lay down your weapons."

O'Malley and Hare followed them but, as the light from the lanterns met with the flames being cast from the team entering at the back of the warehouse, it became all too clear to Gillespie that they'd been duped.

"It's empty back here, sir," one of the sergeants yelled as his team advanced from the rear of the building. Gillespie was left standing alone with his thoughts at the centre of the barren warehouse, his men grumbling in hushed tones amongst themselves.

Fletcher looked distraught. "I don't understand it, Captain," he protested. "How could he have known we were coming?"

"How indeed?" Gillespie muttered, turning to face Hare, who held his steady gaze.

"This has nothing to do with me," the Irishman said.

Before Gillespie could answer, he heard his name being called by a silhouetted figure standing in the open warehouse doorway.

He jogged back across the empty floor to opening to find Sergeant MacLeod hunched over as he tried to regain his breath.

Gillespie had left the old sergeant back at the nearest police station to await further instructions or to lead a back-up team if it was needed. He knew the situation must be urgent for the old nightwatchman to have left his post.

"What is it, MacLeod?" he asked. "What's happened?"

The old man slowly regained his composure and managed to raise himself back to what passed for his full height.

"It's Hare's house, sir," MacLeod wheezed. "It's ablaze."

15

Hare ran out into the yard like a man possessed, the four police officers struggling to keep pace with him as he sprinted to reach the waiting police carriage that had been brought to the front of the warehouse.

Gillespie, O'Malley and Fletcher followed Hare into the back of the coach, leaving MacLeod to empty the police officers out of the warehouse and reseal the doors. The four men sat in silence as the driver whipped the horses into a near-gallop as the carriage raced along the dock road towards the rows of terraced houses that were home to the navvies and their families.

They smelt the all-too-familiar scent of fire as the ash and soot from the burning timbers of the house drifted up into the night's air and invaded their nostrils as the carriage drew closer and closer to the source of the conflagration.

The driver pulled the horses to a halt at the end of the street and called down to Gillespie that he couldn't get any closer.

Hare was the first out of the carriage and led the charge down the street, weaving in and out of the fire appliances that littered the road. Fire fighters continued to forge a losing battle against the flames in a vain effort to stop the fire from engulfing the houses on either side of Hare's former home.

"No," yelled Hare as he stood in front of what was once his house and stared at the empty spaces in the window and doorway. Where once a door and glass panels protected the house's occupants from the outside world, now only lay vacant gaps. The soot-blackened bricks of the house's front wall stood in stark contrast to the reds, oranges and yellows of the flames that licked the inside of the building and shone through the empty window and doorway.

Gillespie grabbed the arm of a passing police officer who was running up the street to help the fire crew man-handle one of their hoses.

"What happened?" Gillespie asked. "How did the fire start?"

"We don't know, sir," replied the officer, shouting above the noise of the groaning timbers and the yells of the frightened residents gathered outside in the street.

"One of the neighbours raised the alarm with an officer on night patrol through the docks. When we got here, it was just the one house that was ablaze but now it's spreading faster than the boys can douse it."

"I understand, get back to work," Gillespie nodded as the policeman ran to join the fire crew. "Wait," he turned and called after the officer. "What about the occupants?"

The officer stopped dead in his tracks and his shoulders visibly fell as he sighed. "There," he said, pointing further down the street.

Gillespie followed the direction of the officer's outstretched arm and nodded his understanding. But Hare had been watching the exchange of words between the two policemen and reached the three black woollen blankets before Gillespie.

The captain ran and arrived just in time as Hare knelt down and pulled back the corner of the blanket covering the first of the three crumpled forms laid out on the cobbled street.

"No," he screamed as he looked at the body of his son, one side of his face burned black by the flames. Hare quickly crawled on his hands and knees across William's body to reach the second blanket, which he cast aside to reveal the corpse of Tilly, his daughter. The fire had obviously set light to her nightdress, the remnants of which barely covered her naked form. Burns covered most of her tiny body but her face had escaped the worst of the flame and, for a fleeting moment, Gillespie looked at her perfectly preserved face and thought the child might only be sleeping.

But the wail of pain that Hare emitted told its own story and Gillespie watched helplessly as the Irishman reached the end of the line of bodies and tore back the blanket to reveal Molly's body. Like William, the fire had consumed half of Molly's face but Hare still bent down and scooped up the charred remains of his wife in his arms, cradling her head and shoulders against his broad chest. He tenderly stroked the pale skin on the undamaged side of Molly's face, running his fingers across her forehead and down her cheek before slowly patting the singed hair on the side of her head.

"Why?" he bellowed. "Why?"

Then came the sobbing; heart-wrenching cries of pain that wracked his whole body and made his shoulders shake uncontrollably. He let Molly's dead body fall back to the cobbled street and lent back on his haunches, freeing a terrible scream into the night's sky and its uncaring stars staring down from above.

Slowly Hare rose to his feet and turned to face Gillespie.

"This was your doing," he shouted, running towards the captain. "You killed them, you bastard. You murdered my family."

Hare quickly covered the few paces between the bodies and where Gillespie stood but O'Malley and Fletcher were ready for him and each of them grabbed one of his arms from behind, pinning his shaking fists at his side.

"Murderer," yelled Hare, his face red with a rage that Gillespie had not seen cross the Irishman's features since they had been reunited in Boston.

Hare continued to struggle against his captors until his sobbing started again and soon his anger ebbed away and he sank to his knees in fits of tears. He crumbled in a heap on the cobbled road and wept for his lost family.

Gillespie signalled for his two lieutenants to back off and he slowly lowered himself to the ground in front of Hare on one knee.

"I promise you, I had nothing to do with this," Gillespie whispered softly, so that only Hare could hear him. The sobs slowed and Hare raised his face to look into Gillespie's eyes. "I didn't do this," Gillespie repeated. "But if you help me then we can find out who murdered your family and, if I'm right, who killed the navvies too."

Hare's red-rimmed eyes held Gillespie's stare, a degree of composure returning to the Irishman's face.

"What choice do I have?" Hare spat. "I've got nothing left."

CARLISLE, 1835

"For thine is the kingdom, the power and the glory, for ever and ever, amen," said Hare as he finished his prayer and stood up from the altar where he had been kneeling. The church was deserted but Hare didn't feel alone as he turned and sat on the front pew, content to pause and gaze up at the crucifix in front of which he had meditated for countless hours over countless days for the past five years. A crucifix he had carved himself out of wood from the nearby forest.

Outside, the weak winter's light was fading and two tall candles on the alter began to cast their long, flickering shadows across the small chapel as the snow continued to silently fall past the modest stained-glass windows before peacefully settling on the ground.

Hare let out a deep and contented sigh as he reflected on the good fortune that had brought him to the chapel five years earlier. Fleeing London, Hare had instinctively headed north, not sure where he was going but knowing he couldn't return to Edinburgh or Ulster. He had wandered through the countryside for months, stealing food and sleeping under the stars. With no one from London or Edinburgh pursuing him, Hare led the life of a vagabond, drifting aimlessly across the rolling hills and fields of England as he slowly pondered his next move.

But the autumn's rain had forced him to start seeking shelter, making him rest in barns and unlocked outhouses on farms or in small villages. As the rain fell and the sky darkened, Hare's mood took a turn for the macabre. While the roofs of the barns sheltered him from the rain, nothing could protect him from the torment of Burke.

"*Running, running, running,*" *his ghostly companion chanted.* "*Always on the run. Running from Ulster, running from Edinburgh, running from London and running from me. When are you ever going to learn, you'll never shake me, Hare, I'm a part of you now.*"

Hare's wanderings led him further and further north until he reached a small, darkened chapel nestled on the edge of a tiny village among rolling hills. The tall house that sat next to the church looked deserted and so Hare decided to try the door to the small chapel. It opened without protest, the parishioners not bothering with a lock in such a rural setting.

"Desecrating holy ground now are we, Hare!" Burke asked as he followed his fellow Irishman into the unlit church.

"Sanctuary," Hare muttered under his breath. "Come unto me, all ye that labour and are heavy laden, and I will give ye rest," he repeated slowly, clinging to an old memory that had surfaced at the back of his mind.

"Huh, so you've found religion now have you!" Burke mocked. *"The only way you'll find religion is when the priest gives you the final rites. Then the executioner will hang you, just like he hanged me. I'm not done with you yet. I still want my revenge."*

"Vengeance is mine, I will repay, saith the Lord," Hare barked, childhood memories flashing through his mind of his mother taking him and his siblings away from his abusive father and off to mass on a Sunday morning.

"Oh, God will have his vengeance too, make no mistake about that. You'll burn right next to me here in Hell for the crimes you've committed, for the lives you've taken. Your father and your brother and all those paupers and ragamuffins from the West Port will line up to accuse you before God," Burke snarled, dancing from one foot to the other in front of the alter.

Hare collapsed down onto the wooden pew in front of the altar and began to weep.

"He hath delivered us from the power of darkness, and hath translated us into the kingdom of his dear son, in whom we have redemption through his blood, even the forgiveness of sins," Hare cried, the tears rolling down his filthy and unshaven cheeks.

"Are you saved, Hare!" Burke cackled. *"Has God prepared a space for a miserable sinner like you in Heaven! You're going to rot in Hell, just like your brother and just like your father and just like me."*

Hare cried himself to sleep on the pew that first night as Burke's bitter laughter carried on ringing in his ears.

The morning's bright light broke through the clouds and shone down on Hare as he stirred the following day. Opening his eyes, he felt some relief having sunk soundly into the deepest sleep he had enjoyed for weeks – but his tormenter still stood before the altar, ready to curse him again.

"What now, Hare?" Burke spat. *"What's the plan? A day spent hiding here in this church? Or another day on the run, stealing food just to survive?"*

"The Lord will provide," Hare shouted back, his strength returning and his voice booming through the empty church.

"The Lord?" Burke sniggered. *"One night in a chapel and you think you're saved?"*

"Get behind me, Satan," Hare yelled at the top of his lungs.

"I would young man, but it appears I already am behind you," came a voice from the back of the church.

Hare froze. While he had been railing against Burke, he hadn't heard the door to the church creak open or the plump figure of the vicar edge his way inside. The Irishman spun round to see the clergyman slowly walking along the aisle between the pews to the front of the church, where Hare stood alone.

Hare jumped backwards, colliding with a wooden lectern and knocking it to the floor.

"I'm sorry, Father," he muttered. "I didn't realise anyone else was here."

"Father?" the priest chuckled. "I'm no one's father, young man. Nor, I hope, am I Satan, so I pray you'll stop your remonstrations, no matter how heartfelt they may be."

Hare looked blank and the vicar chuckled again.

"You're early for the service," the minister remarked, ignoring Hare's confused look.

"Service?" Hare frowned. "Is it Sunday?"

"Why yes, of course it is my boy," the vicar smiled as he picked up the lectern and laid the Bible he had been carrying on top of it, flicking the pages open to that day's reading. "That's why you're here isn't it?"

Hare looked away sheepishly and avoided the minister's gaze. The priest frowned and then looked down at Hare's stolen coat on the front pew, where he had used it as a blanket the night before.

"Ah, I see," the minister nodded.

"I'm sorry, Father," Hare said again, hanging his head in shame.

"My son, I may be a priest but I'm no Roman Catholic," the vicar shook his head. "So less of this father business. Reverend, or Mister Porter will do nicely. Now, will you be joining us for the service?"

"It's been a long time since I went to mass," Hare muttered.

"Mass?" Porter laughed, his rounded belly shaking. "You will be waiting a long time if you are expecting a mass. I am a minister of King William's Church of England. No one in these parts would be found practising the old religion," Porter shook his head.

Hare smiled nervously, remembering what Thomas had told him about the persecution of the Irish.

"But you would be made more than welcome here in my church," Porter smiled, as the first of the parishioners began to file slowly into the church and take their seats.

"Perhaps if you stay then we can talk some more after the service?" Porter offered, as he helped Hare gather up his coat and retreat to a pew near the back of the church.

And so Hare had stayed. He had remained in his seat when all the other worshippers had formed a line for communion, filing slowly forward along the central aisle to share in the Eucharistic supper.

After the service, Porter had taken him back to the grand, stone-built manse that stood next to the more-modest church and fed Hare with bread and cheese and cold meat. Hare gorged himself on the feast, even sharing in a glass of the vicar's thin and tannic red wine.

Once Hare's hunger and thirst were sated, Porter began to tease out his story. Hare was guarded at first but after a second glass of wine his words began to flow until he couldn't stop himself from revealing the most intimate details of his despair as he had trudged across that countryside over the previous few weeks and months.

Later, back in the small church, as Porter began blowing out the candles following the evening's vespers, Hare swallowed hard and asked: "Father, will you hear my confession?"

Porter smiled his large, warm smile again.

"We have no confession in our church," he replied. "Only you can confess your sins to God. If you truly repent then the Lord will wash away your misdemeanours. There is no penitence that I can hand out to you that will cleanse your heart – only our Lord Jesus Christ's death on the cross can save you."

"Please, Father," Hare pleaded, sinking to his knees and holding out his hands.

Porter could see the Irishman was clearly becoming more and more disturbed and so he relented, kneeling down in front of Hare.

"I'm listening," he whispered.

And slowly, hesitantly at first but then getting faster and faster, Hare poured out his heart to Porter, listing the crimes he had committed and the lives he had taken.

Porter turned paler and paler as Hare recounted his story, but the minister remained kneeling with him, knowing that if Hare had meant to kill him then he had already passed up many opportunities to do so.

After Hare had finished speaking and lapsed into silence, Porter coughed to clear his throat.

"Your father abused you and your brothers and sisters and your mother?" he asked gingerly.

Hare nodded.

"And your brother was beating his wife before you took his life?" the minister questioned.

Again, Hare confirmed the assertion with a nod of his head.

"And you were arrested for your heinous crimes in Edinburgh? But they let you go free?"

"Yes," Hare replied quietly.

"Then confess your sins to the Lord," Porter said, pointing to the small wooden cross perched on the altar, "and pray for forgiveness from the Lord God Almighty. I will pray too for you, begging Our Lord Jesus Christ to intercede for you as he does for all sinners."

The pair turned to face the altar and Hare began praying out loud, slowly and falteringly to begin with but then guided in his words by Porter, who knelt beside him.

When they had finished praying, Hare looked up and felt a weight being released from his soul, as even Burke's evil laughter began subsiding in his ears and eventually faded away to nothingness.

Five years later, Hare founded himself sitting again on that front pew, looking up at the cross he had fashioned for the church as an act of thanksgiving. He had stayed at the manse, acting as the minister's gardener and handyman, growing vegetables in the garden behind the manse and tending to the flowers that grew in the beds on either side of the front door.

Hare fed and watered the minister's horse, which Porter used to visit the households of his parish, both the rich landowners and the poor tenant farmers alike. Porter had introduced Hare to Simmons and Hopkins, two other waifs and strays who the minister had taken into his care. The pair eyed Hare suspiciously but begrudgingly worked alongside him, happy to have another pair of hands to help them with their chores.

"Lost in thought, my boy?" asked Porter from the back of the church as he watched Hare sitting on the front pew.

"Reverend Porter, welcome back, sir," smiled Hare, rising up to greet the minister with a hug and a shake of the hand. "How was Carlisle?"

"It may only be an hour away but it may as well be a different country," Porter beamed. "It makes me glad to be back in God's own land again in our fair countryside. And the Dean was in agreement with my plan," the minister added, which drew a frown from Hare.

"What plan, sir?" he asked.

"To make you my verger," Porter replied. "Your service to me and this church has been exemplary over the past five years, William, and I feel it should be rewarded."

"But sir, you already feed me and clothe me and see to all my needs."

"Yes William, but you are always far away, in the background. As verger, you will be at my side."

Porter could see that Hare was looking hesitant.

"William, you have put your past crimes behind you. It is time for you to play a fuller role in the life of this community and of this church."

"Being more prominent means people will ask more questions," Hare protested. "Now they know me as William but if I'm the verger then my name will be in your record books and people may start asking where I came from and what right I have to be a verger."

"No one will question my motives, William," Porter soothed. "They have seen the hard work you do here at the church and in the manse. But perhaps you would feel happier if you took on another name?" the minister asked.

Hare nodded slowly. "That may help," he smiled.

"Good," grinned Porter. "Just as Simon became Peter and Saul become Paul, so William Hare will take on a new name to mark his rebirth as a servant of the Lord. Have you thought about a name you will use?"

"Laird," Hare replied simply.

Porter nodded, having heard Hare tell the story a number of times about his wife, Margaret Laird, who Hare had married following the death of her previous husband.

"A fitting name," Porter said. "It will remind you of the wife and son who are separated from you and who one day you may get to see again."

"I do hope so, sir," Hare replied.

"Now, let us retire for some supper so that I can rest these weary legs of mine," Porter grinned, clasping Hare by the shoulder and leading him out of the church and to the manse.

The scene that greeted the pair as they stepped over the threshold and into the vast hall of the manse was one of utter chaos. The table in the hall had been overturned and the vase of flowers shattered across the floor.

"What the devil has happened here?" Porter asked.

"I don't know, sir," Hare replied nervously. "I've been in the church praying for the past two hours. I didn't hear a thing from the house."

"Marjorie?" Porter called out, trying to summon his housekeeper.

"Annette?" he added, trying his scullery maid instead.

Hare and Porter edged their way past the staircase and into the large dining room, where the massive oak table had been upended and the Welsh dresser thrown from the wall and left lying across the bare floorboards, its crockery smashed into shards.

The pair moved through to the lounge, where they found Marjorie's body lying in front of the fireplace, her skull split in two and blood oozing out over the carpet. Hiding behind a large stuffed chair, they found Annette, the eight-year-old scullery maid, whimpering quietly to herself.

"Annette, my love, what in heaven's name has happened here?" Porter asked the young girl.

"It was Mr Simmons and Mr Hopkins, sir," Annette cried. "They hit Mrs Yates with a poker when she wouldn't tell them where the house keeping money was hidden."

Hare's blood ran cold.

"Where are they now, Annette?" he asked.

"Upstairs," the young girl moaned. "I heard them turning over the bedrooms."

"Run Annette," Porter commanded. "Go out the back door through the kitchen and don't stop running until you get to the village. Find the Constable and tell him to bring help."

Annette nodded her understanding and then followed the men back out into the hall.

"And where do you think you're going?" came a loud voice from the top of the stairs. Hare, Porter and Annette froze in the hallway as Simmons and Hopkins descended the stairs, Simmons carrying a bloodied poker in one hand and Porter's shooting pistol in the other, while Hopkins aimed the minister's hunting rifle at the party in hallway.

Simmons cocked the pepperbox pistol and took aim at Hare, the gun's menacing five barrels trained on his chest.

"What have you boys done?" Porter pleaded. "Stop this madness now and we will let you go with the money."

"No chance," Simmons spat. "The moment we're out that door you'd have the Constable and half the local hunt after us. No, Reverend, this ends tonight and this ends here, nice and quietly like."

"And what about you, Hare?" Hopkins asked. "Why don't you come with us? There's enough silver and gold in here and in that chapel to fetch a pretty price in Carlisle or Penrith or Liverpool. I've seen you breaking up fights down at The Fox. You'd be a pretty handy man to have around in a scrap."

"Never," Hare spat. "My place is here with the Minister. And you two will burn in Hell for what you've done tonight."

"Burn in Hell?" Simmons snorted. "Sounds like Reverend Porter here has got well and truly inside your head, Hare."

"You always were his favourite," Hopkins snorted. "Always the first he called on. Always the first he praised."

"Is that what this is all about?" Porter asked. "Did I not love you boys enough when I took you in?"

"Nah, it's simpler than that," Hopkins smirked. "There's only so much tough meat and cold porridge a man can take while you swan about with your rich parishioners, with their aged claret and prime beef."

"Shut up, Hopkins, we don't have time for this," Simmons snapped. "Now turn around you three so I don't have to see the look of fear on your faces when I finish you off."

Porter and Hare slowly complied with their captors, while Annette looked frantically between the two for some hope of salvation.

"Annette," Porter hissed quietly. "When I say so, you run out that front door and don't look back."

Annette silently nodded and began sucking in short gasps of breath.

"Now," yelled Porter as he turned and threw himself at Simmons.

His actions caught the gunman off guard and he dropped the poker but he kept the revolver level and squeezed the trigger as Porter barrelled into him, getting off one shot that sliced through the top of the minister's chest below his left shoulder. But Annette did as she was bid and didn't look back as she bolted out of the still-open front door.

Simmons threw Porter's body to the floor where the minister gasped in agony from his wound and turned to level his aim on Hare again. Simmons stepped over Porter's prone form on the floor and stole a quick glance out of the front door to watch Annette dashing across the snow-covered driveway and onto the grass of the lawn, heading down the hill towards the fence and the village beyond.

"Hopkins, take her down," he ordered, stepping back inside and letting his accomplice pass by. "We can't let her reach the village."

"Help," Annette began shouting as she neared the bright lights of the village pub. "Help me, please help."

Hopkins stepped out into the porch and slowly raised the hunting rifle to his shoulder, taking aim as he had practised a thousand times during the afternoons when he should have been chopping firewood but had instead been toying with the minister's rifle.

Cocking the hammer back, he looked down the sight and marked his target as she ran away from him.

Annette never knew what hit her. Even at the hundred or so yards across the lawn, the high-velocity round still sliced through the back of her skull and exited from the centre of her forehead, staining the white snow red with her blood as her still warm body cooled against the cold blanket on the ground.

But her efforts had not been in vain for the door to The Fox swung open and a group of men looked up the hill to the lights in the manse doorway.

"What's going on up there?" they shouted. "Who's that in the snow?"

"Shit," muttered Hopkins, stepping back inside the hallway, where Hare was cradling the dying minister in his arms and Simmons had his revolver trained on both of them. "They saw me," Hopkins told his partner as Simmons shook his head.

"We'll take the minister's horse then," Simmons decided. "It'll get us far enough away that we'll be able to pick up fresh rides."

Hopkins nodded. "Finish these two off and we'll be away."

Hare looked into Porter's face as the light began to fade from the old man's eyes. "God has forgiven you, William," Porter spluttered as a thin trickle of blood slid down the corner of his mouth. "Don't throw your soul away again."

Standing over Hare's shoulder, Burke's ghostly apparition reappeared.

"You can't let them get away with this," Burke hissed. *"It's either*

your life or their's."

Rolling back onto his heels, Hare launched himself at Simmons and catching the man in his midriff, sent him collapsing backwards against the banister of the stairs. Simmons cracked his head off the thick wooden railings and sank dead to the floor, while Hare snatched up his revolver and aimed it at Hopkins, who had reloaded his rifle and had it trained on the Irishman.

"Looks like a stalemate, Hare," Hopkins said. "Who's going to blink first?"

The noise on the snow-covered gravel outside grew louder as the crowd of men from The Fox raced up the driveway, brandishing burning torches to light their paths and weighing their pistols and rifles.

An idea flashed across Hopkins' face.

"In here," he called to the men outside. "Hurry quickly before Hare gets away."

Hare's eyes widened as he suddenly realised what Hopkins had done.

"He's in here," Hopkins screamed as the local police constable led a party of men into the hallway, their faces reddened by the run up the hill and the beer they had been drinking all night.

"What the hell happened here?" the police officer demanded. Hare slowly edged his way across the hall towards the door, all the time keeping the revolver trained on Hopkins, but his escape through the doorway was blocked by the number of men trying to push their way into the manse.

"It was Hare," Hopkins replied. "He must have killed Marjorie Yates. When we arrived back with Reverend Hopkins, Hare shot him with his own revolver. Simmons and me were trying to stop him when he shot wee Annette stone cold dead on the lawn."

"He's lying," Hare barked. "He's a lying coward. I swear on my own life that it was Simmons and Hopkins who were trying to rob the Reverend when we caught them in the act."

"Why would we do a thing like that?" Hopkins countered. "We've been with Reverend Porter since we were boys. But what about you? What do we know about you, Hare? You've lived here for years but no one knows the first thing about you."

"Put the gun down, Hare," the constable ordered. "Drop that weapon and give yourself up."

Hare's eyes widened. "You believe him?" he asked incredulously.

"If there's trouble then seldom's the case that there's not an Irishman involved somewhere along the line," the constable nodded.

"You'll pay for this, Hopkins," Hare spat.

But Hopkins just laughed and raised the rifle again at Hare.

Taking his final chance, Hare squeezed the trigger of the revolver and planted a bullet square in Hopkins' face, slicing through his nose and destroying his brain.

Before anyone could stop him, Hare threw himself through the nearest window, shattering the wooden frame and thin panes of glass as he crashed out onto the drive. Picking himself up and ignoring the burning pain in his shoulder from the impact, Hare raced across the snow-covered gravel to where the minister had tied up his horse. The Irishman quickly mounted the stead and grabbed its reins, forcing it into a fast canter away from the house.

"Don't let him get away," the constable yelled to the other men who had accompanied him to the manse. Three members of the local hunt had their rifles at the ready and fired after Hare but their shots flew high, missing his head by inches.

Gripping on to Hare's coattails on the back of the horse, Burke hissed in his ear: "Take them down, Hare, don't let them get you."

Hare fought off the temptation, the revolver still gripped tight in his hand but, after another hail of bullets grazed past him, he tilted in his saddle and twisted round, emptying the other three chambers of his revolver before tossing its useless carcass aside as the horse galloped on into the night. Hare didn't turn round to see his bullets had each found their mark, injuring two of the riflemen and the village constable who had been chasing him.

The morning's sun rose slowly above the horizon as the port of Liverpool disappeared in the distant east. Leaning against the railing of the cargo ship, Hare slipped his brother's stolen pipe from his mouth having finished smoking the end of the tobacco he had bummed from one of the sailors. He pocketed the pipe and gazed out to the south as the boat passed the northern tip of the Isle of Man and headed further out into the Irish Sea.

Ahead of him, the coast of Ulster came into view and Hare began to imagine Margaret and young William, far inland in his home town of Newry. He could still picture Margaret's plump cheeks but he couldn't imagine the wee boy into which baby William would have grown by now.

Hare stood for what felt like an age, watching the Irish coastline passing by. Great Britain and Ireland held nothing for Hare now; wherever he had gone, he was no longer welcome. Crossing the Atlantic for a new life in the United States felt like all that was left to him.

But as the final stretch of Ulster passed him by, Hare couldn't stop himself from sinking to his knees and pushing his head against the railings. He wept as the boat forged by his homeland and headed out into the deep Atlantic.

PART FOUR
BOSTON, 1863

16

The police coach dropped Gillespie off at the door to his house but, as soon as the carriage pulled away and disappeared around the corner, the captain knew that something was wrong. Even in the pale gas light from the street lamps, he could see that the wood around the lock had been scored with a metal implement.

Though the door was closed and locked, Gillespie knew he would not be alone in his residence. He turned the key in the lock and returned it to his pocket before slipping his revolver out of its holster and pulling back the hammer to arm the Colt. He threw open the front door and then slowly made his way down the hall, kicking the heavy wooden door shut behind him.

He entered the parlour and was astonished to find a fire burning in the hearth and a woman sitting in one of the high back chairs he kept arranged in a semicircle around the fireplace.

"Well, I must say that's no way to greet a lady," complained Amelia Proctor as she stood to welcome the captain.

Gillespie's gaze quickly swept the rest of the room.

"Oh, don't worry, we're quite alone," Amelia offered, watching his practiced eye assessing the situation.

"After my man picked the lock, I sent him home in my carriage. I've been waiting for you for some time now," she added, teasing him to respond.

Gillespie rolled the hammer back into place to disarm his weapon and slipped the Colt back into its holster.

"You won't need that," Amelia shook her head. "Do I look dangerous to you?"

Gillespie stared hard at her for the first time. She was wearing her long red hair down so that it fell past her shoulders. She had changed out of the high-necked dress in which he had seen her at the mayor's rally at the docks but still wore a black outfit. This time, she had paired a long flowing skirt with a full-sleeved blouse. Only the pale skin of her hands, neck and face was visible.

"I must admit, you don't look like any assassin I've seen before," Gillespie smiled. His mind whirled, trying to work out why the industrialist's widow was sitting in his front room.

Gillespie's question was answered instantly as Amelia took a step towards him and pulled his face down to hers by slipping her pale hand behind his neck. Her lips were soft and moist as they kissed, betraying a warmth that seemed at odds to her pale skin and mourning-clothed attire.

After three days with little sleep and an evening spent chasing shadows and murderers around the city's docks, Gillespie didn't stop to question Amelia's presence or her actions but instead surrendered himself to his own desires; desires that Amelia obviously shared.

She stroked the back of his neck as she kissed him, setting every hair on his body on end and sending quivers of pleasure through his nerves. She slowly began working her fingers up into his salt and pepper hair, pulling his head down closer to her mouth while his hands found their way around her narrow waist and down onto the broad hips beneath her long black skirt.

His temptress brought her hands down from amongst his locks of hair and rested them on his shoulders before pulling away from their kiss. She slowly unbuttoned his long military-style greatcoat and let it slip onto the floor before working her way down the buttons of his dark suit jacket and waistcoat. Amelia slipped off his suit garment and began teasing him out of his once-white shirt, now stained with soot from the fire in Hare's home and soaked in his own sweat from the heat of the fiery street.

Amelia tossed the ruined shirt over her shoulder, pulling off the detachable high-necked collar as she went, and then planted kisses along his collar bone and upper arms before slowly working her way down his chest. Her lips passed over the scars from knife and bullet wounds that traced out his long years with police forces on both sides of the Atlantic and his spell in the United States' army.

At first Gillespie let his muscles relax as Amelia worked her magic, permitting himself to enjoy the sensation of intimacy with a woman, a feeling he had not experienced for more years than he cared to count. Then his muscles clenched and tightened once more as Amelia unbuckled his belt and tossed it off to one side before unbuttoning his trousers; she betrayed no sense of surprise that he wasn't wearing any undergarments beneath his shirt and trousers.

Gillespie then grasped Amelia's wrists with his hands and held her arms up above her head as he kissed the pale-skinned woman first on her mouth and then on her high cheek bones and then down her neck.

When he reached the high collar of her black blouse he let go of her wrists and slowly began unbuttoning the garment while Amelia kept her arms high above her head and threw her head back as she sighed with pleasure. She wore no corset or bodice under her blouse, allowing Gillespie to plant a succession of quick kisses across her naked breasts.

His eyes fell across Amerlia's bare chest as his hands descended lower down her body and worked her skirt from her waist to her hips and then let it drop to the wooden floorboards below. He took in the paleness of her skin; the white of her face was clearly her natural pallor and not the result of powders or potions. He noticed the small brown freckles that littered her cheeks were also present across her collarbone and the tops of her shoulders. Gazing down her chest, Gillespie admired how the deep pink colour of her erect nipples and wide areolas stood out against the pale whiteness of her large breasts.

Amelia stepped forward out of her skirt and undergarments and pushed her body hard against Gillespie's naked form as the couple shared another passionate embrace. The police captain swept her up in his arms and turned her round so that he could lay her down on the sheepskin rug in front of the roaring fire. Amelia had lit the two candles sitting on the broad mantelpiece above the hearth and their soft candle light cast its weak glow over the lovers as Gillespie lowered himself on top of Amelia. She moaned softly and then wrapped her arms around his torso, digging her nails into the flesh across his shoulder blades. Gillespie let out a cry part way between pain and ecstasy as she scratched his back.

The pair soon found a natural rhythm as their bodies became one but, just as Gillespie could feel himself reaching the end of his exertions, Amelia sat up and, pushing against the rug with her feet, spun their bodies around so that she sat astride Gillespie. His moans of pleasure matched her high-pitch gasp and then scream of delight.

Later, they lay in front of the fire together on the sheepskin, a grey woollen rug covering Amelia to aid her warmth. She had brought a bottle of wine with her and had proceeded to pour them a glass each before returning to the fireside. As he sipped on the smooth red liquid, he could feel a wave of tiredness crash over his aching body. Amelia seemed to sense it too and swivelled her body around to face him, letting the blanket fall away to reveal her naked breasts once more.

"Shhhh," she whispered as Gillespie began to murmur. "Sleep, we can talk later."

No sooner than she had finished saying the words, Gillespie felt his body relaxing as his vision went dark and his head fell on to the deep white strands of the woollen rug beneath him.

When he awoke, the flames in the fireplace had died away, leaving only the red glowing coals in the grate. Both candles on the mantelpiece had burned down to the final portion of their wax but still cast enough light for Gillespie to read the clock face and see that it was after midnight. He raised himself up from the floor and stretched his stiff muscles. Looking around the parlour he quickly discerned that he was alone again and he began to wonder if his encounter with Amelia had all been a dream.

But then he saw the grey woollen blanket neatly folded on one of the high-backed chairs and the empty bottle of wine on the parlour table and he knew that he hadn't imagined her visit.

The sight of the empty green glass bottle made Gillespie realise how dry his throat was and what a thirst had taken hold of his body. After quickly searching and finding no other drink in the house, he threw on his clothes from the day before and headed out the door.

17

O'Malley had been awoken from his sleep on many occasions during his long career with Boston's police department and its preceding nightwatch. He had often risen to find a junior uniformed policeman standing at his door, urging O'Malley to follow him down to one of the less salubrious taverns that lined the dockside.

But never before had O'Malley been dragged from his sleep in order to confront a senior officer who, according to the flatfoot running ahead of him along the dock road, looked like he was only minutes away from starting a bar room brawl.

The young policeman led O'Malley straight into the dockworkers' inn, much to the shock of the barman, who came round from behind his bar to remonstrate with the officers, fearing that they had found out that he had no license to be operating into the early hours of the morning.

But the Irishman calmed the publican with a wave of his hand. "There's no need to worry, Harry, I'm not here to close you down."

O'Malley turned to face the junior officer. "Wait here," he instructed, pointing to the door to the bar. The lieutenant turned back around and led the barman over to his counter again.

"One of your regulars tipped off that patrolman that there was a fight brewing," O'Malley explained. "He said there was a 'gentleman' involved and I think he might be a friend of mine."

The barman visibly relaxed after finding out his drinking den wasn't about to be shut down.

"He's through the back," the tavern owner nodded, hitching a finger over his shoulder to a heavy velvet curtain that separated off the back room from the main saloon bar. "There was a lot of shouting over a game of cards so I moved them through there out the way. Where they won't cause trouble for the rest of my customers."

Even at such an early hour of the day, the bar was still full of dockworkers drowning their sorrows and avoiding the trip home to their wives.

O'Malley nodded his understanding. "What are we looking at here?" he asked. "Has this friend of mine been knocking the drinks back all night or what?"

The barman shook his head. "That's the worst of it," he snorted. "He's been nursing the same drink all night. Looks like he hasn't touched a drop of it either. I'd go out of business if they were all like him."

O'Malley frowned and headed for the deep red of the velvet curtain. He drew back the drape to be confronted with a cloud of thick blue cigar smoke. Four figures were sat hunched over a card table while a further three leaned against the walls of the cramped back room. At the sight of O'Malley, the trio of onlookers straightened up and the Irishman noticed the trigger fingers of two of them twitching for their guns.

But the lieutenant was quicker than all of them and already had his Colt drawn and cocked before they were able to move.

"Evening gents," he said in a mocking tone. Three of the players at the card table looked up at the interruption to their game and began pushing back their chairs but the fourth remained seated with his back to O'Malley.

"No need to get up on my account," O'Malley signalled with the barrel of his revolver for the players to retake their seats. "Boston police department. I just need a word with your friend here."

Slowly, Gillespie twisted around in his seat to get a good look at O'Malley. The Irishman clocked the still-full glass of dark bourbon on the card table, sitting next to the hand of cards that Gillespie had laid face-down on the green felt.

"Now you listen to me," Gillespie began as he rose from his chair.

But O'Malley was ready to cut him off; he uncocked his revolver and dropped it into one of his deep coat pockets and smacked his hands against each side of Gillespie's head, boxing his ears and instantly disorientating the police captain. As Gillespie crumpled from the blow, O'Malley grabbed him under the arms and half-dragged him away from the table.

"Carry on," he called back over his shoulder as the other card players looked on in surprise.

As he passed the junior policeman at the door of the bar, O'Malley came to a brief halt.

"Not a word of this to anyone," he hissed. The patrolman vigorously nodded his understanding before holding the door open for O'Malley as he dragged Gillespie outside. The lieutenant signalled for the flatfoot to fetch the police coach from where they had left it standing at the end of the dock road, before throwing Gillespie roughly down onto the cobbled street.

"What the hell do you think you're playing at?" O'Malley yelled at his superior officer. "Drinking alone at this time of night? On the verge of starting a fight? Playing cards with men who would shoot you dead in a moment if they knew who you are?"

Gillespie slowed picked himself up from the street, swaying on his unsteady legs as he stood to face his accuser. Even in the pale light cast out through the windows of the tavern, O'Malley could see that the captain's eyes were red rimmed and his cheeks were stained with tears of anger.

"Me?" Gillespie spat back. "It's you who has the explaining to do, Lieutenant. Assaulting senior officers now are you, you piece of Irish scum."

O'Malley balled his hands into fists and huffed loudly to dissipate his anger.

"If you were any other officer then I'd throw you in the drunk-tank for the night and let you sleep this off," the Irishman hissed. "But you didn't even touch your liquor. What the hell's going on, Sandy?"

At the sound of his first name, Gillespie stopped seething with anger for a moment. Shaking his head, he looked at O'Malley standing in front of him, as if for the first time.

"I..." he began to reply. "I don't know. I was with a woman and I drank then," he stammered. Even through the foggy haze that had engulfed his mind, Gillespie knew that mentioning Amelia's name to O'Malley could only lead to more trouble.

"A woman?" O'Malley shouted. "A woman? You watched three charred bodies being laid out from a house fire tonight and you still have an appetite to go out and feed your carnal needs?

"We spend the day on a wild-goose chase to corner this body snatcher and all you want to do is get laid?"

"We don't all have a family to go home to at night," Gillespie snapped back. "We don't all have a woman like Maddie to nurse our woes and bear our children."

"Listen to yourself," O'Malley shook his head. "You're out womanising and gambling while there's a madman out there killing dockers and threatening the war effort.

"Hare may be a murderer but he's the one acting the most human out of all of this. I left Fletcher guarding him down at St Patrick's. He's not left the altar since we took him down there. He just kneels there, praying for mercy for his dead wife and kids."

The black police coach pulled up behind him and O'Malley threw open the door before roughly shoving Gillespie inside.

"You need to get yourself cleaned up," he said, after giving the driver the captain's address.

The carriage pulled away, leaving O'Malley shaking his head and cursing the downfall of his commander and friend.

18

Even though all of the tiered benches were empty, Professor Seymour Cartwright's lecture theatre at Harvard University's Massachusetts Medical College still felt crowded to Gillespie, mirroring the state of his mind the morning after the incident with O'Malley at the dockside tavern.

The fog that had permeated his head was beginning to clear, aided by the cloth soaked in cold water that he was holding to his temple. But his thoughts were still clouded by the events of the past few days as he tried to work out who was killing the dock workers and why they always appeared to be a step ahead of his investigation.

As well as O'Malley and Fletcher, Hare had been brought along to the medical college, where they joined the professor and his assistant, Jamie Taylor.

Cartwright pursed his lips and nodded as he sniffed at the yellow liquid in the glass beaker he held before his face.

"Hmmm, leaf mulch and asparagus," he muttered as he swirled the liquid around in the vessel and took in another whiff of its scent.

"Just as I suspected – turbatium," the professor concluded as he laid the beaker down on his desk and began adding a mixture of two white powders into a glass of water, where they fizzed and then immediately began to dissolve.

"Turbatium?" Gillespie asked.

"A type of truth serum," Cartwright explained, using a spoon to stir the mixture before handing it to the captain. "There's no doubt, Sandy, you were poisoned."

"And you can tell that from just smelling his piss?" Fletcher frowned.

"Oh yes, Lieutenant," Cartwright nodded. "The only trace that the chemical leaves is the smell in the victim's urine. Fortunately, it shouldn't leave you with any lasting damage and this concoction of mine should help to relieve the grogginess and the headaches," he added, turning back to Gillespie, who nodded his thanks and glugged down the mixture in one fell swoop.

"You were lucky, Sandy," Cartwright chided. "A larger dose and turbatium can have some very strange affects on the human body. To the untrained eye, someone who has swallowed more of this substance can appear for all intents and purposes dead. They will appear not to breathe nor have any trace of the pulse that pumps blood through their veins."

Each member of the group was lost in his own reflections for a moment.

"Well that explains a lot then," nodded O'Malley, breaking the silence. The Irishman had spared Fletcher, Hare and Cartwright the details of the previous night, save to tell them that Gillespie had been unwell and that he wanted to be taken to see the professor.

The captain laid the beaker down on Cartwright's desk and perched himself on the corner as he began to feel his head clearing. O'Malley and Fletcher sat on the front row of the lecture theatre's benches but Hare remained standing, his sullen gaze not moving from the white sheet that covered a body on the nearby trolley. Taylor stood behind it, waiting for instructions from Cartwright.

Gillespie sighed heavily. "What about the body?" he asked the professor.

Cartwright moved across to Hare.

"I'm so very, very sorry for your loss," he said, resting a hand on the Irishman's shoulder. Although Gillespie had told Cartwright the full story about Hare – from his crimes in Edinburgh through to Gillespie's suspicions about his involvement in the latest series of murders – the old doctor could still find the compassion to treat him as if he were any other patient. Gillespie watched his friend's actions and longed that he could show the same kind of grace that the academic displayed.

"From my examination of your wife and children's bodies, it's very clear to me that they were still alive when the fire was started. The heat from the flames had warmed the air and burned the inside of their throats and lungs. If, as the police told me, they were found tied to chairs then I believe they may have been overcome by the smoke before the inferno reached their bodies."

Hare looked up and locked his eyes – one green, one blue – on Cartwright, fixing him with his cold stare.

"And if they didn't?" he asked tonelessly.

Cartwright sighed heavily. "Then I fear the flames would have consumed them while they were still conscious."

The men in the room remained silent, each lost in his own thoughts.

"No," screamed Hare as he lunged forward and ripped the white sheet from the trolley. Molly's naked body lay exposed. Just as one side of her face had been burned away by the fire, so too had half of her torso along with one arm and one leg. The heat of the flames had caused her skin to blister and char, boiling the fat inside her breast and thigh and distorting the line of her abdomen.

Hare turned to face Gillespie.

"Are you happy now?" he yelled. "Are you happy now I've lost everything? Has your twisted sense of justice been served?"

"Get him out of here," Gillespie muttered, shaking his head. Fletcher, who had been staring at the deformed corpse, shook himself free of his revere and grabbed Hare by the shoulders, dragging him out of the lecture theatre.

"What a horrible business," Cartwright said sadly after Fletcher had escorted his prisoner away from the body. Taylor busied himself covering up Molly's remains again.

"Are you any closer to catching the killer?" the professor asked Gillespie and O'Malley.

"No," Gillespie sighed. "But Hare is the key to all of this, of that I have no doubt."

Cartwright nodded. "It would seem that you were getting close to the truth if someone wanted to get to Hare like this."

"Were they sending him a warning though?" Gillespie mused. "Were they telling him that if he talked then he'd be next?"

Cartwright turned to help Taylor straighten the blanket. O'Malley got up from his seat on the bench and gathered up his hat and coat ready to leave.

"Thank you for last night," Gillespie said to his lieutenant.

"Just doing my job, Inspector," O'Malley replied. Each of them knew that no more needed to be said.

"Any clues at the scene of the fire?" Gillespie asked.

"None," O'Malley replied. "I led the team that sifted through the wreckage this morning. There was nothing to help us in amongst the embers."

Both officers fell silent, mulling over their next move. Their reflections were interrupted by Fletcher pushing the door to the lecture theatre open.

"Hare's back in the carriage with MacLeod," the lieutenant explained.

"So what now?" Cartwright asked them. "Where do you go from here?"

"We continue with our plan," Gillespie said firmly. "Laying a trap for the killer seems to be the only way that we will catch him.

"After all this," he added, with a wave of his arm towards the trolley, "I think Hare will be ready to cooperate fully."

Cartwright shook his head. "Sad but true," he agreed. "Well, if I can be of any further help then please just call."

Gillespie turned to leave when a thought suddenly struck him.

"Actually, there was one other thing professor," he said. "O'Malley, do you still have those bullets we found on the body when our office burned down?"

O'Malley rummaged in his pocket for a moment before producing the three chunks of metal that had once been fired from a revolver. Gillespie's faithful lieutenant handed the bullets to his boss, who in turn passed them on to Cartwright.

"Is there anything you can tell me about these bullets?" the captain asked.

The professor turned them over in his fingers and then crossed over to his desk, retrieving a large magnifying glass from one of the top drawers.

"Hmmm," he frowned. "They certainly aren't like any of the bullets I see here in Boston," he began. "The mixture of metals looks different, even to the eye."

A loud groaning sound caused Cartwright and the two police men to spin around. Taylor, his tall and gangling frame affording him several inches of height above Cartwright, had been peering over the professor's shoulder at the bullets.

"What is it, Jamie?" Cartwright asked.

Taylor signalled for the professor to hand him one of the bullets and the magnifying glass.

"What? What's he seen?" asked Fletcher, craning his neck to see.

The research assistant passed the bullet back and forth between his fingers, examining what was left of its shape through the magnifying glass. After several minutes of silence, he began moaning again, though this time his mood was obviously agitated.

"What, Jamie? What have you seen?" Cartwright asked.

"Oh come off it," Fletcher frowned, opening his hands out in a sign of exasperation. "We're not gone to trust the opinion of this mute idiot now are we?"

"Jamie is no idiot," Cartwright snapped. "He was the brightest of my students before this infernal war began and he's served me impeccably despite his injury."

"Go on, Jamie," the professor added, "show us what you've seen."

Taylor brushed past the police officers and stood before the giant black chalkboard at the front of the lecture theatre. He danced around looking for a piece of chalk on the shelf beneath the board before lurching back over to Cartwright's desk and plucking a stick of the white material from in amongst the mess of papers and textbooks.

The three police officers and Cartwright gathered behind Taylor as he slowly began working the chalk across the board.

They drew a collective sharp intake of breath as the mute scrawled the word "Confederate".

19

The cold wind from the harbour whipped around the dockside, forcing O'Malley to pull the collar of his greatcoat higher up against his neck. The lieutenant stood beside Hare at his foreman's lectern, a large ledger book lying open in front of him, full of instructions from the engineers who had designed Boston's latest canal. Below them, workers were digging out the bottom of what would become the canal basin, linking the docks to some of Tate's factories further inland.

O'Malley mused as to how easily the workers had accepted the return of their foreman – and his new "deputy" as Hare had introduced him to the navvies working on the project. The lieutenant's Irish accent helped with the pretext and allowed him to watch Hare night and day. Although Gillespie wanted to use Hare as bait to find whoever had been abducting and killing the canal workers, O'Malley knew that his captain still didn't fully trust his former foe. Hare had been back at work more than a week now and – except for the mutterings amongst the navvies about the misfortune of losing his family in a fire – the workers had asked few questions about Hare's absence.

But while life may have returned to normal for the workers, O'Malley could see the change that had come over Hare. Instead of the calmness that he had portrayed while in custody, Hare's actions were now those of a man fighting against his inner turmoil. After his long shifts at the canal side, O'Malley would follow the Irishman back to St Patrick's church, where Hare would kneel praying for hours on end, before the lieutenant would drag him away back to the docks, to trawl the bars and poker dens in search of a contact who may want to buy bodies. Having never worked a beat near Tate's docks, which was far away from Henry's tavern where he had found Gillespie, no one recognised O'Malley, much to the police officer's relief.

But while the Irishman watched Hare's spiral into despair at first

136

hand following the murder of his family, O'Malley could also observe the change that had come over Gillespie. Although the lieutenant could spend little time with his captain, O'Malley had lugged himself and Hare along to certain rendezvous points to report on their progress. Despite the lack of contact, O'Malley could see a sparkle returning to Gillespie's eyes that he hadn't seen for many years. The inspector was on the trail of a murderer and the Scotsman could sense he was getting close to his quarry.

A loud whistle sounded, breaking O'Malley out of his reflections and Hare slammed the ledger closed on the lectern before scooping the heavy leather-bound book up and carrying it back across to the small storage shed that doubled-up as the foreman's office. O'Malley followed, ready to guide Hare back to the taverns. Between them, O'Malley was sure they could find whoever was killing the navvies.

The breakthrough came later that week, while Gillespie was sat reading the day's *Boston Post* in front of the fire in his parlour. He threw down the newspaper, casting aside the headlines about a sixth body being found, and dashed to answer the knocking at his door. His heart had leapt as soon as he had heard the commotion outside, thinking it might be Amelia Proctor returning.

He hadn't seen her since the night they had spent together, a night during which Gillespie knew he had been drugged. He could still feel her scratches across his back when he rolled his shoulders.

The captain had not confronted her about the incident, lacking the evidence to charge her and choosing not to approach Blackstone with his suspicions for fear of the police chief's reaction. Having rubbed the mayor and Tate up the wrong way, Gillespie wasn't sure how many other Boston blue-bloods he could insult or accuse of involvement in murder before Blackstone brought his inquiry crashing down around him.

The captain threw open his door to find O'Malley and Hare waiting for him on the doorstep, with Fletcher standing behind them on the street beside a black police coach.

"We've got him," O'Malley said simply as Gillespie showed the three men inside. Huddled around Gillespie hearth, O'Malley outlined how he and Hare had made contact with a man who claimed to be in the market for buying fresh corpses.

"We've arranged to meet him tomorrow night," the Irish officer explained. "I've chosen a spot for the meeting where you can be ready with a squad of officers to surprise him."

Gillespie could see that even Hare had more life in his appearance that night, buoyed by the chance of putting the whole episode behind him.

"No, not this time," the captain shook his head. "It'll be just you two and me and Fletcher. We meet him alone, rather than advertising our presence with a hoard of armed officers."

"Okay," O'Malley agreed. "As long as he comes alone then I think we could easily take him."

"But we have to take him alive," Gillespie cautioned. "If we pull this off and he talks then we can find out who's been buying these bodies and that could lead us to the murderer too."

"If it's not this guy," Fletcher added. "For all we know it could be him that's killing the navvies and he's eyeing up O'Malley here as his next victim."

The Irishman glared at the New Yorker. "He swallowed our story, I can tell he did," O'Malley said firmly. "Without sounding too macabre, with everything that's happened with Hare, he could see we were desperate to make some cash and get out of Boston."

Gillespie nodded at how O'Malley had executed his plan so well and stole a glance across at Hare. The light from the fire cast strange shadows across the Irishman's face that made it hard to read his expression but Gillespie knew that Hare hadn't been out of O'Malley's sight and couldn't have double-crossed them. The captain began sensing victory was at hand.

"Tomorrow night it is then," he nodded, rising from his seat to show his companions out. "Let's get ready to nail this bastard."

20

Gillespie's feet ached as his boots pounded the cobbled lanes running between the red-brick warehouses along the dockside. His lungs felt like they were on fire with every breath that he hurriedly sucked in as he careered down alleyway after alleyway in pursuit of his prey.

Though he was still in remarkable physical shape for his age, Gillespie knew the number of times he could run like this were severely limited. Not for the first time, he envied Blackstone and his comfortable seat behind the chief's desk.

The police captain cursed himself for not bringing more men; while he wanted to capture the suspect without drawing attention to himself, he now knew that his plan had one major flaw. Even bringing Fletcher as well as O'Malley and Hare to the rendezvous had not been enough man power and, almost as soon as the man in the long woollen greatcoat had seen that O'Malley and Hare didn't have any bodies with them, he had taken off down the nearest lane.

Gillespie had anticipated the move and his men were drilled to give chase but the captain couldn't help but think that the way in which the suspect was fleeing had some pattern to it. As his chest heaved with the effort of keeping up with the chase, the thought ran through his head that the suspect was using some form of technique to evade capture.

Ahead of him, Gillespie could see Fletcher – who was leading the police chase – pull to a halt and quickly draw his Colt revolver from its holster on his belt. Gillespie used what little breath he could muster to scream "No" but, before he could reach his lieutenant, the young officer had let off a shot.

Even though Fletcher's aim was off and the bullet soared high over its target, the suspect still ducked as the projectile hit the wall above him.

Gillespie elbowed Fletcher in the upper arm, knocking the weapon out of his hand and nearly knocking the junior officer to the ground.

"You fool," he yelled. "We need to take him alive."

Fletcher's hard stare met Gillespie's for a moment before he replied.

"I only meant to wound him, sir," said Fletcher, almost spitting out the final word. "We need to bring him down or he's going to get away."

"I don't think so," O'Malley panted as he and Hare drew level with where Gillespie and Fletcher had paused. "He's doubling back on himself."

"You saw it too?" Gillespie asked.

O'Malley nodded. "It took me a minute to realise it."

"It's the same technique we were taught in the army," Gillespie explained.

"We could cut him off," Hare said simply, pointing down an alleyway that led off to their left.

Gillespie quickly weighed up his options as he watched the suspect reach the end of the lane and turn left.

"Ok, Fletcher, you take Hare down this alley and then turn left in pursuit," he ordered. "And for God's sake man, keep your gun holstered."

Fletcher glared at his commanding officer and then took off after the suspect again. Hare paused for a moment and looked at Gillespie.

"I don't suppose you'd consider giving me a gun too?" he smiled.

The joke caught Gillespie off balance and he frowned at Hare for a moment before he caught on to the Irishman's sarcasm.

"No chance," Gillespie snorted as Hare set off after Fletcher, while O'Malley led the way down the alley on the left. They reached the end of the lane just in time to block the suspect's escape route.

As he turned to see Fletcher and Hare coming up behind him, the suspect whipped his hand into the open flaps of his greatcoat and produced a set of revolvers, hoisting and cocking them in one fluid, practised action so that he stood side-on to his captors, one weapon drawn at Gillespie and O'Malley and the other pointed at Fletcher and Hare. The three police officers quickly raised their own weapons before he could get a shot off.

"Two guns against three, that hardly seems fair," snarled the suspect.

Gillespie took a good look at him for the first time, having previously hidden behind a crate with Fletcher while O'Malley and Hare had rendezvoused with the suspect. The final weak rays of the waning moon had emerged from behind the clouds, adding an eerie luminescence to the equally meagre glow of the street lamps at either end of the lane.

The man was maybe a decade younger than Gillespie, with long hair and a shaggy beard, its base black colour already flecked white and grey with age. But the man's arms didn't waver as he held out his weapons. Despite the long pursuit around the docks, he held himself fully-upright, seemingly none the worse for the run.

"Lower your guns and then we'll talk about fair," Gillespie replied.

"I tell you what," the man called to the police captain. "How about you lower your gun and call off these dogs and then I'll think about lowering mine."

"No chance," Gillespie replied. "I'll give you to the count of ten and then we'll open fire."

"Sir," O'Malley shouted. "Look at his guns."

Gillespie frowned but did as O'Malley said. The revolvers looked similar to the Colt navies that Gillespie and his men carried but, to the captain's trained eye, he could quickly see the difference O'Malley had spotted.

"Navy revolvers," Gillespie nodded. "Brand new too by the look of them. Who did you steal those from you piece of scum?"

The suspect held Gillespie's gaze for a moment as he appeared to weigh his options. After a pause, he replied: "I'm Major Archibald Tanner, United States Army Bureau of Military Information."

Gillespie sighed heavily and exchanged looks with O'Malley; weeks of work just to capture a spy was another hindrance that his investigation could do without.

"And you are?" Tanner frowned, expecting Gillespie to have replied.

"I'm Captain Alexander Gillespie of the Boston Police Department," he called back. "And I'm going to need proof you are who you say you are."

Tanner visibly relaxed, his shoulders unknotting slightly but his guns remaining trained on the police officers and Hare.

"My papers are in my inside my coat," Tanner replied. "Inner left hand pocket. My orders come from Captain John Babcock, Colonel George H Sharpe's intelligence chief. I report directly to the captain or to Major General Joseph Hooker himself, commander of the great Army of the Potomac."

Tanner cocked the hammer forward on the revolver he carried in his right hand and raised the weapon into the air, allowing O'Malley to move forward at a signal from Gillespie to examine the major's papers. Tanner kept his other weapon levelled at Fletcher, who shifted his weight from foot to foot but didn't take his eye off the major. For his part, Tanner watched O'Malley approach him and reach inside his coat but kept swivelling his head to watch Fletcher, whose itchy trigger finger he knew had fired the shots at him back in the alleyway.

O'Malley handed the papers to Gillespie before raising his weapon and returning his aim to Tanner. Gillespie unfolded the sheaf of papers and quickly scanned their contents.

"Damn it," he cursed under his breath, folding the papers again and slipping them into his own greatcoat pocket. "You understand my chief will have to have these papers authenticated," he added, turning his attention back to Tanner.

"Now, if you're army, why did you run?"

"I had no idea who you were," Tanner replied evenly. "I'd arranged to meet the foreman and his deputy and then you two appear as well. I thought it was an ambush."

"It was," Gillespie snorted. "And it seems it would have worked too, if it wasn't for the fact we got the wrong man. Why were you looking for dead bodies?"

"Let's not talk here," Tanner suggested. "Take me with you."

Gillespie nodded his agreement. "You're right. Let's get him off the streets before the dock workers start pouring in here."

Fletcher and Gillespie holstered their guns, as did Tanner, but O'Malley kept his levelled on the army officer.

"Just a precaution you understand," the Irishman explained in response to Tanner's raised eyebrow.

21

"His story checks out," Blackstone said, tossing the telegram across the desk for Gillespie to read. "I wired Hooker's office in Washington first thing and this reply came back from the Major General himself."

Blackstone cleared his throat and shuffled in his chair so that he was sitting fully upright.

"Gillespie, you are hereby authorised to offer any and all assistance necessary to Major Tanner here in the course of his inquiry into Confederate activity in Boston. Those are my express orders and you'll have them in writing once I have briefed the Mayor later this morning."

"You know there's no need for that, sir," Gillespie sighed as he read the telegram confirming Blackstone's statement. "We'll help Tanner in any way that we can. But first, I need to know why you tried to buy dead bodies from my men."

Tanner shifted his weight as he lent casually against the sideboard in Blackstone's office, helping himself to a glass of bourbon without being asked. His pose against the furniture was the same as Fletcher always adopted in the office and, without fail, the lieutenant was there by Tanner's side. He made to pour himself a glass but was stopped in his tracks by a glare from Blackstone, who was obviously uncomfortable enough with their army guest helping himself. Gillespie idly wondered if adopting such a casual manner in a senior officer's presence was something taught to all New Yorkers at private school or if it just came naturally to them.

Like Fletcher, Tanner obviously came from a well-to-do Manhattan family and, having managed to bathe and clean himself since being brought to Blackstone's temporary lair, Tanner's cultured accent became more apparent.

Despite the flowing locks and beard – which had obviously been grown to disguise his appearance and allow him to more easily slip by enemy lines without being noticed – Tanner carried himself with an air of authority that Gillespie had never been able to groom, no matter how hard he had tried.

"Chief Blackstone, please forgive me for operating in your city without making you aware of my presence but my mission is of the upmost importance to the war effort," Tanner began.

Gillespie rolled his eyes at O'Malley but a glare from Blackstone stopped him dead.

"Four weeks ago we intercepted a communiqué from the Southern command to one of its agents here in the North, arranging a rendezvous here in Boston for tonight."

The police officers were stunned by the news.

"A Confederate plot here in Boston?" Blackstone exclaimed. "But it's not possible. Boston is a powerhouse of the Union war effort. We produce the guns and the shells and the boats that are winning us the fight against the South."

"Those same routes that take arms out of Boston can also be used to bring Confederates into the city," Tanner interrupted. "Neither your force nor the State's militia have been made aware of this plot because we don't have enough information to stop it. I was sent to infiltrate the plotters and find out what I could about the rendezvous."

"I refuse to believe this," Blackstone shook his head.

"Sir, we have evidence that might support Tanner's claim," Gillespie informed him. The captain signalled to O'Malley who, on cue, produced the remains of the Confederate bullets from his pocket and let them roll across the polished surface of Blackstone's broad mahogany desk.

"What are these?" Blackstone asked, picking one up and holding it to the light between his thumb and forefinger.

"Confederate bullets," Gillespie explained. "We found them in the bodies of our dead men at the burned-out office. One of the assistants at the university identified them for me."

"And why wasn't I told about this?" Blackstone yelled. "You should have brought this to me straight away, Gillespie."

"I have only just learned of the bullet's origin," the captain defended himself.

"Confederate gunmen operating here in Boston," Blackstone sighed.

"These aren't standard bullets," Tanner remarked after carefully examining what remained of the lead pellets.

"These are hollow shells, distributed only to the Secret Service Bureau within the Confederacy's Signal Corp," he continued. "Gentlemen, these bullets belong to my opposite numbers in the Southern army and, if they are indeed operating here in Boston then we need to find them and stop them."

"But why the bodies?" Gillespie pressed, desperate to know if or how the plot might fit in with his own investigation.

"The message we intercepted made reference to the procurement of corpses," explained Tanner, reaching into his greatcoat pocket and producing another sheaf of folded papers.

"Let me see," Gillespie held out his hand. The major handed the bundle over to the police captain with a smirk on his face. Gillespie unfurled the documents and quickly scanned over them.

"But they're in code," he protested.

"Of course," Tanner grinned. "All enemy communiqués are encrypted so that only other Southern agents can read them. But we broke the cipher and have been decoding messages such as these for months."

"Then why haven't you shared this information until now?" Gillespie said, throwing his hands up in exacerbation.

"Like I said, we didn't have enough information about the plot."

"Then what do these messages say?" Gillespie continued. "What do they say about corpses and how can that form a Confederate plot?"

"They talk about the need to find fresh bodies so that they can prove what the doctor is telling them and then some obscure reference to 'an army of the dead', which I think must either be a mistranslation or more likely a code for a broader Confederate plot."

"But what do they say exactly?" Gillespie sighed, becoming more frustrated with the way in which Tanner was avoiding his questions.

Blackstone signalled for the captain to be quiet with a wave of his hand. "Never mind that now, Gillespie," he said. "We need to concentrate on stopping this Southern mischief in Boston."

"Agreed," nodded Tanner. "By infiltrating the dock workers' community, I have been able to identify the men who are procuring these bodies and I have arranged to meet them tomorrow night. It is essential that I can continue with my plan without further interruption."

"But if you already have a rendezvous arranged then why did you meet with O'Malley and Hare?" Gillespie asked.

"I needed to be sure I had the right agents," Tanner replied sharply. "When your men turned up offering to sell bodies I needed to make sure they weren't connected with this plot."

"If you're quite finished interrogating our guest then we need to get moving," Blackstone snapped at Gillespie. "What assistance can we offer, Major?"

"Let me be on my way and keep well away from the docks," Tanner replied.

Gillespie leaned back in his chair as a smile spread across his face.

"Just a moment, Major," he said, as Tanner turned to the door. "How exactly are you going to deal with these agents when they rendezvous with you? If they're Confederate spies then they won't come quietly. If you kill them then you'll be no further along with your inquiry into this plot."

A flash of doubt passed across Tanner's face.

"What do you have in mind?"

"Take us with you – if we bring fresh corpses along with us then your scheme will seem more believable and we can give you the extra man power to pull off your plan."

"But where are you going to find dead bodies?" Tanner frowned.

"I know someone who can help," Gillespie replied.

22

"This has to be one of the most stupid schemes I have ever heard," Professor Cartwright exclaimed as he ran his fingers through his thick white hair for the umpteenth time since Gillespie and the others had entered his laboratory. Unlike the airy openness of the lecture theatre, Cartwright's lab space felt more private and allowed Gillespie to outline the plan to his old friend.

"Please, Seymour, it's the only way for this to work," Gillespie pleaded.

"This is such a dangerous route to go down," Cartwright shook his head. "Is there really no other way?"

"We need to convince these agents that Tanner and O'Malley and Hare are serious about selling them corpses," Gillespie spelled out patiently. "We need to make the deception seem as real as possible or they may smell a rat. This could be our only chance to catch these killers and put a stop to this Confederate plot."

Cartwright looked across the lab to where Hare stood silently. Gillespie watched as Cartwright remembered the charred corpses of Hare's wife and children and imagined that he could almost see the mutilated bodies of the dead dock workers who he had examined passing before his eyes.

After a lengthy pause and barely audible sigh, Cartwright shook his head again.

"I'm so sorry, Sandy, I just can't do it," he replied.

"We haven't got time for this," protested Tanner. "We only have a matter of hours before I'm due to meet these agents. If this man can't perform a simple task to help us then I need to put my plan into action."

"Young man, tinkering around with the boundaries between life and death is no mere trifle," Cartwright spat, his booming voice adapting the tone he would use with a petulant student. "I have healed men for decades on both hospital wards and the cold battlefield and now I teach others the art and science of medicine. I cannot simply turn my back on all my training to take away the life of my dear friend and his colleague."

"It would only be for a short time," Gillespie interrupted. "As you said so yourself, the turbatium will only give the appearance of death. And we only need to use it for a short time – once the ruse has been completed then we can be injected with your antidote."

Cartwright sighed heavily. "'Thy dead men shall live, together with my dead body shall they arise: awake and sing yee that dwell in dust: for thy dew is as the dew of herbs, and the earth shall cast out the dead.'"

Gillespie smiled at his old friend. "Then you'll do it?"

"I pray you know what you're doing, Sandy," Cartwright replied as he turned and rummaged in a cabinet full of bottles containing coloured liquids. He selected eight bottles and took them over to a workbench, where he quickly began mixing the chemicals together in two separate beakers; one for the turbatium and one for its antidote.

"Clear those two benches," Cartwright said, pointing to the nearest two worktops and then to O'Malley, Tanner and Hare.

"Jamie," he called. After a moment, his mute assistant, Jamie Taylor, appeared in the open doorway.

"Jamie, I'll need two of the long hessian sacks we use for the corpses," Cartwright instructed. "Go and fetch them for me and avoid contact with anyone else on the way if you can. Now run along, there's a good man."

Taylor looked puzzled when he caught sight of the array of half empty bottles that sat in front of Cartwright on the bench. He turned to Gillespie, as if seeking the policeman's permission to carry out the professor's strange orders.

"It's ok, Jamie, do as he says," Gillespie smiled and nodded.

Taylor disappeared from view and the group could hear his footsteps echoing down the polished tiles of the university's corridors beyond the laboratory.

"We will need to be quick about this," muttered Cartwright, loading the mixtures into two long glass syringes and then fixing large brass plungers to the end of the phials. "If the Dean catches wind of this then

I'll be out on my ear."

"Let's get it over with then," said Fletcher, hoisting himself up on to one of the empty bench tops and rolling up the sleeve of his right arm. He leaned back so that he was lying flat as Cartwright walked round to stand by his side.

"Are you sure you're ready?" the professor asked softly.

"Do it," the lieutenant replied firmly.

Cartwright slipped the needle into a vein on Fletcher's outstretched arm and quickly depressed the plunger, sending a dose of the mixture into the policeman's body.

Gillespie had expected Fletcher to convulse in agony but the chemicals got to work quickly and the lieutenant simply closed his eyes and appeared to fall to sleep. But very quickly his lips began to turn from a deep life-filled pink to a much paler tone and then to a chilling shade of blue. The colour quickly drained away from his skin too, leaving his flesh a ghostly shade of white.

"You're next," Cartwright told Gillespie after checking for signs of a pulse in Fletcher's neck and finding none.

Slowly Gillespie raised himself up onto the empty workbench next to where Fletcher's body lay; while the young New Yorker had effortlessly vaulted onto the bench, Gillespie's aching arms and shoulders made it harder for him to clamber up onto the surface. He slipped off his jacket and rolled up his shirt sleeve before lying back on the worktop. As Cartwright prepared his syringe, Gillespie gazed up at the ceiling and let his mind wander.

The laboratory sat behind the wall at the front of the lecture theatre and shared the same glass ceiling. The wrought-iron metalwork in between the glass panels reminded Gillespie of the orangery at the Mayor's house, which in turn caused his thoughts to turn to Amelia. Despite having spent only one night together – and even that night had been cut short by her abrupt departure – Gillespie still couldn't get her out of his head.

He began to consider what would happen if the drug Cartwright was about to administer didn't work as intended and instead claimed his life. The thought brought Gillespie up short – he had faced death many times in the line of duty and during his spell with the army but to die without seeing Amelia again filled him with sorrow. He had always carried out his inquiries with a stoic certainty that if today was to be his final day on this earth, then so be it.

While he would miss the friendship of O'Malley and Cartwright, it was the loss of Amelia that concerned Gillespie the most. That and the thought he would never look out over the Edinburgh skyline again from the approach to the castle. Though he had been gone for decades, he still held a secret desire to return to his homeland.

His train of thought was interrupted by Taylor dragging two heavy hessian sacks into the laboratory. The professor's assistant was clearly disturbed by the sight of Fletcher laid out on the bench, motionless and apparently murdered.

"It's ok, Jamie," Cartwright cooed. "He isn't dead, simply drugged."

From where he lay on the bench, Gillespie could see that Taylor was still unsure of what was taking place in the lab but he helped O'Malley and Tanner lower Fletcher's body into the first of the sacks and started tying up the lace on the front with a practiced hand.

"Are you sure about this, Sandy?" Cartwright asked quietly, so the others would not hear him.

"Aye, Seymour, there's no other way," the captain replied. "Besides, it seems to have worked okay on Fletcher."

"Fletcher is... how can I put this? Somewhat younger than you or I," Cartwright looked stern. "His body will react in a different way to yours. I cannot be sure if your body will be able to fight off the effects of the turbatium in the same way, especially as you have so recently been exposed to it."

"Please," Gillespie pleaded quietly. Cartwright paused for a moment more and looked down at his friend before clearing his throat loudly.

"Ready?" he asked.

"All set," Gillespie replied.

He felt the prick of the needle as Cartwright punctured his arm and hit a vein. Almost immediately Gillespie could feel a queer chill taking hold of his body, spreading from his arm throughout his torso and into his gut as his vision grew dim and then turned to black.

As his world faded into nothingness, Gillespie was sure he caught a glimpse of Amelia's face passing before his eyes – followed immediately by a ghostly image he hadn't seen for thirty-four years.

INTERLUDE

"Hello, Inspector," Burke hissed as Gillespie slowly opened his eyes. The Irishman's face filled Gillespie's full field of vision, blocking out any sign of life or form beyond him.

"What's going on?" Gillespie rasped groggily.

"Well, it looks suspiciously to me as if you're dead," Burke brayed, throwing back his head in laughter. "How else could you be seeing me again, Alexander?"

"How do you know my name?" Gillespie frowned. "We never met while you were still alive."

"Come now, Inspector, there's nothing I don't know about you," Burke replied dismissively. "When your friend the hangman had his evil way with me, I realised that death wasn't the end but just the beginning of my time on Earth. Hare has provided me with sport ever since. I've lived the life that I was denied through him, walking in his steps, sharing in his thoughts."

Gillespie frowned again.

"Well, maybe not 'ever since'," Burke corrected himself. "Hare has managed to go nearly thirty years without me bothering him. Until his path crossed yours, that is. Oh yes, Inspector, you've awoken me from my slumbers and I can't say dear old William will be pleased to see me again. I've been there at the edge of his vision, but I think it might be time to burst back out on to the stage. What do you think?"

Gillespie ignored Burke's ramblings and tried to take in his surroundings.

"Where am I?" he asked, trying to peer through the thick brown haze that had enveloped his body.

"Why, don't you recognise your own home town?" Burke gasped in mock surprise.

Gillespie squinted and slowly the fog began to clear, affording him a view of a starry sky above his head and the soft gas lights of Edinburgh spread out beneath his feet. The policeman gasped and threw his arms out to steady himself, but found he was floating quite freely above the city.

"Takes a bit of getting used to, doesn't it, Inspector?" chuckled Burke cruelly as he hovered next to Gillespie, their bodies floating effortless in the air.

Gillespie looked down and saw Edinburgh Castle directly below him, a pair of soldiers patrolling along the parapet and the Union flag fluttering softly in the night's breeze.

"Can they see me?" Gillespie asked. Burke sniggered.

"Help, help me," Gillespie shouted. But the two soldiers carried on their patrol, undisturbed by the phantoms floating high above their heads.

"Don't worry about them," Burke shook his head. "There are far more interesting things for you to see."

Burke reached his arm out in front of him and, before Gillespie knew what was happening, the pair were floating forwards, following the Royal Mile down into Edinburgh's Old Town.

Gillespie watched as the spires of the Old Town churches passed beneath his feet, the wind whipping past his face as they floated onwards.

"Down there," Burke said as he pointed to an old man hobbling along a cobbled street. "Recognise him?"

Gillespie strained his eyes but the figure didn't come into focus so he shook his head slowly.

"So you don't recognise Jeffrey Matheson, your old sergeant?" Burke said.

The figure on the street became more defined and Gillespie saw his former commanding officer, aged by the ravages of time but still looking stern and gruff, ready to clip a young patrolman behind the ear if he gave him cheek.

As Gillespie watched, two figures emerged from the shadows and grabbed Matheson, throwing him to the ground and beating him with the iron bars they carried.

"No," yelled Gillespie but his words passed noiselessly above the pair's heads as they bent down and removed the old man's wallet and watch from his coat pockets and left him to bleed to death on the dark street.

"Look at the filth you left behind in Edinburgh," Burke tutted, as Matheson's body convulsed and then fell dead and limp against the cobbles. "While you've been playing soldier and copper in America, this city has gone to the dogs."

Again Burke thrust his arm forward and the pair soared higher into the night's sky, up above the tenements of the Old Town and out across Princes Street Gardens, the landscaped park built on the land created by the draining of the Nor Loch. They banked to the right and Gillespie watched as steam trains pulled in and out of the three stations – General, North Bridge and Canal Street – that were clustered together in the valley, the smoke from their engines belching out into the night's sky.

"You think all of Edinburgh's problems were solved when the New Town was built?" Burke asked as they banked left again and flew out over the wide streets and clean sandstone buildings erected in the neo-classical design Gillespie had watched taking shape during his youth.

Beyond the rigid grid of Princes, George and Queen streets, Gillespie could see that the regimented schemes had been extended since his time in Edinburgh and Burke guided him down to one of the plush Georgian terraces that had sprung up around the central core of the New Town.

"Who's this?" asked Gillespie, as he saw a solitary figure approaching from the other end of the gas-lit street.

"You don't remember your old school master, Mister Thompson?" Burke sniggered. "He was the one who pushed you to join the police, the one who taught you right from wrong. Perhaps, more than anyone else, he's the one who made you, the one who shaped you, Inspector," the Irishman hissed.

"He saved his salary for years and finally retired to this New Town, leaving the squalor and the slums behind to find salvation among the aristocrats and the merchants."

The old man lent heavily on his cane as he slowly made his way back from the public library to his modest flat. But, just as Matheson had fallen prey to fiends in the Old Town, so Thompson was set upon by a pair of dock workers piling out of a tavern. Gillespie watched helplessly as the blade of a knife glinted in the gas light before being plunged into Thompson's chest, puncturing his heart before being drawn back out. The dockers didn't even bother to remove the old man's purse but instead just left his body on the pavement as they ambled back down the streets to their hovels in Leith.

"No more," Gillespie moaned. "You've shown me all that I can bare to see."

"But wait, there's one more thing you need to see," replied Burke, spinning Gillespie around so that he could see what was happening at the other end of the street. A well-dressed gentleman was climbing the stairs to his front door when a figure walking on the pavement called to him. The man turned and descended back down the stairs to greet the newcomer with open arms, as if to welcome the return of an old friend.

But Gillespie watched as the friend pinned the gentleman's arms to his sides and, out of the shadows, an accomplice stepped forward and smothered the gentlemen with a sack over his mouth and nose. While the friend looked smartly attired in the latest fashionable suit from Italy, his accomplice was dressed in a simple working man's suit, his clothes ridden with dirt and grime.

"You," Gillespie mouthed. "You and Hare. But how can it be? You're dead and he's in Boston."

"Not us," Burke shook his head. "But it's nice to see we left our mark on the world. It's always nice to have something named after you," the Irishman smirked.

"But I don't understand," Gillespie protested. "If they're not you then who are they?"

"Scum," Burke spat. "The kind of scum you won't be able to stop if you leave the police behind. These are a new breed of criminal, Inspector. I knew I was doing wrong and I confessed my sins right there in the gaol before you led me out to the gallows.

"But these two; these two are different. They don't kill for money – they kill for pleasure. These are the kind of scum that are roaming the streets of Edinburgh now. The city that gave birth to the Enlightenment thinkers and scientists has now spawned a new wave of crooks and criminals.

"And soon they'll be spreading – to London, to New York and to your beloved Boston too."

Gillespie scowled at Burke as his words sunk in.

"Industry gives rise to free time and the devil makes work for idle hands," Burke finished with a flourish, sweeping his arm in an arc in front of him and sending the pair of them back up into the air.

"But what can I do to stop all of this?" Gillespie pleaded as they hovered above Edinburgh Castle again, their journey ending where it had begun.

"You can't do anything if you leave the police," Burke shrugged.

"But I can't do anything to help Edinburgh if I stay in Boston," Gillespie mused.

"First thing's first," Burke warned. "You need to work out if Hare is up to his old tricks again."

Gillespie glared at the ghostly figure of Burke.

"You know, don't you?" he said. "You know who's behind these killings."

Burke returned his gaze, chuckling to himself.

"Tell me," Gillespie yelled. "Tell me."

"You'll see," cackled Burke, as the brown haze enveloped Gillespie once more and his vision faded back to black.

PART FIVE
BOSTON, 1863

23

O'Malley was beginning to develop a deep-seated hatred for Boston's docks. Even at night, the intertwined smells of dead fish, burning coal and human sweat failed to dissipate from the wharfs and quays. The stench crept into his nostrils and further hampered his progress as the lieutenant lugged his bulky load along the cobbled lanes of the dockside.

In his hands, he cradled the head of the sack containing Gillespie's body. Even though he was beginning to form a grudging respect for the man, he still didn't trust Hare with the precious cargo and had pushed his fellow Irishman out of the way to claim his place carrying Gillespie. MacLeod, who had been waiting for them in the police carriage outside the medical college, had been enlisted to lug the captain's legs, while Tanner and Hare hobbled alongside them, carrying Fletcher's body in an identical hessian sack.

Each man had his hands full with their load and so no-one carried a torch, making their progress even slower as they stumbled across the uneven cobbles. Tanner's rendezvous had been arranged for a derelict area of the old docks where the abandoned warehouses did not warrant the new gas lighting that had been installed elsewhere. The lack of any moonlight added to their problems.

Having spent so much time at the docks – with Hare and with the two failed attempts to catch the serial killer on the loose – O'Malley was hoping this would be his last trip to the harbour for some considerable time to come.

"Third time lucky," he muttered under his breath.

As they rounded the corner of the penultimate warehouse in the row, the group carrying the bodies could pick out two flaming torches in the shadow of the final warehouse. While most of the structures in the row had retained their roofs, the final warehouse in the line was totally derelict. Its roof had been removed or had caved in and most of the panes of glass were missing from its windows.

"Is this one of Tate's warehouses?" O'Malley hissed at MacLeod as the old sergeant staggered in front of him.

"Yes," MacLeod replied in a hushed tone over this shoulder. "You'd think he'd keep it in better condition – the rest of his property is immaculate."

O'Malley nodded and put the thought from his mind as they neared the two men holding the torches. In the flickering light, O'Malley was able to tell that one of the men was tall and broad with ginger hair and a beard to match, while his companion was shorter but equally as well-built, as if the pair had spent time labouring on the docks or in one of the city's factories, building muscles and toning their bodies through hard work. Even though there were four men in his group and only two of them, O'Malley didn't fancy his chances if a fight broke out.

"Right on time," lanky said, greeting Tanner with a nod.

"The boss'll appreciate not being kept waiting," added shorty.

O'Malley immediately clocked the pair's Irish accents but kept quiet to let Tanner lead.

"I always deliver," the major replied, returning to the coarse accent he had first used when Gillespie and O'Malley had captured him. "And there's plenty more where these came from. I want to talk to your boss about bringing him more corpses like these."

Shorty and lanky exchanged looks before lanky nodded his agreement.

"All right," the shorter man said. "It sounds like the boss'll be needin' more bodies anyway and it's been getting tougher and tougher for us to get 'em with all those police pigs crawling their way around the docks."

Tanner laughed and the others joined in. "Don't worry about the police," he said. "I have ways of getting round them."

"Let's be having a look at 'em then," commanded lanky. Tanner unlaced the sack containing Fletcher and let lanky lean in to inspect the face of the body.

"Looks nice and fresh," lanky nodded. "And the other one?"

O'Malley slowly unlaced Gillespie's bag and was taken aback to see the ghostly pale face of his captain.

Lanky nodded his approval and O'Malley laced the sack up again. "Right, let's get these corpses stowed away and we'll take you to see the boss," he said, taking the end of the sack containing Gillespie's legs away from MacLeod and effortlessly hoisting it over his shoulder.

"My man will come with us too," Tanner added, as he and Hare edged forward with Fletcher's body still suspended between them.

A scowled passed across shorty's face.

"I don't want no trouble, fellas," Hare muttered but loud enough for the pair to hear his Irish accent.

The two body snatchers exchanged looks and nodded at each other.

"Ok, he's all right with us," shorty said. "Now let's get a move on."

A flash of panic spread through O'Malley and he nervously fingered the syringe in his pocket. Why was Tanner taking Hare and not him?

Seeing the moment was slipping away from him and that Tanner was being watched by the two Irishmen, O'Malley quickly sidestepped across to Hare and dropped the syringe into his coat pocket. Hare glanced at him and gave him an almost imperceptible nod, acknowledging what he had to do.

"Off you go, boys," Tanner instructed O'Malley and MacLeod. "I'll see you two later."

"Where are they taking them?" MacLeod muttered as he and O'Malley backed away from the derelict warehouse and the body snatchers disappeared inside through a door-less hole in the wall.

"I don't know," replied O'Malley. "If their boss is inside then we need to stand ready."

"Look!" shouted MacLeod. "What the hell is that?"

O'Malley followed MacLeod's outstretched finger and turned his gaze back to the roofless warehouse.

"Sweet Mary mother of Jesus," he swore as he watched a giant black shape emerge from the top of the warehouse and glide off into the dark sky. Though O'Malley couldn't tell what he had just seen rising out of the warehouse, his eyes had picked out two words etched in white paint onto the side of the dark shape: *The Resurrectionist.*

24

Hanging high above the streets of Boston, Hare dared himself to glance over the side of the basket in which he found himself suspended and gazed down at the city spread out before him. Hare had heard of balloons and knew that some were being used for reconnaissance on the frontlines of the civil war but never in his wildest dreams had he ever believed he would one day find himself flying in one of them.

As the black canvas of the balloon's skin continued to rise into the air, Hare could feel a second motion creeping in to the aircraft's trajectory. Slowly at first but then getting faster and faster, the balloon began edging forward until it was not only rising but also speeding out towards the edge of the city.

Eventually, the balloon finished climbing and eased out into level flight, charting a straight course for the Massachusetts countryside surrounding Boston.

"Pretty impressive contraption you have here," Tanner remarked as the balloon levelled out.

"This airship is the boss's pride and joy," shorty replied, as he let go of the series of ropes that controlled the balloon's flight. "He's been milling his metal finer and finer until he could make this balloon."

"But how are we moving?" Tanner ventured.

"Propeller," lanky replied, pointing to the back of the basket. "Steam driven, just like you'd get on an ironclad."

"But much lighter," shorty chipped in again.

"And the lift?" Tanner asked, pointing up to the black balloon from which their basket was suspended.

"It's full of some gas," shorty replied. "Hydrogen he calls it. Lighter than air he says."

Tanner's mind was reeling. Could the Confederacy have built such a machine without the Bureau of Military Information even catching the faintest wind of it?

"So who is this boss of yours?" he tried.

Lanky and shorty exchanged looks again.

"You'll see," lanky replied. The group fell silent and Hare watched as best he could in the dark of the night as the street lights of Boston faded away and the balloon set out across a vast swath of farmland. He could feel the cold night's air sweeping through his hair as the balloon gathered speed. After what felt like hours but could only have been a matter of some twenty minutes, shorty took up the ropes again and the balloon began its descent.

Below them, Hare could begin to make out the shape of a large stone-built country manor house, complete with a tall central tower. But where Hare would have expected to see sculptured gardens and lawns laid out behind the house, instead he could see a large structure with a glass and metalwork roof, which reminded him of the roof above Professor Cartwright's lecture theatre and laboratory. In the light cast out from the windows of the house, Hare could just make out the glint of two sets of railway tracks leading up to the structure connected to the back of the manor house.

As the balloon slowly glided in on its approach to the house's central tower, lanky grabbed a pair of coiled ropes from around his feet and tossed the first of them over the side of the basket where it was caught below by a man standing on the balcony that encircled the top of the stone tower. Lanky threw down the second rope, which the man below tied to the metal railing surrounding the balcony and shorty guided the balloon into dock with the tower.

Hare could hear the hiss of steam escaping from the propulsion system as shorty vented some power from the system and kept the balloon in check as it hovered, suspended next to the tower. The man on the balcony slid across a wooden plank, which lanky secured in place as a boarding ladder between the balcony and the balloon. The taller of the two body snatchers then hoisted Gillespie's body back onto his shoulder and effortlessly climbed out of the basket and on to the balcony. Tanner and Hare gingerly picked up the sack containing Fletcher and made their way across the plank, followed by shorty, who was unsteady on his feet and practically scrambled his way to the tower.

Hare didn't know the face of the man who had tied the balloon up on the tower but he instantly recognised the navy blue greatcoat and peaked cap that the man wore.

Lanky led the way down the tower's spiral staircase as Tanner and Hare struggled behind with Fletcher's body. Shorty brought up the rear, whistling tunelessly as they descended.

When they reached the bottom of the stone staircase and were out of earshot of the man on the balcony, Tanner made his move.

"Well, you gentlemen have been so helpful," he said.

Lanky looked confused for a second but then his head exploded in a shower of brain and bone fragments as Tanner pulled one of his Colt revolvers from beneath his greatcoat and fired a bullet straight into the body snatcher's forehead.

Hare didn't miss a beat and swung his elbow into shorty's face, breaking his nose and sending the man crashing back against the stone wall of the tower. In the cramped confines of the staircase shorty was unable to fight back and Hare was quickly upon him, landing blow after blow against either side of his skull.

"Clear!" Tanner yelled and Hare dodged to his right as the army major fired a shot into shorty's head. The body snatcher's limbs twitched and then fell limp as the sound of the second revolver round reverberated around the tower.

Tanner paused for breath and turned his head from side to side as he listened for footsteps above them. Hearing nothing, he holstered his weapon and relieved lanky of his revolver, before doing the same to shorty.

Hare held out his hand, expecting Tanner to hand him the gun.

"No chance," Tanner shook his head swiftly.

"If Gillespie was right about you then there's no way I'm handing a loaded gun to a murderer," he added.

"That was a long time ago," Hare protested.

"You handled yourself pretty well just now," Tanner replied. "I'm not going to end up with a bullet in the back of my head if I can help it.

"Now let's get these bodies hidden before someone comes looking for them."

Tanner edged open the heavy wooden door at the bottom of the stone staircase and peered down either end of the corridor beyond. When he didn't see or hear anyone, he began dragging lanky's body. Throwing open the first door he came to, he found a cupboard filled with bed linen and quickly cleared a space on the floor for lanky's corpse. Hare followed behind, dragging shorty as he went and the pair tossed the body snatcher's corpse on top of his companion. They then returned to the tower and retrieved the sack containing Gillespie, where it had fallen against the wall when Tanner had shot lanky.

After trying several locked doors along the corridor, they found one that opened in to a bedroom. Depositing Gillespie's sack on the bed, they returned to the tower to retrieve Fletcher and brought him into the bedroom too, before dumping his sack next to Gillespie's on the bed. The two brown sacks and their ghostly contents seemed at odds with the powder pink curtains and sheets on the bed.

"You have the syringe?" Tanner said to Hare in more of an instruction than a question. The Irishman glared at the army major before fishing the medical instrument out of his coat pocket.

"Hurry up man, we don't have time to lose," Tanner said as he tore at the laces on Fletcher's sack.

Tanner pulled back the sides of the sack to let Hare find his mark on Fletcher's bare arm before turning his attention to Gillespie. Hare stuck the needle into Fletcher's arm and depressed the plunger halfway, saving half of the serum for Gillespie.

After a moment's pause, Fletcher sat bolt upright gasping for breath before his body was racked by a wave of coughing that resulted in him leaning over the side of the bed and vomiting noisily. Satisfied that the lieutenant was awake, Hare rounded the bed and turned his attention to Gillespie. He slid the point of the needle into one of the veins on Gillespie's arm and emptied the remainder of the syringe.

Hare stood back, expecting the captain to revive as quickly as Fletcher had. But when first one minute and then a second passed without any sign of life from Gillespie, Hare began to suspect that something was wrong.

25

"Inspector," Hare said, shaking Gillespie's shoulders. "Inspector, wake up."

"We don't have time for this," Tanner repeated. He grabbed a pitcher full of water from the bedside table and threw its contents over Gillespie's face.

The shock of the cold water had the desired effect and Gillespie's eyes opened in a flash and he rolled over on to his side and began throwing up over the side of the bed. His convulsions were so severe that he rolled off the bed and remained crouched on all fours on the floor long after his vomiting has subsided.

"Get up, Gillespie, we have work to do," Tanner barked. Hare hoisted Gillespie up off the floor and their eyes met for a brief moment. Gillespie held Hare's gaze and simply said: "Thank you".

Hare nodded his understanding and helped the captain to his feet as Fletcher picked himself up off the bed and gave a violent shake of his head.

"That was the strangest feeling," he moaned. Looking around, he took in his surroundings. "Why did you bring Hare instead of O'Malley?" he asked.

"I needed someone to know where we'd been taken," Tanner explained. "That MacLeod looked liked a gormless buffoon so I needed O'Malley to stay behind and follow us if necessary."

"Where are we?" Gillespie asked, pinching the bridge of his nose to ward off the headache that was spreading through his cranium.

"A country house outside the city," Tanner replied.

"How long were we out?" Fletcher asked.

"Only a matter of hours," said Tanner. "They brought us here on an airship."

"A what?" Gillespie frowned.

"A balloon, but with some kind of propulsion system that frees it from being idly blown in the wind," Tanner explained quickly. "We need to get hold of that machine. If it's been developed by the Confederacy then the Union army needs a similar tool in its arsenal."

"First thing's first," Gillespie coughed. "We need to find out who would want to bring dead bodies to a country house."

"Let's go," Tanner said, wrestling the initiative back from Gillespie. He handed Fletcher and Gillespie the revolvers he had taken from shorty and lanky and then led the way back out into the corridor.

"Once we find out where we are then we need to get word to either the police or the Boston militia," Tanner told the others. "That airship must be at the heart of the Confederate plot and we can't let it get away."

"But why the bodies?" Gillespie repeated. "It just doesn't make sense. I can't see a connection between the airship and the murderers in Boston."

"There'll be time for that," Tanner snapped. "First we need to work out where we are."

"I saw a large structure sticking out the back of the house," Hare said. "Maybe there's a clue there."

"It's as good a place to start as any," Tanner muttered, retracing his steps and guiding the group back past the door leading up into the tower and instead towards the rear of the house. The corridor ended in another heavy wooden door, which Tanner gingerly prised open before leading the way through onto a metal walkway that encircled a vast hall. Edging their way along the gantry, the four men took up position behind a row of wooden packing crates, which afforded them a view of the events going on below but would hide them from prying eyes.

Gillespie began taking in his surroundings, looking at the group of men below being led to a platform in the centre of the hall upon which stood a table surrounded by a bank of machines from which a loud electrical hum was emanating.

As he peered down for a closer look, Gillespie heard a familiar voice filling the vast space below.

"Colonel Drummond, welcome, I'm so pleased you could join us tonight for our little demonstration," said Amelia Proctor.

26

Gillespie's mind raced as he watched Amelia embrace a man dressed in the uniform of the Confederate States of America's army, with gold insignia on his lapels identifying him as a colonel.

"Delighted, Mrs Proctor," replied Drummond in his deep Southern drawl, kissing Amelia once on each cheek. "I just hope your demonstration will have been worth our trip. I would much rather have conducted these proceedings at Richmond."

Tate, decked out in a black suit and top hat, shook hands with the colonel and then with three officers from his entourage who he introduced in turn. Gillespie made a quick count and worked out that there were around two dozen Confederate soldiers and their officers in the hall below, along with around the same number of Tate's men, all wearing the same navy blue greatcoats and peaked hats. Gillespie noted the Confederate soldiers were armed with rifles, while each of Tate's men wore a pair of Colt revolvers on his belt underneath their open greatcoats.

"Herr Professor van der Waal was more comfortable conducting our business behind Union lines for the time being," smiled Amelia. "Please, will you take a seat for the demonstration?"

Drummond and his officers sat down on chairs that had been laid out in a semi-circle to give an unobstructed view of the apparatus set up on the stage. Tate slipped into a chair at the edge of the circle next to Drummond.

"You're in for a real treat," Tate told the colonel in a mock stage whisper.

"Since the dawn of warfare, the main obstacle to a general's – or even a colonel's – success has been the rate of attrition of their army," Amelia began. Her voice was loud and commanding, holding the attention of her audience and sending an involuntary shiver up Gillespie's spine as he watched her from his vantage point hidden behind a crate. He soaked up the image of her standing on stage, dressed once more in her familiar high-necked black dress and matching long-sleeved gloves.

"Soldiers die on the battlefield from many types of injury, often before they can receive medical aid," she continued. "But what if those lives could be sustained until an army surgeon could arrive to stem their bleeding or the injured soldier could be ferried from the battle to receive attention in a field hospital?"

There was a murmur of interest from the assembled officers, which Amelia silenced by raising one of her black-gloved hands.

"Gentlemen, Professor Kristophe van der Waal, the noted Prussian physicist, has perfected a method that will reanimate lifeless soldiers on the field of combat, buying doctors the time they need to administer their life-saving treatments. Your army's numbers will be swelled as troops recover and then rejoin the fight against your foes."

"But that's madness," exclaimed Drummond. "You're talking about the resurrection – only our Lord Jesus Christ can bring men back from the dead."

"Not back from the dead but merely reanimating those who have fallen," Amelia corrected. "The professor's experiments have proven that only those who have very recently died can be reanimated using his technique."

"Poppycock," spat one of Drummond's officers, who wore the epilates of a major in the surgical corps on his shoulders. "Van der Waal died in Prussia over six months ago. There's no way he could have perfected what you're talkin' about before he died."

"When I read of Professor van der Waal's work, I immediately saw its – how can I put this? – commercial applications," Tate offered. "I convinced him to join me here in Boston to complete his experiments."

"But his lab burned down," the Confederate field surgeon stated.

"My little insurance policy," Tate explained. "That was the only way to make sure that we were the only players with the professor's technology or the ability to replicate it."

"So those pieces of Yankee scum don't have wind of this?" Drummond asked suspiciously, stroking one end of his bushy moustache.

"Neither the Prussians nor the French nor the British nor the Union have any clue as to how the professor's technique works," Tate nodded.

"But why are you trying to sell this to me?" Drummond pursed his lips. "Surely you're a loyal Union man, Tate?"

"Let's just say I can see some remarkable business opportunities in importing and exporting cotton and other raw materials if the Civil War continues," Tate offered.

"Surely you mean the War of Northern Aggression, dontcha?" Drummond corrected him with a booming laugh. "Ah heck, let's be hearing this then, Tate. Where is this van der Waal and his gizmo?"

"Professor," Amelia called. "Please begin the demonstration for our guests."

From out of Gillespie's field of view, a short man in a white laboratory coat walked into view along with two assistants wearing white tunics and pushing a trolley with a sheet draped over it. The medical orderly lifted the trolley on to the stage and wheeled it over so it stood next to the table.

"Gentlemen, the first thing I must teach you is about the human heart," said van der Waal in heavily accented and haltering English. "Just as Morse sends electrical signals down your telegraph wires, so the heart sends out electrical pulses along with every beat that pushes blood around the body."

The murmuring had started again among the Confederate officers.

"You are not believing me?" van der Waal asked. "Then you will allow me to demonstrate."

Stepping aside he flicked a switch on the nearest of the machines set up around the table and the needle that sat against a large dial sprang into life, tracing out a semi-circular arc against the dial before bouncing back and resting flat in the horizontal position again, emitting a single loud beep as it did so.

"I can demonstrate these electrical signals to you on this dial and with this accoustoscope," van der Waal explained. "Now, for this demonstration, I need you, Hans, to remove your tunic. We must have bare skin for this to work," he added, indicating that one of his assistants should remove his top.

"No, wait," Drummond commanded, standing up from his chair. "I want you to demonstrate on her," he added, pointing to Amelia, who stood off to one side of the equipment on the stage.

Amelia narrowed her eyes at Drummond but then a smile spread across her face.

"As you wish, Colonel," she said, gathering up the hem of her dress and giving a low courtesy. Without taking her eyes off Drummond, who by now had retaken his seat, Amelia moved to the centre of the stage and slowly began unlacing the high neck of her dress. She carried on pulling the lace through its loops until the front of her dress lay open, exposing the upper portion of her milky-white chest but leaving the dress bunched up under her arms so as to keep her breasts covered. The titillation brought a chorus of wolf whistles from Drummond's soldiers and officers and even from the colonel himself, who clapped his hands together. Up on the walkway, Gillespie swallowed hard.

"Yes, yes, very good, now if I may?" van der Waal tutted impatiently, the sight of Amelia's décolletage lost on him. He drew a pair of wire leads out of the side of the machine and dipped their ends in a pot of glue before placing them against Amelia's chest. The dial on the machine flicked to the right again before falling back down to the left and emitted a loud beep that filled the hall. Each time Amelia's heart pumped blood around her svelte body, the machine released another beep and the needle flicked its way across the dial before returning to its starting point.

The Confederate officers clapped politely and, after several minutes, van der Waal removed the electrodes from Amelia's chest and she laced her dress up again.

"Well, that's all well and good, but how does this have anything to do with this fancy reanimation stuff?" Drummond drawled.

"That brings me to the second part of my demonstration," van der Waal intoned. "Hans, Helmut, place the body on the table."

Van der Waal's assistants pulled the white sheet off the trolley to reveal the body of a young man, naked to the waist. They lifted the corpse on to the table and wheeled away the trolley.

"This man has been dead merely for a matter of hours," van der Waal explained. "I will now demonstrate my method for the reanimation."

The professor proceeded to add more glue to the end of the electrodes before sticking them on either side of the man's upper chest, halfway between his nipples and his collarbone. The machine behind him began emitting a loud continuous beep.

"The sound signifies the absence of the heartbeat," van der Waal said, raising his voice to be heard above the noise of the machine. "I will now restore that heartbeat."

"Let me see," called the Confederate surgeon, as he climbed up on to the stage. He proceeded to snatch a stethoscope from one of the professor's assistants and thrust the bell of the instrument against the man's naked chest. Satisfied there was no heartbeat, he then felt for a pulse at the neck and on the wrist but found none. The surgeon returned to his seat while van der Waal stood shaking his head.

After flicking the switch on another machine, the professor slipped on a pair of long rubber gloves that reached up to the elbows of his white coat. From the top of the workbench, he took up a pair of metal discs fitted with wooden handles. The disks were connected to the second machine by a similar length of wire to the electrodes on the corpse's chest.

"Hans, we will start with the one-hundred joules setting," van der Waal instructed. One of his assistants adjusted a dial on the front of the equipment and the machine began emitting a loud whining noise. The whirring sound reached its climax as a needle on one of the machine's dials reached the one-hundred mark.

The professor lent forward over the patient's body and pressed the metal discs against his chest, one on his sternum between his pectoral muscles and the other below his left nipple against the wall of his chest. Van der Waal then depressed two buttons, one at the end of each handle, completing the electrical circuit and sending the current pulsing through the corpse.

The man's chest shook with the charge from the machine but the heart monitor continued to emit its dull monotone.

"My equipment has been fitted with several settings," van der Waal explained, leaning back and pulling the metal discs away from the corpse's chest. "If the first amount is not enough then we will hit him with more of the electricity. Two-hundred joules, Hans."

The machine whirred louder as the setting was increased and van der Waal resumed his position leaning over the dead body, slipping the metal discs back against his chest. After the whining of the equipment reached a peak, the professor let the current loose through the patient's body.

The corpse's chest was raised off the table this time, but landed back on the cold surface with an audible thud and the heart monitor continued to sound its single monotonous tone.

"No matter, the third setting will be enough," van der Waal reassured his audience, who were by now shifting in their seats. Without waiting for his instruction, Hans flipped the dial up to the three-hundred-and-sixty joule mark and the whining noise started afresh.

The professor placed the discs against the patient's chest again, easily finding his mark from the two large red welts swelling up on the man's naked chest where the discs had been placed. As soon as the machine had finished charging, van der Waal pushed the paddles hard against the man's chest and pressed the release button, sending the charge coursing through his heart.

The corpse's chest was raised into the air, his hands flopping open before his torso crashed back down onto the table. But the dull monotone was this time replaced with a regular beeping sound and the man gasped for air. He rolled to his side and vomited loudly onto the floor and all over the feet of van der Waal's assistant, Helmut.

"Bravo, professor, bravo," cried Amelia as she led the round of applause from the Confederate party. The Southern surgeon made his way back onto the stage and helped the man to lie flat on the table again, after which he proceeded to examine him with the stethoscope once more.

"Remarkable," he muttered. "How do you feel, son?"

The man shook his head and mumbled something inaudible.

"Patients can take some time to recover the power of their senses but he will be quite fine," van der Waal offered, flicking the switches to silence his machines.

"Now Colonel Drummond, as you have seen we have kept our part of the bargain – what of your contribution?" Amelia said, addressing the Confederates from her position on the stage.

"Young lady, you have yourself a deal," Drummond called back. "Show her the money boys."

Two of Drummond's soldiers set about unclasping the latches on half-a-dozen trunks that had been laid out behind the semi circle of chairs. They threw back the lids of the chests to reveal hundreds of thousands of gold coins.

"One million of your Yankee dollars," Drummond shouted.

"Excellent," Tate exclaimed, warmly shaking Drummond's outstretched hand. "Professor van der Waal has ten of his units ready to ship immediately and they will be included in my next shipment heading for the Confederacy. A further ninety units will be ready to ship by the end of the month."

"Now Colonel Drummond, perhaps you'd like to join me in my study for a brandy before our airship takes you back to your vessel?" Amelia cooed as she descended from the stage and looped her arm around Drummond's outstretched elbow.

"Lady, there's only one thing we'll be drinking to celebrate this occasion and that's the South's finest whiskey," Drummond yelled as Amelia led him to the rear of the hall and back into the mansion house. "Now, how much for that airship contraption of yours?"

Gillespie let out a sigh of relief as the main body of the party disappeared out of sight and Tate's men set about loading the trunks of coins into the carriage of a waiting train. He heard two large barn doors being opened to let the trains rejoin the tracks outside at Amelia's command.

"We need to get word to Boston," hissed Gillespie, turning to Tanner.

"We've got hostile soldiers on Union soil, a mad industrialist doing deals with the enemy and a Confederate army of the dead being mobilised to move against our front line," Tanner spat back. "Fuck Boston, we need to get word to the President."

27

Tanner and Gillespie remained crouched behind the crates on the walkway as Fletcher and Hare crawled over to them.

"We need to get word to one of the Massachusetts regiments and get some serious firepower up here," Tanner said. "Did you clock any telegraph wires coming into this place when we flew over?" he asked Hare.

The Irishman thought for a moment before nodding. "One set of wires, coming into the hall near those two railway sidings," Hare said, pointing down to the two locomotives and their coaches, which were slowly inching their ways out of the hall and onto the tracks outside.

"Good," Tanner nodded. "Now, have you worked out where we are yet?" he hissed at Gillespie.

"It's obvious from what Amelia Proctor was saying that we're at her former husband's mansion, Rosebank Hall" he replied.

Tanner nodded again. "Right, let's find that telegraph room."

"And how do you propose we do that?" Fletcher asked.

Tanner tapped his fist against the crates behind which they were hiding. The other three looked at where he was indicting and saw the word "Uniforms" stencilled on the container. Levering the lid off, they found more of the navy blue greatcoats and peaked caps worn by Tate's men and quickly slipped into their disguises.

By the time they found the metal staircase leading down from the gantry, the hall was almost empty, save for a few of Tate's men having a smoke down by the two steam engines. As the group made their way across the hall in search of the telegraph transmitter, Hare paused and stood staring at the van der Waal's equipment.

"Molly," he muttered as he walked towards the machines.

"What the hell's going on?" Tanner hissed as Gillespie trotted after Hare.

Hare stood holding the two metallic discs in his hand as the other three men crowded around him.

"We haven't got time for this," Tanner said.

Gillespie slipped the discs out of Hare's hands, watching the pain in the Irishman's eyes as he remembered his dead wife and children.

"It would never work," Gillespie said quietly. "They've been dead for too long."

As he went to slip the discs back onto the workbench, a glint of silver on the surface of one of the discs caught Gillespie's eye. He lifted the disc closer to his eye and found a tiny needle protruding from the disc, with a plunger built into the handle on the back of the metal. He instantly recognised the white liquid left in the syringe.

"The son of a bitch," he said. "It looks like van der Waal had the Confederates fooled."

Tanner inspected the syringe rigged into the metal disc.

"Or more like Tate double-crossed them," he said. "He's just sold a contraption that doesn't even work to the Secessionists for one million dollars."

"Maybe we should just tip off Drummond that he's been duped and let him sort out Tate and Proctor," Gillespie smiled.

"I'll still need some back up to take on those Southerners," Tanner nodded grimly. "Let's find this telegraph and send for help."

The small telegraph booth at the front of the hall near the doors for the rail tracks was empty as the four men slipped inside. Gillespie slid himself into the operator's chair and flexed his fingers ready to tap out the necessary message on the control button in front of him.

"You know how to operate one of these units?" Tanner asked.

Gillespie nodded. "As long as this terminal is connected to the main exchange in Boston and not to Proctor or Tate's offices in the city then it should work fine."

"Right, send to Boston militia," Tanner began.

"I can't let you do that, Major," said Fletcher simply as he raised his revolver and shot Tanner once through the head at point blank range.

The spy crumpled to the floor instantly as a sheet of blood and cranial matter showered the rear wall of the telegraph booth in a spray of red and grey.

Fletcher turned his gun on Hare but the Irishman was too quick for him and jammed his elbow up into the lieutenant's arm, sending his aim high and the bullet off into the ceiling. Hare quickly thrust his fist into Fletcher's belly, making him double up in pain and then knocked the revolver out of his grip and sent it rolling across the floor. The Irishman forced Fletcher to the floor and clamped his hand around the lieutenant's mouth. Fletcher began struggling, writhing his arms and legs around to try and free himself.

"Help me," Hare yelled at Gillespie. "Pin him down. Crush his chest. If we fire another shot then someone's bound to hear."

Gillespie sat frozen in his seat, unable to take in the scene before him, unable to comprehend why one of his officers had just shot an army major. But deep down he knew it made sense; he had instinctively sensed that something had not been right with Fletcher.

"Help me," Hare repeated as Fletcher's struggles became wilder.

Gillespie slowly raised himself from the chair and stepped across to where the pair were struggling on the floor. He knelt down and looked into Fletcher's eyes, hoping to see some sign that his instincts were wrong. But the lieutenant just glared back at Gillespie and continued to struggle against Hare's grip.

Before he knew what was happening, Gillespie found himself throwing his arms across Fletcher and pinning him to the floor to stop his arms from flailing about and to squeeze the breath out of his chest.

Slowly the New Yorker's struggles lessened as the lack of oxygen took its toll on his body as he strained to take a breath that he couldn't due to Hare's vice-like grip across his nose and mouth. Finally his energy ebbed away and his body flopped lifelessly against the floor of the booth. Hare's eyes met Gillespie's for a brief moment across Fletcher's body.

Gillespie rolled back on his heels as the enormity of his actions sunk in. He had killed a man, one of his own officers, in the same way in which Hare had slaughtered sixteen souls in Edinburgh's West Port. He had played the role of Burke for Hare. Gillespie felt the bile rising in his throat moments before he knelt down and vomited in the corner of the booth.

He gasped for breath after dry retching for several moments and then rolled over and leaned back against the wall.

"How did you know?" he panted.

Hare looked at him for a moment, as if choosing his words carefully.

"It was Fletcher who threw the gunman from the city hall construction site," Hare offered.

"But why didn't you tell me?"

"Would you have believed me?"

Gillespie looked away, barely able to bring himself to look at either Hare or at Fletcher's body.

"Besides," Hare added, "I'd bet on Molly's grave that it was this piece of shite who torched my house and murdered my children."

The Irishman's attention was suddenly snatched away by the sound of slow hand clapping coming from the rear of the booth.

"Bravo, Hare, bravo," came an all too familiar voice. *"It's nice to see you haven't lost your touch."*

Hare turned pale.

"What is it?" Gillespie asked. "What's the matter?"

"What's the matter, Hare?" asked the voice. *"Don't you remember me? Don't you remember your old friend William Burke?"*

Hare gasped as the ghostly apparition he hadn't seen for nearly thirty years faded into view sitting on one of the spare seats in the telegraph booth.

"You can see him, can't you?" asked Gillespie, looking down at Fletcher's body and then remembering his own time floating above Edinburgh while he was drugged. "Can you see Burke?"

But before Hare could reply, Gillespie heard footsteps outside, growing louder as they headed towards the booth.

"Bolt the door," he yelled at Hare, as he swung back into the chair at the telegraph transmitter.

"This should be good," grinned Burke, rubbing his hands together *in glee.*

A loud thud reverberated throughout the booth as a heavy body launched itself against the door.

"What's going on in there?" came a shout from outside. "We heard gunfire."

Gillespie turned to the transmitter and began frantically tapping out a message in Morse code.

"Open up before we break this door down."

Gillespie's finger bashed away at the transmitter as the banging on the door grew louder and more frantic. He got the final character away as the door splintered away from its hinges and collapsed into the booth, leaving Gillespie and Hare staring down the barrels of six Winchester rifles.

28

The laughter being shared by Amelia, Tate and Drummond's officers was brought to an abrupt halt as Gillespie and Hare were marched into the drawing room. Burke took up his position leaning against the fireplace, looking longingly at the drinks and cigars being enjoyed by the Confederate party.

"Captain Gillespie, what an unexpected pleasure," said Amelia as she rose from her chair beside the roaring log fire. "To what do we owe this surprise visit?"

"I see you can't keep yourself away from my foreman," snorted Tate, who remained seated and sipped at his whiskey. Drummond, who had risen from his chair when Tate's men had entered the room with their prisoners, picked up his whiskey from a side table and lowered himself back onto the sofa in front of the fire.

"And who are these two clowns?" the colonel drawled in between slugs of liquor.

"Captain Gillespie is Boston's finest police officer," Amelia cooed. "And Mr Laird here, oh sorry, Mr Hare, was his chief suspect for the murders being committed all along Boston's docks. Won't you join us in a whiskey, Captain?"

"I'm afraid I only drink proper whisky – I'll take a Scotch if you have one?"

Tate and Drummond both scowled but Amelia giggled at Gillespie's insult.

"Murders?" Drummond snorted. "What murders?"

"Well, we had to find bodies for Professor van der Waal to perform his experiments," Amelia smiled. "Poor Captain Gillespie here was always just two steps behind."

"You?" Gillespie asked.

"Oh, don't look so surprised, Captain," Amelia pouted. "Mr Tate and myself would even join Callaghan and O'Leary on the hunt some nights. Speaking of which, any sign of those two yet, Fraser?"

"No, ma'am," replied one of the men who had dragged Gillespie and Hare into the drawing room. "The airship docked but there's been no sign of them since."

"You two wouldn't know anything about that, would you?" Amelia asked.

"We found these two with them" Fraser added. He snapped his fingers and two more of Tate's men entered the drawing room, dragging behind them the bodies of Fletcher and Tanner, who they dumped on the rug in front of the fire.

"Oh, not blood on the axminster again," Amelia said with mock horror. "Now who do we have here? Oh, poor Lieutenant Fletcher. He had such as promising career ahead of him."

"Good bent policeman are so hard to find these days," said Tate dryly.

Gillespie found it hard to conceal his surprise.

"Oh yes, Captain, didn't you guess?" Amelia tilted her head to one side. "That's how we were able to keep one step ahead of you – with our man on the inside. All that time there you were suspecting Mr Hare and it was really Lieutenant Fletcher who was feeding us information about your inquiry."

"Who's the other one?" Tate asked, draining the last of his bourbon and rising to refill his glass.

Drummond leaned forward from the sofa and gave the body a kick to turn it over, so he could inspect its face.

"Major Archibald Tanner, of the Union Army's so-called Bureau of Military Misinformation," he offered. "Our paths have crossed more than once. Pity he's already dead or I would have killed the son-of-a-bitch myself."

"I'm sure the feeling was mutual," quipped Gillespie.

"So let me see," Amelia mused. "A bullet hole to the head would indicate that Fletcher shot this Tanner character. But no gunshot wound on Fletcher so... Oh, Captain Gillespie, you didn't? You didn't help Mr Hare practice his old trade did you?"

"Oh, he did, he did, he did," Burke mocked, drawing a hard stare from Hare.

"Stop playing with them and kill them now," Tate spat as he lowered himself back into his chair.

"We found them in the telegraph booth," Fraser offered. "All four of them."

The smile fell away from Amelia's face and she glared at Tate's men.

"You fools," she screamed. "You didn't think to tell me that first."

Drummond sat bolt upright in his seat and his officers rose from their various perches on the furniture around the room, shaking off the effects of the whiskey to rouse themselves and become fully alert.

"Telegraph?" Drummond barked. "A telegram to the fucking Yankee army?"

"Who did you send that message to, Captain?" Amelia asked, stepping over the corpses on her rug to stare up into Gillespie's face. "Hmm?" she pressed. "No matter. I couldn't get a word out of you even when you were drugged," she snarled. "Well, no words, just moans of pleasure," she added, with a wink.

Gillespie screwed his face up. "Burn in hell," he muttered.

"Gentlemen, the time may have come to take our leave of one another," said Amelia as she led the way to the door. "Fraser, ready the airship."

"And how do you propose to get us out of here?" Drummond snapped as he and his officers followed Amelia and Tate from the study and down the corridor. Tate's men bundled Gillespie and Hare along in pursuit of the main party. Amelia's voice echoed back down the corridor: "Don't worry, Colonel. One of the advantages of owning half the railroad company is being able to move our own trains about without question. Take your men and board the first of the locomotives. Mr Tate and myself will take the airship and meet you at the docks once we have secured Professor van der Waal and his equipment on the second train."

The group entered the large hall at the rear of the house and Drummond's men started making their way down to the first of the trains.

"What about these two?" asked Fraser as he drew his revolver and pointed it at Gillespie and Hare.

"As fun as it's been, Captain, I think our evening together has reached its end," laughed Amelia. "Kill them," she added.

But even as the words were leaving her lips all hell broke loose as one of the side walls to the hall collapsed in a deafening explosion and gunfire echoed through the smouldering remains of the rubble.

LOWER CANADA BORDER, 1837

Hare cursed the saddle quietly under his breath as his horse continued to trot slowly along the forest path, its rider doing his best to dodge the low-slung branches obscuring the edges at either side of the track.

He tried to shift his weight from side to side to make himself more comfortable but the rough leather continued to chaff against his breaches as the smell from the wet pines overwhelmed his nostrils. The drizzle that had followed the small patrol all morning had finally begun to ease, but the collection of rain-drenched soldiers still couldn't wait to be out of the claustrophobic forest and out onto the openness of the plain again.

Hare felt the fear building up again in his gut, unable to free himself from the feeling that the small troop was being watched from the undergrowth all around them. He shook his head to try to clear his thoughts, trying to push his mind onwards through the damp air and back to the mission beyond.

"Where to next, Sergeant Laird?" asked the young soldier who rode alongside him.

Hare looked up. "Fort Andrews, Roberts" he told the soldier, the youngest member of the platoon. "Once we finally get away from these God-forsaken trees."

"Calling it a fort is making it sound a bit too grand, don't you think, sarge?" snorted Jamieson, who turned around in his saddle to cast the comment over his shoulder.

Hare smiled. Jamieson, the only other Irishman in the troop, was the closest he had to a friend. "I'd forgotten you'd been there before too, Jamieson," Hare said. "There's no pulling the wool over your eyes."

"Aye, although I'd be glad of anything to keep this rain out of my face," Jamieson laughed.

"Why isn't it a proper fort?" Roberts frowned.

"It's a frontier post," Hare explained. "Little more than an ammunition dump for the army, where a few fur trappers and lumbermen have set up home."

"Quiet back there," came the call from the head of the line, where Lieutenant Adam Pierce was leading the tramp through the forest. "Laird, keep your men in check back there."

"Aye, sir," Hare barked a reply.

Jamieson gave Hare a mischievous look before swinging back round in his saddle again.

Hare cursed Pierce under his breath. The commissioned officer encapsulated everything Hare had grown to hate about the fledgling United States Army over his past two years of service. A Boston blue-blood from the upper echelons of a well-to-do family, Pierce's commission in the army owed more to his standing in polite society than his abilities as an officer.

Having failed to find work when he had disembarked in New York on the ship from Liverpool, Hare had headed up the coast, roving from town to town until he found himself in Boston. With no options left, he had spied a recruitment poster and enlisted at the nearest army camp.

Thirty long months later and Hare was still regretting the decision. The army had taken him up and down the eastern seaboard of the United States of America, using rifle and field gun to suppress uprisings and slaughter the continent's native inhabitants.

Though Hare hadn't abandoned his beliefs while fleeing from England, the actions of Simmons and Hopkins had further dented his faith in humanity. Yet every bullet he fired in what his commanding officers laughingly called the protection of the United States forced Hare into the realisation that what he was doing was ultimately wrong, taking human lives to satisfy the white man's greed for the land.

Now, on patrol along the country's northern boundary with Lower Canada, Hare found himself alone with his thoughts, protecting an empty border land that he thought would never be attacked. By night, his dreams were filled with the faces of those whose lives he had taken; the Indian braves and their squaws; his brother Thomas and their father, both grinning crookedly at him through the night's darkness; and the men, women and children he and Burke had slaughtered in Edinburgh.

And by day, Burke's face gave him no rest.

"What's the matter, Hare?" the spirit asked him as he sat on the back of Hare's horse, leaning backwards and not bothering or needing to wrap his arms around Hare's waist. *"Cat got your tongue? Are you going to let that stuck-up, snooty-nosed toff talk to you like that?"*

Hare growled under his breath, loud enough to ward off Burke but not with enough volume to rouse the suspicions of the soldiers around him.

Moments later, the column of riders reached the edge of the forest and Pierce raised his hand for the soldiers to stop at the top of the slope that led down to the plain.

"Laird," he called, signalling for the sergeant to join the lieutenant at the head of the column. Hare squeezed his heels into the side of his stead and the horse edged forward.

"Laird, form the men into three columns for the trot down to Fort Andrews," Pierce instructed, pointing to the modest wooden structure on the plain ahead of them. "I want the good frontiersmen to see that their soldiers are here to protect them and provide security for them in this wild land."

Hare nodded slowly, indulging yet another of Pierce's monologues.

"Look, they've even lit the camp fires for us already," Pierce laughed, pointing to the column of smoke rising up above the fort.

Hare paused for a moment and squinted at the fort, before dipping into his saddle bag and removing a simple brass telescope. He held the instrument up to his eye and surveyed the scene below them on the plain.

"Sir," he muttered, "something's wrong at the fort."

"Give me the spyglass," Pierce commanded, holding out his hand and then snatching the telescope away from Hare. The lieutenant looked down at the fort and gasped when he saw that, where the stars and stripes should have been rippling in the wind, a green, white and red horizontal tricolour hung fluttering from the flagpole.

He whipped the telescope around, taking in the burning wagon just outside the fort's open gate and the absence of anyone along the ramparts.

"Shit," he hissed as he lowered the telescope.

"Form ranks," Hare bellowed at the soldiers. "Attack formation, lads. Load rifles and fix bayonets. Those fucking Frenchmen have taken the fort."

The soldiers shook off the fatigue of the long morning's trek through the forest and sprung to life, loading their rifles and screwing on the metal bayonets. The soldiers from the richer families also loaded the revolvers they kept tucked inside their greatcoats and Hare did the same, sliding bullets into the weapons he had purloined from dead comrades on the battlefields of Florida.

Once their weapons were loaded, the soldiers formed two rows of chevrons, with Hare at the centre of the first arrowhead and Pierce leading the band behind him. Without the need for another word, Hare led his well-drilled patrol down the slope and onto the plain, building up speed to a charging canter as they went.

But as the platoon neared the fort, the resistance Hare had expected from the French Canadians didn't materialise and the soldiers reached the open gates to the wooden stockade without a single shot being fired.

"Secure the perimeter," Hare barked as he dismounted and looked around the empty centre of the fort. A circle of small wooden huts surrounded the bare earth in the middle of the encampment, with a platform built into the side of the stockade above the huts, allowing defenders to fire at any attacking force.

"Find any survivors," Pierce commanded, taking charge of the situation. "We need to find out what happened here."

The soldiers dispersed, poking their rifles and then their heads into the wooden huts. Pierce headed for the largest building in the compound, a simple chapel with a cross hung above the door.

"What the hell is going on here, Laird?" Pierce asked. "Where is everyone? Where are the men who were supposed to be defending this —"

Pierce's words died in his mouth as a bullet ripped through his chest and sent the dying officer collapsing to the floor of the chapel. Hare ducked out of the way as a bullet flew past his left shoulder and crouched on the ground as he looked for their attacker.

A young man with lank black hair ducked back down behind a pew to reload his weapon but Hare was too quick for him, speedily closing the gap between himself and the rows of wooden seats and shooting the assailant once through the head.

Hare didn't bother retracing his steps to check if Pierce was dead but instead crept forward to where a moaning sound was coming from the front of the church. He wheeled past the wooden altar, draped with a deep green cloth, and threw open the door to a full-height cupboard off to one side. The man who had been leaning against the inside of the door fell out onto the floor of the church, his trousers down round his ankles.

"*Merde,*" he swore as Hare cocked his revolver and pointed it square at the prone man's chest. But before Hare could interrogate the Frenchman, a howling banshee flew from the cupboard and began kicking the man as he lay on the floor. Hare watched with a half-smile on his face as the young woman let fly with a series of kicks to the Frenchman's torso.

The girl was short and couldn't have been much older than sixteen, the dirty blond ringlets of her hair bouncing around her face as she bent over and landed a series of punches to the man's face, which he tried to protect by drawing up his hands. Hare was mesmerised by the look of determination on the girl's face, knowing she was ready to tear the Frenchman limb from limb. She pounded away at him with her fists, either unaware that Hare was watching her ample breasts jiggling up and down under her torn white nightdress or not caring to hide her modesty.

"That's enough," Hare barked, grabbing one of the girl's outstretched arms and effortlessly pulling her off the Frenchman, all the time keeping his revolver trained on his prisoner.

The woman glared hard at Hare. "I suppose you'll be wanting to have me and all," she spat, the firing continuing to burn in her eyes. Her Irish accent caught him by surprise.

Hare looked confused. "It was me who rescued you," he frowned.

"You wouldn't be the first to want me," she spat, gathering the sides of her torn nightdress and wrapping them across her chest. Hare slipped his greatcoat off his shoulders and tossed it across to her. She looked at the coat for a moment and then back at Hare, before picking up the outer garment and quickly burying herself deep inside the giant woollen coat.

Hare grabbed the battered Frenchman by the arm and pulled him to his feet. The man brushed himself down and grabbed his breeches and pulled them back up, all the time keeping his gaze fixed on the woman in case she attacked him again.

"What's your name?" Hare asked her.

"Molly," she replied simply. "What's yours?"

"Edward Laird," Hare replied, the lie coming so easily to him now after nearly three years of practice. "Now come along, Molly. You and your friend here have some explaining to do," he added as he led them both from the church and out into the centre of the fort.

"Corporal Jamieson, report," Hare barked as he emerged back out into the weak sunlight that was penetrating the gathering rain clouds.

"The fort is secured, sir," Jamieson replied, crossing the dirt to join Hare outside the church. "We found about a dozen survivors hiding in the huts, some of them injured. About twenty bodies all told, including women and four children too."

Hare shook his head.

"It's a massacre," he muttered. "What happened here, Molly?"

"Why are you asking her?" spluttered one of the fort's inhabitants. A group of men had followed Jamieson and were now gathered around Hare. "There's no use asking the town whore. She's got nothing to tell you."

"I've got more to tell him than you have, Samuel Pike," Molly snapped. "Where were you when those men were attacking the fort? Where were you when our men were dying all around us trying to defend our homes?"

"All right, that's enough," Hare said calmly. "One of you needs to tell me what happened here."

"These scumbags came from nowhere," Molly said, silencing Pike with a glare. "They attacked at first light yesterday. They must have waited for us to open the gates to let the trappers out to catch their beavers. They slaughtered men and women in their beds and then hoisted that monstrosity up there," she added, pointing to the Lower Canada flag fluttering in the gathering breeze.

"Where are the rest of the Canadians?" Hare asked.

"They only left those two," Molly replied. "This one here was trying to rape me while the other was out here. He must have gone inside the church when he saw you coming."

"Where's the other one?" asked Jamieson. "Come to think of it, where's Lieutenant Pierce too?"

"Dead," Hare replied simply. "The other Frog shot Pierce before I could get off a clear round."

Jamieson and Hare exchanged a look; the two Irishman knew that there was no love lost between either one of them or Pierce, but Jamieson didn't have time to ask if the lieutenant had died from one of the raider's bullets or one from Hare's own gun.

"They'll be back," Pike muttered. "These two were only left here to keep an eye on things while the raiding party gathered more men."

"What did they want with Fort Andrews?" Hare asked.

"Gunpowder," Pike nodded, indicating the stack of barrels stored inside one of the huts. "The army's been resupplying forts up and down the border all spring in case the government decides to back those separatists in Canada."

Hare turned his attention to the Frenchman, who had stood silently, eyeing the soldiers suspiciously.

"When will your men be back?" Hare demanded.

The Frenchman gave a Gallic shrug of his shoulders and began babbling in his native tongue. Hare sighed and drew his pistol again, levelling the barrel at the Frenchman's head.

"You're Canadian," he barked. "I know you speak enough English to answer my questions and if you don't I'll blow your God-damned head off."

The Frenchman's eyes narrowed and he sighed.

"You're Irish?" he asked in heavily-accented English.

Hare nodded.

"Then you'll know why I don't use the language of our oppressors," the Frenchman spat. "Too long we have been kept at heal by those English dogs and now we will rise up and free our lands from the assembly and the council and the governor."

"Why attack these people? Your quarrel isn't with us?"

"You have the gunpowder and the weapons," the Frenchman answered. "We cannot wait any longer while your government in Washington hums and hahs over whether it will aid us or not. We must act now. We must free our lands."

"And what about this girl?" Hare asked. "Are you going to free your land any quicker by raping an innocent woman?"

Pike smirked. "Innocent? Didn't you hear me, she's nothing but a miserable prostitute. I'm sure she got what she deserved."

"That's enough from you," Hare snapped, before turning back to the prisoner.

"Now tell me when the rest of you arseholes will be back?"

"Arseholes?" the Frenchman spat. "We are patriots."

Hare turned his gun around and swiped at the prisoner with the butt of his pistol, smacking him hard against his left temple. The man recoiled and rubbed his bruised head as he answered.

"Before sunset," he muttered. "They crossed the border to bring wagons so we could move the powder."

"Shit," Hare cursed. "We've not got long to get these people out of here."

"What do you mean?" Pike demanded. "You've got to stop them. You can't let them steal these supplies."

"I don't have the numbers we need," Hare replied.

"What? How many men do you have?" Pike frowned.

"With the lieutenant dead, we're down to twelve," Hare replied.

"Oh my God," Pike explained. "We're done for. When those Frogs get back they're going to lay waste to you and your men."

"What do you want to do, Laird?" Jamieson asked. "You're in charge now," he added with a smirk.

Hare ignored his friend and looked around, desperately trying to force a plan to form in his mind.

"So this is where it all ends," Burke snorted. *"Hare's last stand, here in a miserable frontier fort at the hands of a rag-tag bunch of French rebels."*

Hare spun round, ready to shout abuse at Burke, but controlled his temper.

"Just run," Burke taunted him. "Just run like you always do. This isn't your fight. Take your men and get out of here before you get cut down like these trappers and loggers and their whores did."

"Pike," Hare began, "Do you have bows and arrows in the fort for hunting?"

"Of course we do," the trapper scowled. "But that ain't going to be any use against those raiders' rifles."

"I don't need them to be," Hare replied. "Go get as many bows and arrows as you can find and start dipping the tips in pitch. We're only going to get one shot at this."

"At what?" Pike frowned.

"Never you mind for now," Hare replied, a note of anxiety creeping into his voice. "Just go and take the other survivors and get it done."

He turned his attention to his men.

"Jamieson, take every man we've got and bring those barrels of powder out of the store. I want them spread out here in the centre of the fort," he added, sweeping his arms out in a circle around him.

"Grab everything you can find that will burn. Blankets, straw, wood, anything that's not bolted down we need out here on the bonfire."

"Bonfire?" Jamieson asked. "What the devil have you got planned, Laird?"

"You'll see," Hare grinned. "And keep an eye on him?" he added, pointing to the prisoner.

"Is there another way out of here? Besides the gate?" Hare asked Molly. She thought for a moment and frowned.

"There's the drain," she replied slowly.

"Is it big enough for a man to squeeze out of?" Hare asked.

Molly nodded. "But why do you want to know that?" she asked.

"Because it just might save my life."

The sun had just started setting when Hare heard the sound of a bugle in the distance. He dropped the bundle of straw he had been carrying out of the supply store and weaved his way between the gunpowder barrels and up the ladder that led to the battlements behind the fort's stockade.

Jamieson was standing with the telescope, which he handed to his superior officer as Hare approached.

"About forty of them," Jamieson reported. "All of them on horseback. Leading two wagons by the look it."

Hare followed where Jamieson was pointing and raised the telescope to his eye. Across the plain and closing fast, he could see the Canadian rebels galloping towards Fort Andrews.

"Get the men out of here," Hare ordered. "Leave me two of the best shots and then take the rest with the townsfolk and get them out into the scrubland away from here. When I give the signal, you know what to do."

Jamieson looked grim. "Is this going to work?" he asked.

"I hope so," Hare smiled and patted his friend on the shoulder. He followed Jamieson down the ladder and then grabbed the captured Frenchman and pushed him up the stairs to the ramparts.

"I want you up here where they can see you," Hare hissed. "The closer they get before they suspect something's up, the better."

"You're really going to do it, aren't you?" Burke frowned. "You're going to make a final stand. You're going to try and save these people."

"I've had enough of running," Hare snapped back, ignoring the strange look the prisoner was giving him. "I've drawn a line in the sand, Burke. This is where it ends. This is where I stop running."

"You fool," Burke laughed. "If this is where you stop running then this is where you'll die, not at the hands of Edinburgh's police, not at the hands of a London mob but here in a frontier fort that no one cares about and no one will remember."

"If that's the case then, with a bit of luck, this is where you're going to die too," Hare replied, watching as a look of horror crossed Burke's face. "I die, you die," Hare added, turning to watch the approaching horsemen.

The bemused Frenchman lent against the wooden stakes and peered out at his comrades, galloping towards the fort, one of them carrying the Lower Canada tricolour, another letting off blasts from his bugle.

"Wave to them," Hare commanded as the party of Canadians began drawing closer. "Slowly," Hare added as the Frenchman began waving his arms. "You're telling them that everything's ok."

Down below, Hare could see that the last of his men had left via the gate, which they left open as they had found it. He breathed hard, praying silently for God to give him victory.

As the Canadians drew closer, the prisoner began shouting at them in French, waving both arms and becoming more and more agitated with every word. Hare realised that the prisoner was trying to warn them away and so he quickly cocked his revolver and shot the Frenchman once through the head, leaving the corpse to fall forward over the stockade and smash down into the dirt of the plain below.

The approaching rebels saw what had happened and quickened their pace, just as Hare had hoped.

"Get ready, they're coming," Hare shouted to the two soldiers he had left on either side of the gate. "Fire at will, but remember I want to draw them into the fort."

The two marksmen began letting off their rifles, taking down two riders at either side of the approaching column and then dropping to their knees to reload. Hare unshouldered his own rifle and let off several rounds before the first shots from the approaching guns began splintering the wooden stakes on either side of him.

"Let's get out of here," he yelled, signalling for the two snipers to leave. They raced down the ladders with Hare in hot pursuit and quickly crossed the centre of the fort and dropped down into the drain. The murky water, thick with human excrement and slop from the kitchens, ran in a shallow channel under the stockade and out onto the plain. The metal grill for catching the large pieces of detritus had already been removed and so the two soldiers easily ducked through the gap in the stockade and climbed out of the ditch at the other side before racing across the plain to take cover behind a bank of bare trees in the scrub just beyond the fort.

Hare turned to see the Canadian riders racing through the gates, first twenty then thirty and then all that remained of the forty horsemen piling into the fort to find out why one of their comrades had been executed. The wagons were left on the track outside, blocking their exit.

Hare quickly dropped down into the cesspit and dragged himself under the stockade and out the other side. Panting heavily from the exertion, he grabbed his sergeant's whistle from the top pocket of his uniform and, with what was left of his strength, gave a loud blast on the tin instrument.

"That's the whistle – open fire," screamed Jamieson from his position behind the row of archers. All of the huntsmen who could wield a bow had been lined up for action and dipped their pitch-covered arrows into the brazier that Jamieson had set up in front of them. Yanking back their bows, they let slip a flight of arrows that flew high above the wood stockade and came thundering down onto the array of barrels and kindling in the centre of the fort.

The early evening's twilight was lit up as the gunpowder barrels ignited, blasting apart in a cacophony of explosions that ripped through the fort, destroying the outer stockade and sending splinters of wood raining down on the plain all around.

Hare shielded his head as the wooden stakes came crashing down around him. He lay there in the cinders as the last of the barrels blew itself to pieces and then slowly freed himself from under the rubble. All around him, the acrid smell of burned flesh, both human and horse, filled the air.

As Hare shook his head to try to clear the ringing from his ears, he stopped and paused for a moment, looking all around him. But instead of the charred timbers and mangled limbs of the rebels, Hare's gaze searched for the familiar image of Burke, his constant companion for so long. But the other murder's visage was gone and Hare was left alone. He had never felt more alive.

Hare slowly clambered through the debris and emerged to be greeted by Jamieson and Molly, who came running towards him.

"Those were some fireworks," Jamieson laughed, slapping Hare on the shoulder. "Looks like we don't need any fancy lieutenants when we've got a sergeant like you."

Hare grinned and wiped some of the soot from his face. Molly threw her arms around his chest and pulled him down to her. She planted a kiss across his lips, which Hare returned, splitting her lips open and forcing his tongue into her mouth.

Jamieson coughed loudly to break them up. "There'll be time for that later," he chided. "Time to get out of here before any more of those rebels cross the border. I bet you can see our handy work all the way to Montreal."

"Come on," Hare said, pulling away from Molly. "Time for us to go."

Molly didn't let go and pulled Hare closer.

"You saved my life," she smiled. "I'm never going to leave your side again."

PART SIX
BOSTON, 1863

29

Gillespie couldn't tell how long he had been lying on the floor following the explosion. He slowly became aware of vague shapes moving at the edge of his blurred vision as the bodies lying around him began moving again. With a shake of his head to clear the dust from his eyes and try to stop the deafening ringing in his ears, Gillespie raised himself up onto his elbows and surveyed the scene around him. Tate was helping Amelia back to her feet and the pair appeared to be barking orders at their men, who were gathering their fallen weapons and heading to repel the dozens of Union soldiers who were pouring through the giant hole that had opened up in the side wall.

Hare tugged at Gillespie's elbow and slung his arm around the captain's shoulders as he raised him up off the ground and guided him to safety behind the overturned table on the stage as a hail of bullets rained down on Tate's men, striking three and forcing the rest to take cover where they could find it.

"You all right?" Hare asked. The Irishman's voice sounded distant and Gillespie shook his head again to try to overcome the ringing.

"I've had better days," Gillespie coughed as he peered over the edge of the table.

"Better get rid of these," Hare suggested, pushing the navy blue greatcoat he had used as a disguise off his shoulders.

"Good thinking," Gillespie nodded as he followed suit. "We need to signal we're on their side."

Just then a familiar voice began calling out over the sound of gunfire.

"Captain Gillespie," called Sergeant MacLeod as he edged his way through the rubble, a pair of infantrymen flanking him and offering occasional volleys of rifle fire by way of protection.

"Over here, MacLeod," Gillespie yelled, waving an arm above the table.

"Sir, thank God you're all right," MacLeod said, joining his senior officer in crouching behind the overturned table.

"How did you find us so fast?" Gillespie asked, surprised at how quickly the troops had attacked the mansion house following his telegram.

"When O'Malley and me dropped you off at the docks, we saw that big balloon rising up out of the warehouse," MacLeod began. "O'Malley worked out the general direction you were flying in. When we got to the police station nearest the docks he telegrammed Chief Blackstone and he contacted the Mayor. Eventually, I was dispatched with half the Boston militia regiment out on the road to Cambridge. When your telegram came in, Chief Blackstone sent a fast rider after us to tell us where you were. Lieutenant O'Malley has taken the other half of the militia regiment to the docks to find out what Tate was up to."

"It's not just Tate," Gillespie said. "Proctor was in on it too. They were stealing the bodies to try and bring them back to life."

The colour drained from MacLeod's face. "Did they succeed?" he asked nervously.

"No," Gillespie shook his head. "But that didn't stop them duping the Confederacy into buying the technology from them. They faked their results."

"Confederate soldiers in Massachusetts," MacLeod said. "I never thought I'd live to see the day."

MacLeod frowned for a moment and then asked: "But where are Major Tanner and Lieutenant Fletcher?"

"Fletcher killed Tanner," Gillespie replied. "It turns out the Lieutenant had been working for Proctor ever since he came to Boston."

"That's how they always stayed a step ahead of us," MacLeod nodded slowly. "Where are Tate and Proctor now?"

"A good question," Gillespie nodded, peering over the edge of the table and glancing around the room, trying to locate his foes.

"There," Hare pointed.

"That's strange," Gillespie mused. "They're heading back into the mansion."

"Should we go after them?" MacLeod asked.

"Aye," Gillespie nodded. "But we're going to need some cover."

"Armstrong, Miller, over here," MacLeod called to the two soldiers who had provided cover fire as he had entered the hall. "Give the Captain here your revolvers and then cover us, we're heading for that staircase over there."

The two troops did as they were instructed and each handed a revolver to Gillespie who checked the chambers and then cocked each of the weapons.

"What about me?" Hare frowned. "That pair killed my family."

"I need them alive, Hare," Gillespie said. "I can't let you kill them."

"Shooting them would be too quick – I want them to suffer, I want to see them hang for what they've done."

Gillespie stared long and hard into Hare's eyes. Could he trust this man? Could he trust this murderer who he had chased through the streets of Edinburgh? Gillespie could see the fire that burned within Hare's eyes and the look of anger that demanded revenge. He shook his head slowly.

"Not this time," he told Hare, who scowled back at him.

"Ready?" MacLeod asked.

"Ready," Gillespie replied, signalling for the two soldiers to lead the way across the hall.

Armstrong and Miller fired a volley in the direction of the nearest group of Tate's men as the two police officers and Hare began following them across the hall. The group reached the bottom of the metal staircase leading up to the gangway on which Gillespie and the others had hidden to watch van der Waal's demonstration just in time to see Tate and Amelia reach the top. Fraser and two of his men turned at the top to fire down on the group pursuing them. Gillespie and his men took cover either side of the staircase and Fraser's bullets flew wide of their mark. Once Fraser had fired the six shots from his revolver and his two companions had fired their rifle shots, Gillespie led the charge up the stairs, crashing into Fraser at the top of the stairs and knocking the man off his feet and onto the mesh floor of the metal gantry.

Miller and Armstrong were right behind him but didn't reach the gangway in time before Fraser's two men had reloaded. The pair of Union soldiers caught the blasts from the weapons full on in their chests and crumpled down onto the gangway. But Hare was quicker, jumping over their bodies and closing the gap between him and the two men before they had time to reload again. He careered into the first of them, knocking him off his feet and over the side of the gangway to fall crashing down on to the floor of the hall below. The second man Hare head-butted, knocking him off balance before a single punch sent him back against the wall, cracking his head open as he slid down.

Gillespie meanwhile wrestled with Fraser on the floor of the gantry before MacLeod stood over his shoulder and calmly fired a single shot from his revolver into Fraser's head, sending a spray of blood across Gillespie's shirt and face.

"Sorry, sir," MacLeod muttered as he helped his captain to his feet. Gillespie looked up in time to spot Hare grabbing the rifle from the grip of the guard he had just killed.

"Not this time," Hare snarled at Gillespie as he set off in pursuit of Tate and Amelia. Gillespie and MacLeod gave chase along the gantry and then through the door leading back into the mansion house. They ran down the hallway after Hare and spotted him pause outside an open door.

While Gillespie and Macleod thought Hare had pulled to a stop on his own, the Irishman stood staring at the image of Burke, who stood in front of him with his arm pointing to the open door and staircase beyond, an evil grin spread across his ghostly features.

The three stood listening to the sound of footsteps echoing round the flights of stone stairs that led up the tower.

"Up here," Hare spat as he led the charge up the tower. Gillespie panted to keep up with the Irishman, who ran like a man possessed, a look of hatred flashing across his face as he chased down his prey.

Gillespie felt like his lungs would exploded as he ran up the stairs and he could hear MacLeod's desperate panting falling further and further away behind them. But Hare didn't let up his pace for a moment, climbing higher and higher up the staircase until Gillespie could feel the cold night air biting into his face as they raced up the final flight of stone stairs.

Hare and Gillespie burst through the doorway and out onto the balcony surrounding the top of the tower just in time to see Amelia leaning over from the airship's basket and casting off the last of the rope lines that tethered the balloon to the tower.

"You just don't give up do you, Gillespie?" she said as she took aim and fired her revolver. Gillespie and Hare dropped to the floor as her bullets flew high, to be joined by a barrage of shots from Tate. Gillespie jumped to his feet and returned fire, with his sixth and final bullet striking Tate in the right shoulder. The industrialist gasped in pain and leaned back against the side of the basket.

"It looks like you've outlived your usefulness, Arthur," said Amelia as she shook her head sadly. Tate grimaced in pain and looked up at his accomplice with anguish on his face. But it was too late; Amelia was already upon him, pushing him by the shoulder and bundling him over the side of the basket.

"No," screamed Tate as he fell from the airship and plummeted through the air. Gillespie watched with horror as the industrialist smashed through the glass roof of the hall below. The captain leaned over the edge of the balcony to catch a glimpse of Tate's body splayed across the stage. Gillespie turned just in time to see Amelia goading the airship pilot on, urging him to coax every last bit of speed he could out of the propulsion system as the balloon banked and turned back towards Boston.

"Did she kill him?" MacLeod wheezed from the open doorway, propping himself up against the wooden frame as he watched the airship escape and saw Tate's body lying in the hall below. "She'd kill her own accomplice."

"She's mad," Gillespie said simply. "We need to stop her before she escapes. We need to get after her."

He leaned over the railing surrounding the balcony and sucked in the cold air to try to clear his head. His eyes fell to the hall below and sound of gunfire that continued to be exchanged between the Union and Confederate troops. The two plumes of steam caught his eye.

"The trains," he gasped and led the way back down the tower.

30

Gillespie, Hare and MacLeod reached the hall just after the Union soldiers had formed themselves into ranks and began pushing the remnants of the Confederate force and Tate's men back down the mansion towards where the two locomotives were now stoked and waiting to leave.

The troops grouped themselves into three ranks, with the first firing their rifles then kneeling to reload as the rank behind stepped past them and fired their shots. The soldiers slowly began working their way down the hall, firing volley after volley into the retreating Confederate force.

"This is taking too long," Gillespie yelled at the commanding officer standing behind his troops.

"And who the hell are you?" the officer screamed back.

"This is Captain Gillespie," MacLeod panted, catching up with Hare and Gillespie. "He was being held by Tate and Proctor."

"We need to stop them reaching those trains," Gillespie explained. "We need to cut them off before they can leave."

"We need to do this in a systematic fashion, Captain," the officer sneered, spitting the final word at Gillespie.

"We don't have much time," Gillespie pleaded. The Union commander glared at him for a moment then nodded sharply.

"Bring the field gun back round," he barked. "We'll blast those trains so they can't leave."

"We don't have time for this," Gillespie muttered.

"There, down the other side of the platform," Hare pointed. Gillespie followed his outstretched arm and saw at once what the Irishman meant. A long wooden platform ran between the rails on which the two trains sat. As the Union troops forced the Confederates back down the left hand side of the platform, Gillespie and Hare could use the platform itself as cover as they ran along the right.

"Let's go," Gillespie nodded before MacLeod or the army commander could stop them.

Hare led the way along the tracks at a jog, leaping between the wooden sleepers and avoiding the metal rails. They covered the ground quickly and stopped behind the rear carriage of the right-hand train to assess the situation. Ahead of them, Drummond was yelling orders at his remaining troops as Tate's men finished loading the gold onto the final carriage of the train that sat on the left-hand side of the platform.

"We need to go for Drummond," Gillespie whispered.

"Cut off the head and the snake dies?" Hare hissed back.

"Exactly," Gillespie nodded. "On three. One, two, three."

The men charged along the remainder of the tracks and vaulted up on to the platform, taking the Confederates by surprise. Gillespie's first bullet hit one of the Southern troops in the back of the head, killing him instantly. As his body crumpled onto the platform, it opened up the line of fire for Gillespie's five remaining bullets to hit Tate's three men who had finished loading the gold. His revolver empty, Gillespie charged at Drummond, hitting him square in the chest and forcing his elbow into the Confederate commander's arm, knocking his revolver down onto the tracks below. But Drummond kept his balance and threw Gillespie back off him before drawing his sword from the scabbard hanging from his belt. The police captain looked anxiously from side to side and then lunged at the body of the dead Confederate soldier, quickly turning him over and yanking his sword free from its sheath.

Drummond was on him in a second, thrusting his sword at Gillespie's exposed torso. The captain parried his first blow and then swung round to meet Drummond's second and third lunges.

Hare meanwhile had snatched up a pair of revolvers from two of Tate's dead men and was exchanging fire with three of Drummond's officers who hung out the open door of the penultimate carriage. Hare hid behind the end of the final carriage, using its wooden frame as cover.

Drummond's blows came thick and fierce, forcing Gillespie back along the platform.

"Is that all you've got you piece of Yankee scum?" Drummond taunted as he advanced on Gillespie again.

"Try Scottish," Gillespie spat back as he flicked his blade down and nicked Drummond's left calf with the tip of his sword.

The Confederate commander let out a yelp of agony but then growled and came at Gillespie again, his blood-lust sparked by the police captain's lucky strike.

Just as Drummond was getting the best of Gillespie, the first of the field gun shells exploded behind them, ripping apart the platform and sending a shower of wooden splinters into the air. Both men were knocked to the ground and, as Gillespie groggily got back to his feet, he saw that a large shard of wood had sliced through Drummond's chest, impaling the Confederate commander against the platform. Gillespie stared down into Drummond's face, the Confederate colonel's eyes still wide open and his mouth snarling with hatred as the wooden stake had ended his life. Hare picked himself up off the platform and threw down his pair of empty revolvers.

"Get us out of here," the Confederate surgeon called from the open carriage door, seeing that his commander was dead. The train lurched and pulled away, leaving Gillespie and Hare behind.

"Quickly," Gillespie shouted, "we need to get on the second train."

Gillespie and Hare raced along what was left of the platform and reached the second locomotive, the captain threading spare bullets from his waistcoat pockets into a revolver as he ran. Tate's men had just loaded the gold onto the first train and hadn't bothered with the second, except for the dumpy driver who stood in the cab of the locomotive, fiddling with the steam gauge and pasting down grey tufts of hair that poked out from under his cloth cap.

Gillespie cocked the hammer back on his revolver. "Ready to go?" he asked the driver, who nodded mutely and held his hands up just as Union soldiers began swarming up the platform.

"Uncouple the engine," Gillespie barked over his shoulder.

"Are you sure, sir?" asked MacLeod, who came up behind the troops.

"Do it," Gillespie yelled. "And you," he turned to the driver, "put your hands down and get ready to follow that train."

The driver nodded again and grabbed the lever for the brakes. Gillespie felt the engine lurch beneath his feet as the locomotive began edging forward.

"MacLeod," he called. The sergeant's head appeared again, peeping up into the engine as he broke into a trot to keep up with the slow-moving train. "You need to wire O'Malley at the docks and warn him about Proctor. She's on her way there in the airship."

"But what are you going to do, sir?" MacLeod asked as the engine picked up speed.

"We'll take the train," Gillespie shouted back. "We have to try and stop her getting away."

"Oh good, I do enjoy a good train ride," Burke cackled as he climbed up onto the engine.

Gillespie leaned back into the engine as the locomotive began to gather some speed, slipping out from under the glass ceiling of the hall and out into the cold dark night beyond the mansion house.

Gillespie watched Hare loading two revolvers that he had retrieved from the fallen Confederate soldiers.

"Are you ready for this?" he asked Hare.

The Irishman looked up to face Gillespie and, even in the eerie red glow emanating from the fire raging in the locomotive's furnace, the policeman could see a look of pure evil in Hare's eyes.

"I'm going to kill her," the Irishman spat. "I'm going to have my revenge on her for killing Molly."

"We need her alive," Gillespie scowled. "She needs to pay for all she's done."

"She'll pay all right," Hare snapped. "She'll pay with her life."

"That's my boy," Burke laughed. "That's the old Hare I knew. No more saving people. No more selfless acts. It's time for blood to be spilt, Hare. Either Proctor's or Gillespie's."

31

Gillespie stuck his head out the side of the locomotive's cabin and tried to pick out the tell-tale signs of steam rising up from the track ahead.

"I can't see them," he said, shaking his head as he pulled himself back inside the cabin, shielded from the cold night's wind by the small plate-glass windows built into the engine.

"We need more speed," said Hare, raising one of his revolvers and pointing it at the head of the driver, who was busy shovelling more coal into the furnace.

"We will once we get to the main track," the driver panted as he slung the final spade full of coal into the fire and slammed the wrought-iron door shut. "I can only go so fast in this siding but I'll be able to open her out when we reach the mainline. As long as they've left the points set right."

Gillespie and Hare exchanged looks over the short engineer's head.

"What do you mean?" Hare snarled.

"If those Confederate boys on the train ahead of us change the points then we won't be able to get back onto the main line," the driver replied.

"Can't we move them back?" Gillespie asked.

"Not unless either of you boys knows how to change points," the driver answered, shaking his head.

"I don't believe you," Hare yelled, pushing his forearm into the driver's neck and pining him against the side of the cabin as he jabbed the barrel of his revolver into the man's flabby cheek.

"Leave him," Gillespie snapped. "We need him to get us back to Boston."

"*Come on, Hare,*" hissed Burke. "*Don't let Gillespie push you around. You need to take control here.*"

"We'll find out soon enough," wheezed the driver as he massaged his bruised neck. "We're coming up on the end of the branch line now."

Gillespie and Hare craned their necks around the side of the cabin and, through the pale light cast by the lantern mounted in front of the engine's bulbous funnel, they could just make out the junction ahead. They each held the breath as the locomotive reached the end of the branch line and braked before sliding noisily across the points and onto the rails of the mainline track.

"Phew," the driver bellowed, wiping his brow. "Now we can get up a head of steam," he added, adjusting the dials and levers that regulated the engine's speed and grabbing his shovel again.

"I'll need some help from you boys if we're going to catch them," he added, handing the shovel to Hare. Gillespie nodded and Hare began packing coal from the small tender behind the locomotive into the waiting jaws of the furnace.

"Thought you were past this did you, Hare?" Burke snarled. "Thought your days of manual labour were over now that you've got a nice foreman's job?"

Hare ignored the ghost's taunts and carried on shovelling coal.

Gillespie stuck his neck back out the side of the cabin and studied what little he could see of the track ahead. The lurching arrival on the mainline stuck in his head.

"The points," Gillespie said. The driver looked across at him.

"What about them?" he asked.

"If Tate's men could have tampered with those then what else do we have to worry about?"

The driver stroked the silver and grey stubble on his chin. "More points I guess," he mused. "There's a signal box about a mile down the track, next to the junction for one of the countryside loops. If they send us down that then we'll never catch them."

"How can we stop them?" Gillespie demanded.

The driver shrugged.

"We need to catch them before they make it to that signal box," Gillespie said.

"Then you'd better get shovelling too," the driver smirked, handing the police captain a second shovel. Gillespie stared hard at the driver before snatching the spade out of his hand and joining Hare in his efforts to feed the fire, the men grunting at the effort in the enclosed cabin.

As the engine rounded a long flowing bend in the railway, a light on the line ahead caught Gillespie's eye.

"We're gaining on them," he said, peering through the night at the lights of the train ahead carrying the Confederates' gold. "Wait," he added, squinting against the smoke from the engine. "They're slowing down."

"Why are they –" Hare began but a hail of bullets silenced his question as the glass in the locomotive's small windows was shattered and sent a shower of bright shards across the three figures lying flat against the cramped floor of the engine house.

Outside, three of Tate's men had dropped down from the slow moving train and begun firing at the oncoming locomotive as the engineer from the first train slipped inside the white-painted wooden signal box and began pulling the levers to switch the points.

Gillespie felt the engine lurching as it was forced through the points and on to a different track.

"What's going on?" Gillespie yelled as the noise of the bullets being sprayed against the metal of the engine died away.

The driver poked his head out one of the shattered side windows.

"Looks like they've sent us on the countryside loop," he replied.

"Where is it taking us?" Hare barked,

"Oh, we'll still end up in Boston all right," the driver replied. "This'll still bring us down to the docks with the other train. But we've got no hope of catching them now – this loop will add miles to the journey."

"Faster," Hare spat. "We need to go faster."

"Then you two'd better get shovelling again," the driver shrugged, turning back to the controls for the locomotive.

Hare set about the coal with his spade like a man possessed, leaving Gillespie amazed by how a man pushing sixty could show so much stamina and effort while he was left exhausted from the events of the night. Though Hare was eight years older than him, Gillespie had been struggling to keep up with him and soon his efforts at hauling the coal were put to shame by the Irishman, who kept ladling spade after spade into the furnace.

"*Seems like a lot of effort to me, Hare,*" Burke mused. "*Lot of coal being shovelled into an engine without any carriages. Why didn't we race past that other train I wonder?*"

Hare paused and threw his suit jacket into the corner of the cabin before starting again, throwing fuel onto the fire. After another tremendous bout of fire stoking, he paused and lent on his spade while he wiped the sweat away from his high forehead against the dirty sleeve of his once-white shirt.

"Why aren't we going any faster?" he panted. "I've been shovelling my heart out and we're not picking up speed."

The driver glanced back over his shoulder at Hare but didn't offer an answer. The Irishman threw down his spade and leaned forward to squint at the dials.

"*That's it, Hare,*" Burke said quietly.

"Here, why isn't there more steam?" he shouted, tapping the glass dial with his knuckles. "What are you playing at man?" he snarled, searching about the cabin for an answer to his question. He pushed the driver to one side and saw the levers that controlled the breaks.

"You bastard," he shouted at the driver, pushing him in the chest with both hands and sending him careering back against the side of the cabin. "You've had the breaks half on this whole time."

The driver began shaking his head and protesting his innocence but Hare silenced him with a slap from the back of his grimy hands across his fat jowls. The Irishman reached across and grabbed the lever, pulling the brakes fully off, allowing the engine to run at full speed. There was a lurch as the locomotive started accelerating and Gillespie steadied himself against the side of cabin as Hare turned his attention back to the driver.

"Leave him, Hare, that's enough," the captain cautioned as he slid his revolver out of its holster.

"*Don't pay him any attention,*" Burke shook his head. "*This fat bag of shite had been holding you back.*"

Hare ignored Gillespie's warning and grabbed the driver by the straps of his blue dungarees, dragging him up from the floor and pushing him towards the narrow gap between the end of the locomotive's cabin and the edge of the tender car running behind them.

"Were you going to stop us reaching the docks?" Hare yelled at the driver as he shoved the old man's head out the side of the engine and into the cold wind whistling past at ever faster speeds. "Were you going to lead us away from Proctor?"

"Stop it, Hare," Gillespie yelled over the thundering sound of the engine. "Bring him back inside."

"Go to hell," the driver replied, spitting in Hare's face. The Irishman yelled in fury and, before Gillespie could close the gap of two paces between them, Hare lifted the driver clear off the deck of the cabin and threw him out into the black night. Gillespie watched in horror as the driver's body sailed through the air and hit a nearby tree with a sickening crack that he could hear even above the noise from the engine, before the driver's limp remains crashed down into a wooden fence running along the length of the railway track. The captain chastised himself for not taking a shot at Hare but he knew that with the engine lurching and swaying from side to side as it gathered speed he had just as much chance of hitting himself with a ricocheting bullet as he did of stopping Hare.

"Shit," Gillespie cursed. "What now? Do you know how to control this thing?" he added, pointing to the levers and valves that regulated the engine.

"That felt good, didn't it, Hare?" Burke said. *"Getting your hands dirty again. Just like it did with Fletcher."*

Hare turned to Gillespie and fixed him with the same stare that Gillespie had last seen thirty-four years earlier on a rain-soaked street in Edinburgh, when Hare had stopped himself from taking Gillespie's life. A fire of pure hatred burned in Hare's eyes, the mixed colour of his irises doing nothing to dim the blaze. But, just as quickly as Hare had fixed his look on Gillespie, the Irishman turned away again and began studying the controls to the locomotive.

"He's not worth it. Leave him for now," the voice told Hare.

"We've used steam engines while we've been building the canal," Hare offered. "I think I can tease enough steam out of this beast to get us to the docks."

Gillespie shook his head in disbelief as Hare played with the dials in front of him and the engine shook again as it began picking up even more speed. The policeman grabbed on to rail that ran along the inside of the cabin, his knuckles turning white as he gripped the polished brass. Hare remained impassive, sinking back inside himself as he stood in the centre of the cabin, feet apart to steady his body while he read the gauges and dials.

"You can hear him can't you?" Gillespie asked. "You can hear Burke can't you?"

"Just because I hear him doesn't mean I have to listen," Hare protested, all the time keeping his eyes fixed on the steam gauges.

"Oh, you'll hear alright," Burke shook his head, whispering over Hare's shoulder and into his ear. "It's nearly time, Hare. Nearly time for you to finish the job you started all those years ago in Edinburgh."

Outside, Gillespie started to see the gaslights of Boston adding an orange glow to the low-lying clouds that were covering the city. His mind raced as he tried to work out where the track would enter Boston and whether any obstacles would stand in their way before they reached the docks.

"Can you steer this thing?" Gillespie asked with a worried look spreading across his face. The buildings on the edge of the city began to zip past the empty windows as the locomotive sped past them.

"Steer it?" Hare snorted. "It's on rails, there's only so much steering that can be done."

"Then how about slowing it down?" Gillespie queried.

Hare turned and looked at him. "Why?"

"Because we've only got about two minutes before we hit the docks and unless we slow down then I don't think we're going to stop when we hit the buffers."

A look of realisation passed across Hare's face.

"Then we might have a problem," the Irishman replied. "I don't think I can vent enough steam in time."

The buildings were becoming more closely grouped together now and the streetlights more frequent as the engine roared along the track. Gillespie stuck his head out of one of the windows and could enjoy an unobstructed view of the warehouses and other dock buildings rising up from Tate's yard ahead of them.

"In that case keep her running at maximum," the captain said, a grim look passing across his features. "Ramming the other engine might be our only way of stopping them now."

Hare gave a curt nod and opened the valves to their limits.

"What about us?" he asked. Gillespie knelt down and picked up Hare's coat.

"Put this back on and stuff some of these sacks inside," Gillespie replied, handing Hare his suit jacket and a handful of hessian sacks, which had been absentmindedly thrown into the cabin after their coal had been emptied into the tender. "There are still grassy banks on either side of the line. If we roll down one of those then these sacks might absorb some of the impact."

"Ever the optimist," Hare snorted as he stuffed the sacking inside his coat. The glow from the lights at the dock was becoming brighter as the locomotive drew closer and Gillespie briefly wondered if his plan would work as he threw himself out of the engine's cabin and followed Hare in rolling down the bank.

32

The wailing of the locomotive's engine filled the whole dockyard as the train raced through the opening in the fence surrounding Tate's private quay and careered towards the wooden buffers. The locomotive jumped the tracks and smashed through the buffers in a spray of splinters. The impact was strong enough to knock the engine onto its side but not to check its motion as it slid along the dockside and crashed into the side of the first locomotive that stood in the siding next to it.

Gillespie and Hare's engine smashed into the side of its companion, rupturing the metal shell protecting the furnace and setting off an explosion of steam that sent the funnel of the second train flying high up into the air. Both engines exploded in a shower of sparks that ignited the rear wooden coaches and released a fireball that engulfed Tate's men as they were trying desperately to empty the chests of gold coins out of the rear carriages.

The dockside was lit up in a bright orange glow from the flames of the mangled train wreckage as Gillespie gingerly picked his way along the railway tracks and through the hole in the fence surrounding the docks. He gasped as the pain from his cracked ribs bore into him but pushed himself on, following Hare onto the quayside. The Irishman's fall from the train had not been as heavy as Gillespie's and once again Hare was showing himself to be the more resilient in the face of pain and danger.

"O'Malley," Gillespie yelled, trying to find his lieutenant among the dark shapes running each way across the dockside. He knew his deputy would be somewhere in the melee that was consuming the quay.

"Over here, sir," O'Malley called back, waving his arm above a row of crates that offered some protection from the hail of gunfire that was being exchanged between Tate's men who had been stationed at the docks and the phalanx of Union soldiers and police officers led by

O'Malley.

Gillespie gripped the Irish officer's shoulder as he crouched behind the crates with him.

"Good to see you," Gillespie grinned as Hare slid in next to them.

"You too," O'Malley nodded. "You made quite an entrance," he added, pointing to the flaming carcass of the locomotive.

"Never let it be said that a Scotsman doesn't know how to announce himself in style," Gillespie smiled before sticking his head over the top of the crate to survey the docks. Tate's men appeared to be defending one specific warehouse that hung out over the edge of the quayside. "Did Proctor make it to the train before the explosion?" Gillespie asked. He knew in his head that justice would have been better served if she had died in the fireball but in his heart he still foolishly hoped she had escaped so that he could track her down again.

"She did," O'Malley replied. "That train must have only arrived a few minutes before your engine shot across the docks. Her airship had landed first and moored over by that warehouse. Proctor was supervising the unloading and barking instructions at her troops when the wailing of that locomotive stopped everyone dead in their tracks."

Gillespie nodded his understanding but before he could formulate a plan, Hare interrupted his line of thought.

"Over there," the Irishman yelled, pointing off to the right with one of his revolvers. Gillespie followed his gaze and saw Amelia flanked by the Confederate army surgeon and two of Tate's men as they made their way towards the warehouse.

"Hare, stop," Gillespie yelled as the Irishman began running towards the group.

"She's mine," came Hare's reply over his shoulder.

Gillespie gave chase, followed by O'Malley and the six Union soldiers who had been sheltering with him behind the crate, happy to follow an ex-soldier around a dockside that he knew better than any of them.

Hare began firing his revolver as he ran, striking the Confederate surgeon in the arm and one of Tate's men in chest, sending him sinking to his knees. The group returned fire but Gillespie and the others soon joined in the fire fight, which left Amelia and the Confederate surgeon standing surrounded by the Union soldiers, Hare and the two police officers.

Gillespie took in the sight of Amelia dressed in a long black flowing coat that she wore open, showing the gun holster slung around the narrow waist of the long black dress she wore, laced all the way up the front a high neck. Given a matching hat, she could almost be dressed in her Sunday best for worship at her local church.

"So it comes down to this, Gillespie," Amelia grinned as she lowered the aim of her revolver at the police captain. A second weapon still sat in its holster at her waist. "You shoot me then I shoot you. You kill me then I kill you. Maybe there's a better way out of all this?" she added quickly scanning around for an escape route but all the time keeping her pistol levelled at Gillespie.

"It's over Amelia," Gillespie replied. "You've aided and abetted the Secessionists and murdered Tate's dockworkers. The only place you're going now is the gallows."

Amelia threw back her head and let out a loud cackle of laughter.

"You'll have to catch me first," was all she said as she fired a single shot from her revolver and then crouched down on the ground.

Gillespie frowned as the bullet sailed past his shoulder but he and the others were too slow to realise what was happening as Amelia's bullet struck the central barrel in a row that stood off to their right and ignited the gunpowder inside.

33

The noise was like nothing Gillespie had heard before as the loud whoop of the ignited gunpowder was followed by an almighty explosion when the barrel caught light and set fire to the neighbouring containers in the row. Gillespie and the others were thrown from their feet by the force of the blast as burning barrel fragments came crashing down around them on the dockside. Thick black smoke bellowed around them as the clouds in the night's sky were seared yellow, reflecting the flames that licked in every direction along the quay.

Amelia slipped quickly past their immobile forms as she headed for the warehouse. Gillespie could only helplessly watch her run past him as he rolled onto his side and tried to raise himself up on his elbows. He quickly assessed his limbs and found he hadn't been hit by any of the shrapnel from the explosion – but O'Malley's inert form lying next to him told a different story.

"O'Malley?" Gillespie coughed as he crawled over and shook his friend's shoulder. The captain knew that O'Malley was dying even before he hauled himself up into a sitting position and turned the Irishman over, pulling him into his lap. Gillespie could see the soot caked across O'Malley's face from the explosion and the three chunks of wooden shrapnel that protruded from the front of his coat, soaking the wool in deep red blood and causing the lieutenant's breath to come in short wheezing gasps. O'Malley's eyes fluttered open and he looked up at Gillespie.

"Tell Maddie that I love her," the Irishman managed to croak through his cracked lips.

"You can tell her yourself," Gillespie shook his hand. "Hang on, we'll get you to a doctor."

But before the words had left Gillespie's lips, O'Malley's eyes rolled up into his head and all of the tension ebbed out of his body, leaving his inert form sagging in Gillespie's arms. The captain fought back his tears as he lifted his fingers up and slowly closed O'Malley's eyelids before shifting his corpse out of his lap and onto the wet dockside.

The ringing in Gillespie's ears began to subside and he could slowly begin to make out the shouts of the surviving Union troops as they began organising themselves to mop up the last of the resistance from Tate's men, who continued to defend the warehouse at the edge of the quayside.

Hare slowly walked over to Gillespie, having left the captain to mourn the loss of O'Malley. The Irishman leant down and offered Gillespie his hand.

"Ready for one final roll of the dice?" Hare asked.

Gillespie looked up at him, a man who had lost everything but was still prepared to sacrifice himself in order to catch Amelia. Could he have been wrong about Hare all this time?

"Let's go," said Gillespie, grabbing Hare's arm and hauling himself back onto his feet. "Let's get after her."

Amelia used the chaos following the explosion of the gunpowder barrels to slip through the Union lines and reach the men defending the warehouse. Tate's men recognised her and let her inside.

She ran across the empty interior of the warehouse and down a wooden walkway that led to the deck of a waiting ironclad warship.

"Where's Mr Tate?" asked the ironclad's captain, a frown crossing his face as he stood aside to let Amelia pass through the open hatchway and into the interior of the armoured vessel.

Amelia paused for a moment before turning to face the captain.

"Mr Tate sadly won't be joining us," she sobbed, forcing tears into her eyes to win over the captain. "He died defending me from Captain Gillespie and that dog Hare."

The captain nodded grimly.

"Then we must get you away from this mess," he said, taking her by the hand and leading her through the ironclad to its bridge at the front of the vessel. Amelia smiled behind the captain's back and ran the sleeve of her coat across her eyes to dry the faked tears. They passed row after row of heavy artillery guns being loaded for action, in preparation for fighting their way out of Boston's harbour and into the North Atlantic and safety.

"Is the gold stowed on board?" Amelia asked as they reached the bridge and the captain pulled up a simple wooden chair for her to sit on.

"We managed to get four of the chests on board before the first of the explosions," the captain answered.

"And Professor van der Waal's equipment?"

"The Professor and his machine are stowed safely in the hold. He was mumbling something about taking some of the fallen men with him so that he could perfect his technique," the captain replied with a shake of his head before breaking off to bark orders at his crew.

"Prepare for launch," he yelled. "Retract the boarding plank and seal the hatches. Ready the main guns."

Amelia settled back in her seat as best she could and peered through one of the two forward portholes, just in time to see Tate's men opening the doors of the covered dock to reveal the harbour beyond.

Gillespie couldn't believe his eyes as the seaward doors to the warehouse were drawn open and the ironclad began edging its way out into the harbour. Hare and the Union troops they had rounded up to storm the warehouse stopped beside Gillespie and gaped open mouthed at the ship.

"Tate could have run the war on his own," Gillespie shook his head. "Is there nothing that money can't buy you?"

"An airship, steam locomotives and now an ironclad," Hare nodded. "I guess owning an armaments factory has its uses."

The men watched helplessly as the ironclad began sailing past the dockside, the white skull and crossed-bones of the Jolly Roger fluttering against their black background on the stern as the cold night's breeze whipped around the flag.

A movement from one of the hatches on the ironclad's flank caught Gillespie's eye.

"Get down," he yelled as the gun ports suddenly sprang open and a volley of heavy artillery fire peppered the quayside. The shells rained down on the docks, exploding in a wave behind where Gillespie and the others were standing and igniting what remained of the cranes and barrels scattered around Tate's docks.

Gillespie picked himself up off the ground once more and shook the concussion from his head. He grabbed the nearest of the Union soldiers.

"Get back to the nearest police station and wire the commander of the militia," he barked his orders, pulling the young soldier close to him so that he could shout in his ear. "We need to signal to the shore batteries to open fire on that ironclad and slow it down. We can't let it make it out to open water. Do you understand?"

The soldier nodded and raced off into the night in search of help.

Gillespie turned back to Hare. "We need a boat," he said simply and they set off at a trot along what was left of the quayside in search of a vessel in which to mount their pursuit. Several minutes' searching proved fruitless as they watched the ironclad slowly gaining distance away from the docks as the captain did his best to tease more speed out of its engines.

"It's useless," Hare shook his head. "There's nothing left here that's salvageable."

Gillespie sighed heavily and looked around the remains of the quayside. In the corner of the dock, shielded from the raging battle by the leeward side of the warehouse, sat Tate's airship, its balloon still filled with hydrogen and its basket slowly bobbing up and down against the ground while held in place by a series of ropes.

A grin spread across Gillespie's face.

"You proved yourself more than adept at crashing a steam engine – but how about an airship?" he asked as he led Hare towards the waiting balloon.

34

The airship lurched from side to side as Gillespie and Hare struggled with its series of pulleys and levers to bring the balloon under control in the strengthening winds that had whipped up over the harbour. After casting off the holding lines from the dockside, the airship had immediately been thrust into the air, quickly gathering height and veering off out over the water.

The Union soldiers left on the quayside stood in awe of the flying machine as it passed over their heads and then set off in pursuit of the ironclad, which was making its way out into the main channel of Boston's large harbour.

"Pull that one," Gillespie yelled as Hare made a lunge for one of the steering ropes that had come free in the wind. Hare quickly grabbed the line and tied it off against the basket's railing, bringing the balloon above their heads back under some kind of control. Between them, the two men quickly assessed how to regulate the airship's height and direction before Hare bent down and stoked the small steam turbine that drove the propulsion system, building up a head of steam so that the balloon could follow the ironclad. Gillespie grabbed the rudder and sent the airship out into a wide curve across the harbour, in pursuit of the ironclad below.

"Well this is a first," shouted Burke from his position at the front of the basket. "First horseback then steam train and now a flying machine. You certainly know how to show a man a good time, Hare."

All the way along the harbour, the Massachusetts regiments that were still based in Boston were dragging field guns from their storage sheds and down to the bay, ready to set up temporary artillery positions to bombard the ironclad. Most were too late to catch the boat but five hastily erected gun positions were able to open fire as the vessel reached the end of the Charles River and out into the main portion of the harbour, aiming for the bay beyond. But the commanders of the permanent defensive batteries had received their orders too and were ready for the ironclad as it entered range.

The first of the incendiary shells exploded above the ship, missing their mark but lighting up the night's sky around the vessel and providing the Boston gunners with a target at which they could aim.

"Incoming shell, sir," screamed one of the ironclad's officers as he ducked below a beam and squeezed onto the bridge. "Their range is good but their elevation is all wrong."

"Let's make the most of that while we can," the captain replied. "Return fire. All guns."

"Aye, sir," the officer replied, heading back into the main body of the ironclad.

"Return fire men, take out the gun batteries," he ordered, as Tate's men loaded explosive shells into their cannons and swung open the gun ports ready for action.

The guns rolled backwards along their tracks as they hurled their shells forward and up into the air. Three of the five guns along the ironclad's port flank found their target, raining down on the permanent gun encampment and knocking out one of the coastal defences' weapons. The starboard battery found their mark on one of the walkways along the harbour's edge, destroying the hastily-positioned field gun that had been brought to bear on the fleeing vessel and shattering three of the nearby wooden park benches in the process.

The remaining gun placements along the shoreline returned fire with a barrage of shells that exploded around the escaping ship, sending a wall of spray across the boat's metal defences but leaving its armour unharmed.

High above the ironclad, Gillespie slowly turned the rudder of the airship to bring the nose of the balloon to bear on the armour-plated boat.

"One quick question," coughed Hare as he struggled to breathe in the cold air that whipped against the airship while it sped across the harbour. "How exactly do you plan to stop that iron beast?"

"The guns along the shoreline should do the job for us," Gillespie replied, sticking out his arm and pointing to the row of lights flaring up from the mouths of the field guns mounted along the side of the harbour.

"Once the boat's speed is checked we can bring the balloon down and board her."

"Land on the boat?" Hare asked.

"On the boat," Gillespie nodded.

Hare shook his head slowly as he watched the shells from the Boston guns continually missing their target.

"They'd better get a move on," he mused. "She's heading for open water."

Shells from the shore batteries continued to explode in the air above the ironclad or splash into the water around the vessel but none of the gunners managed to find their target.

"They can't keep up with us, sir," shouted the gunnery officer from the bowels of the ironclad to his captain. "Their aim is all askew."

"Continue the bombardment," the captain bellowed back. "Fire at will."

"You heard the Captain," the officer told his gunners. "Take aim and fire."

A fresh volley of shells erupted from the muzzles of the ironclad's guns peppering the shoreline around the batteries and the temporary gun positions.

The heavy artillery of the Massachusetts regiments returned fire and finally an explosive round found its target, striking the ironclad clean in the centre of its port side. But the shell simply bounced off the boat's thick iron plating and exploded in the air above its target.

A loud cheer went up from the crew inside the ironclad as the loud "thunk" of the shell hitting the armour was replaced by a whistling sound and the explosion high above their heads.

The first shell was followed by a further four that hit the boat in quick succession but each rebounded off its target and exploded harmlessly all around it.

Gillespie watched in horror as the rounds of fire from the shore batteries failed to pierce the armour plating of Tate's vessel as it steamed passed the barrage of fire from the harbour and began to steer its way between the small shingle islands in the sound and head for the bay beyond.

"What now?" Hare cried.

Gillespie shot Hare a sideways glance as he fought to keep the balloon under control. A look of worry passed across the police captain's face as his mind raced to come up with a new plan. Then a sad smile slowly began to spread across his features.

"The gas in the balloon is highly combustible," he said simply. "All we have to do is get close enough to the ironclad's funnel to puncture the skin of the airship."

Hare stared hard at him for a moment and then looked down at the ironclad in the water ahead of them. Slowly the airship was closing the gap on the boat and the image of the vessel was looming larger and larger.

"What happened to trying to take Proctor alive?" Hare asked.

"You wanted your revenge didn't you?" Gillespie parried.

"Aye," Hare nodded slowly. "I'd just wanted to see the look of fear in her eyes first."

Gillespie sighed heavily and began pulling on the ropes and pulleys to bring the nose of balloon down before pushing hard on the rudder to take the airship down onto an intercept course for the ironclad.

The guns along Boston's waterfront continued to fire long after the ironclad had sailed out of range, the orange glow from their explosives lighting up the night as shell after shell of heavy ordinance blew up in the air, trailing behind the fleeing vessel.

Another chorus of cheers broke out amongst the ironclads' crew as they laid down their barrels of gunpowder and relaxed for a moment after the intense fire fight.

The gunnery officer smiled and leaned into one of the two rear gun ports to look back out at his vanquished foes on the shoreline.

"Sir," he screamed. "You'd better take a look at this."

On the boat's bridge, the captain exchanged a worried glance with Amelia before ducking under the beam and back out into the main body of the ironclad, pushing his men out of the way to reach the rear of the vessel. Amelia trotted after him.

"What the hell is that?" the gunnery officer asked, pointing up into the sky behind the boat.

The captain leaned out through the gun port and gazed up at the dark silhouette of the balloon following them, the sky around it lit up by the continuing gun fire from the harbour.

"It looks like Mr Tate's airship," the captain replied. "But how did _"

"Gillespie," spat Amelia, who had pushed the gunnery officer out of the way so that she could lean out of the other gun port. "Captain, we need to bring that balloon down."

"But what harm can that craft do to our vessel?"

"I don't know, Captain, and frankly I don't care. Just blow that God-damned airship out of the sky now."

"Yes, ma'am," the captain nodded.

"Take your stations men," he yelled as he raced back along the narrow passageway between the guns and headed for the bridge. "Right full rudder, bring her around."

"They're turning," Hare yelled as he watched the bow of the boat begin to come around, bringing its lethal array of guns to bear on the unprotected airship.

"Shit," muttered Gillespie. "Hang on, I might need to take some evasive action."

"Evasive action he says," Burke mocked, flailing wildly from side to side. "That doesn't sound good."

Gillespie grabbed at two of the ropes again and began to rock from side to side, making the balloon sway wildly in the air but all the time keeping his leg rammed hard against the rudder to maintain the balloon on course.

His actions put off the aim of the ironclad's gunners, whose shells sailed wide of their mark on each side and lit up the dark sky with their exploding shells.

"Keep firing," Amelia screamed at the gunners as the ironclad's captain struggled to make the boat turn in a tight circle, attempting to keep the airship in range of the guns.

Amelia watched in horror as the airship continued to duck and weave the shells but all the time banking around and getting closer and closer towards the boat.

"It's now or never," Gillespie yelled at Hare as he began tying off the ropes and locking the airship into its deathly course towards the ironclad.

"How do you mean?" Hare looked blank.

"You jump now," Gillespie shouted. The two men stood staring at each other in silence for a moment, each weighing up his desire to jump from the basket into the freezing waters below or face their fate in the fireball that would soon consume the airship.

No words were needed as each man clambered over the side of the basket and plunged headfirst into the chilly depths of the bay.

The balloon's final arc towards the ironclad seemed to play out in slow motion for Amelia. She raced from the gun deck back through onto the bridge in time to see the airship disappearing from view as it passed over the portholes at the front of the ironclad and sailed back towards the funnel.

Amelia turned and stared dumbfounded at the captain, whose head sank in shame as he realised what was about to happen. She managed to scream "No" at the top of her lungs before her whole world was enveloped in a sheet of flames.

The airship seemed to hang for a moment above the ironclad before the jagged edge of the funnel's hot rim collided with skin of the balloon and ripped the thin protective fabric before igniting the hydrogen inside. A massive explosion ripped through the airship, shattered the basket and balloon and sending its flaming carcass crashing down onto the outer deck of the ironclad.

The flames from the explosion shot down through the funnel of the ironclad and destroyed the furnace below, quickly ripping through the engine room and igniting the boat's gunpowder battery.

A chain reaction spread through the ship as the gunpowder exploded, vaporising the crew instantly and puncturing the iron plating from the inside out, causing the ironclad's superstructure to collapse down into its hold and sending the hissing hot metal into the cool waters of the bay.

Gillespie hit the icy surface of the water and carried on falling, sinking deeper and deeper into the inky black water. He tried to control the flow of air bubbles escaping through his mouth as the shock of the freezing water caused his body to spasm and his lungs to ache.

The police officer kicked off his heavy boots and slipped out of his greatcoat as he tried to kick his way towards the surface, fighting every inch of the way against the rising pain in his chest and throughout his left arm. After what felt like an eternity, his head broke through the waves and he gulped into the frigid salty air of the bay.

Once he had coughed up the water from his lungs, Gillespie swivelled his head around and scanned the waters for means of safety. He spotted the shingle beach on one of the small islands that dotted the bay and began stroking towards it, pulling himself forward with his right arm and kicking as hard as he could with his legs. As he edged closer to landfall, he could see Hare's head bobbing up and down in the water a few yards to the right as the Irishman pushed towards the same island. Hare's strokes looked even and measured even in the cold water.

Gillespie's stocking feet reached the shingle as the waves began breaking against the shallows and he sank to his knees and began crawling up the beach. His left arm was pulsing with pain and his ribs ached from the impact with the water. When he reached the small tufts of grass that sprouted up from the island's pebbles, Gillespie collapsed in a heap and gasped for air. As he rolled over onto his back to look for Hare, he was startled to see that the Irishman was standing over him, his revolver drawn and pointing at Gillespie's chest.

"What the hell are you doing?" Gillespie coughed as he stared up at

Hare.

"I'm sorry that it has to end like this," Hare sighed.

"End like what? What the hell do you mean?"

"Thank you for catching Proctor, Inspector," Hare said, ignoring Gillespie's questions. "I'm sorry that this is where our paths must diverge once more."

"There's no way that gun is ever going to work," Gillespie offered, trying to buy himself some time before Hare used the weapon.

Hare didn't reply but simply cocked the hammer back and raised the gun towards the sky, firing off one round with a loud bang.

He brought the gun back down and cocked the hammer again as the barrel rotated to bring the next chamber and its deadly bullet into play.

Gillespie wasn't sure what he was more surprised about – the fact that Hare had pulled a gun on him or the fact that he had managed to keep it dry inside his jacket and coat despite their swim through the cold waters of the bay.

He absentmindedly noticed that the first light of morning was beginning to peek over the horizon as he tried to make sense of what was happening.

"Do it," hissed Burke in Hare's ear. "Do it. You've waited a lifetime for this moment. Finish what you started. Pull the trigger."

"Goodbye, Inspector," said Hare simply as he lowered the revolver, took aim at Gillespie and squeezed the trigger.

EPILOGUE
ULSTER, 1864

The solitary figure stood on the hill staring down at the gravestone. His long black greatcoat whipped around his legs as the wind weaved its way through the deserted graveyard. The simple chapel with its grey stone walls offered little protection from the bitter breeze or the occasional bursts of drizzle that peppered the graveside with rain.

The four grave diggers and the padre had long since left the freshly-covered burial but the man carried on staring at the words on the tombstone, words he had agonised over for days during his passage on the steam ship across the Atlantic.

"Here lies Edward Laird," he read to himself. The lie seemed fitting somehow.

He turned when he heard the crunch of footsteps on the gravel path behind him. A man in his mid-thirties was helping an old woman to walk up the small rise that led from the chapel to the top of the hill where the freshly-dug grave lay. The old woman was dressed in a long black cloak to protect her against the bitter wind, covering her whole body from her hooded head down to the trailing hem around her ankles.

The man wore a dark suit that was too old to be fashionable but had obviously been cared for and still looked neat and tidy. He led the old woman up the hill with her right arm linked through his left, her walking stick trailing from her left hand.

As the pair reached the man standing at the side of the grave, the old woman let go of her companion's arm and shifted her weight onto the walking stick, her dignity demanding that she stumble the final few steps to the graveside under her own steam.

"I stayed away from the service like you suggested," she said without introduction. Her emotions were still raw from their unexpected meeting earlier in the week, memories of nearly forty years ago dredged up and invading the peace and calm of the present. "Did anyone else turn up?"

"No," the man by the graveside replied. "It was just me and the priest and the grave diggers. But it wouldn't have done for you to have been there. If the village has forgotten him then it's probably best to keep it that way."

He looked over his shoulder at the younger man, who stood several steps away, watching the pair of them beside the mound of wet earth. His eyes were red rimmed and it was obvious that he was making an effort to control his emotions and stop himself from bursting into tears again. He kept his eyes fixed on the inscription on the freshly-erected tombstone.

The old woman turned to follow the man's gaze. "My son never knew his father," she offered. "After he left, I raised him myself. Few people in the village remember his father, so when you turned up unannounced after all this time it came as quite a shock for my boy."

"I'm sorry again for all the distress this has caused you," the man told her. "Both of you," he added, addressing her son.

The three figures stood in silence by the graveside as the wind continued to whip the dry brown leaves around their feet.

After what felt like an age, the woman turned and told her son that she was ready to leave.

Before they started making their descent down the hill, she turned to look up into the man's face.

"Thank you," she said. "At least now I know he's at peace at last."

Alexander Gillespie watched Margaret Laird slowly disappear out of sight down the hill and leaned heavily on his own walking stick. The cold and drizzle was doing little for his aching joints and the sharp stabbing pain in his leg had returned. He watched as Margaret and her son left Hare's graveside, still unsure if returning the Irishman's body to his homeland had been the right decision.

Few people in the village of Newry remembered Hare, who had only returned briefly after turning king's evidence and fleeing Edinburgh in 1829. Nearly forty years later, Gillespie had wrestled with the decision to bring Hare home, running the risk of reigniting old hatreds and ruining the peace enjoyed by Laird and her son, William, who Gillespie had learned was the local doctor.

But being buried in his homeland had been Hare's final request on the rain-soaked island in Boston harbour as the sun began to rise. Gillespie had traced Laird and agreed with her that a burial in Newry, Hare's home town, was the most fitting end.

As he stared down at Hare's grave, Gillespie's mind flashed back to that cold night in Boston harbour as he lay shivering on the beach and Hare had lowered his revolver. With the practiced shot of an army marksman, Hare had hit his target, shattering Gillespie's left kneecap in an explosion of pain that nearly caused the police captain to pass out. But Hare had taken a calculated risk.

Gillespie had looked up at the Irishman, the smoke curling away from the muzzle of his revolver as he drew back the hammer and brought the next chamber to bare, ready to fire again.

"Why?" Gillespie managed through gritted teeth as the pain engulfed his leg.

"I can't let you stop me, Gillespie," Hare had replied. "There's nothing left for me to live for now. Molly and the children are dead. I've killed nearly as many men tonight as I did before. I can't take this anymore. Helping you to stop Proctor and Tate was my chance at redemption but I don't know if God will see it that way."

Gillespie's eyes widened as he realised Hare's intention.

"Besides, this is the best thing for you too," Hare added. "This," he said, tipping the barrel of his weapon towards Gillespie's shattered leg, "gives you the excuse you need to leave the police."

Gillespie almost laughed at Hare's perceptiveness. Both men knew that the dockyard murders had been Gillespie's final case.

"Do one last thing for me?" Hare asked.

"What?"

"Bury me in Ulster. I've run a long way from home, but now I think it's time to go back."

The two men stared at one another and shared a final moment of silence.

"Goodbye, Gillespie."

"Goodbye, Hare," the police captain managed as the Irishman raised the barrel of his gun and forced it into his mouth. Without a moment's hesitation, he squeezed the trigger and sent the single bullet slicing through his brain and out through an exit hole in the back of his head.

Hare's corpse sank to its knees and then toppled forward, coming to rest next to Gillespie.

He watched the sun rising above the horizon as his vision slowly faded to black. But just as his world was being swallowed up into nothingness, he saw a ghostly figure standing over Hare's corpse, before it slowly began fading away, like harr melting in the early morning's sun over the Firth of Forth.

The harbour master's rowing boat reached the island less than an hour later, its rescue teams scooping up Gillespie's beaten and bruised body and tightly wrapping Hare's remains in a thick grey blanket.

Professor Cartwright said it was a miracle that Gillespie was even able to walk with the aid of a stick following his lengthy stay in hospital. Cartwright and his fellow surgeons at the Boston Medical College had worked feverishly to save Gillespie's leg and their efforts were not in vain. The captain hobbled down the steps from the college's hospital six weeks later to be greeted by Chief Blackstone, Sergeant MacLeod and the Mayor himself.

Despite protests from Blackstone – who promised Gillespie an administrative role at the nearly-completed city hall – he resigned his commission as a police officer the next day. The proceeds from selling his house in Boston and the money he had saved while working in America allowed him to pay for the return passage back across the Atlantic, with Hare's embalmed body stowed away in the cargo hold of the steamship.

A fresh burst of drizzle stinging his cheek broke Gillespie's revere and brought him back to the present. The weak afternoon light was beginning to fade as the sun sank behind a bank of thick cloud. Down in the village below, a dog started barking and Gillespie could see the shapes of men leaving their work and heading back home or to the local pub. For a moment he was tempted to stay and set up home, letting himself melt into the background as just another nameless old man in a sleepy rural community.

But then his thoughts turned to Edinburgh and the chance to

reconnect with the city of his birth.

"Goodbye, Hare," he said to the gravestone before turning and limping down the hill to the village and then the steamer and then the road home to Edinburgh.